I0653768

Crossroads

Julie DeFisher

Crossroads

Julie DeFisher

©2025 Julie DeFisher

Cover art by C. R. McCormack

NO AI TRAINING: Without in any way limiting the author's exclusive rights under copyright, any use of this publication to "train" generative artificial intelligence (AI) technologies to generate text is expressly prohibited. The author reserves all rights to license uses of this work for generative AI training and development of machine learning language models.

No part of this book may be reproduced without permission from the author except in brief quotations and in reviews.

This is a work of fiction. References to real people, events, establishment, organizations, or locales are intended only to provide a sense of authenticity and are used fictitiously. All other characters, and all incidents and dialogue, are drawn from the author's imagination and are not to be construed as real. Real people did help breath life into characters to give perspective outside that of the authors knowledge base.

"The fiction writer is the ombudsman who argues our humble, dubious case in the halls of eternal record." — John Updike

In Dedication To:

Celtic Blue2U, Izzy Krause, P.A. Power, and C.R. McCormack: Thank you for the encouragement and never letting me give up. Mom would be proud of all of you.

PROLOGUE

Some family traditions run deeper than the rivers or the roots of the oldest forest. While most dissipate or fall to the wayside, there are certain ones that are the core of the high society families. No matter how antiquated, archaic, or even downright cruel they seemed, they would never be anything more than duty to one's family. In Evette Cason's world, you grew up, fell in love, had kids, and continued those very family traditions without complaint.

As the heiress to the Cason Oil dynasty, she knew education had to come first. Though most would say educating her past a few years of college would be a waste of time for a woman that would be expected to raise her children and run her home. She was presumed to fall in love and marry. In the world around her some believed in the sanctity of love and marriage. For some marriage wasn't about love, it was a transaction, a negotiation, a coldly calculated move to solidify family power. She had always known this, but chose, long before it was her time to worry about such things, to go against the grain. She would only be with a man that valued her over family obligations.

For Evette's mother, Betsy, she was the precious jewel of the family that would undoubtedly go to the highest bidder or the oldest money. "You were born to build bridges," her mother often said, her sharp eyes appraising Evette like an investment. "The world will try to tell you otherwise, but never forget: a daughter is her family's prestigious asset. Never let any man make you think less. If it wasn't for us, those poor bastards wouldn't find their way out of a wet paper sack."

Her father, Larry Sr., was an oil tycoon who wielded influence like a king within his court, and rarely spoke of her future. His silence about anything other than business spoke volumes to Evette. This, among other things, had her remaining quiet to the oppressive nature that was her father. While Evette would play by the rules set out for her, she would never stop dreaming of a day when she would be free from the public eye.

Evette had her father's money, her mother's good looks but more importantly she had her grand-daddy's intelligence. With every uncomfortable glance during lavish dinner parties with his business associates, she would pay more attention to the shop talk than the parade of young men brought to sit across from her at the table. Poised and silent, watching every interaction, she learned everything she needed to know.

Unfortunately, this night was no different as she was now sixteen years old and it was now her time to enter fully into society. As Evette stood on the grand staircase overlooking the gardens, a vision in a silver gown that shimmered like moonlight, her anxiety threatened her composure. How was she supposed to walk gracefully in six inch heels, when she had barely made it from her room to the stairs without breaking her neck?

Her mother's hand rested lightly on her back, a gesture that to anyone else might have seemed affectionate, but Evette felt the weight of it, a silent command to move forward.

"Mom." Evette's voice was barely audible but the fear in her eyes spoke the words she couldn't say out loud.

"Your guests have arrived." her mother whispered through clenched teeth, her tone carrying the finality of a judge's gavel.

The sprawling estate, usually a sanctuary of stillness and grandeur, had transformed into a battlefield of subtle politics. Men in dark suits and women in glittering gowns flitted through the marble halls, exchanging veiled threats and promises over the clink of crystal goblets.

All with one thing in common, they wished to know which of the suitors Evette would choose.

Evette's stomach clenched, but she smoothed her expression into one of practiced neutrality. She had spent years perfecting this mask; the face of a daughter born for duty. She descended the stairs, her steps measured and graceful, every inch the obedient daughter. Scanning the crowd as every eye was on her, Evette heard the low murmurs of guests, clinking glasses of champagne, and the faint notes of a violin floating from somewhere in the garden. Her eyes fell on her old friend, Xander Hulston, entering with a smug smile plastered across his face.

The room seemed to shift as the guests parted, revealing a group of men who had entered. They moved with a predatory confidence, their tailored suits barely disguising the ruthlessness beneath. Evette's eyes brightened as she saw nothing had changed in his normal behavior from the upsetting tragic events that caused Xander to lose his older brother, Ethan, earlier that summer.

When her heart began to clench at the thought of Ethan, and the time they had spent together, she knew this was not the time or place to let herself feel those emotions. Looking up through her long lashes as she paused a few steps from the floor, her heart began to flutter at the sight as each man's eyes turned to her, especially Xander's cool blue eyes that seemed to be fixed on her.

He was taller than she'd remembered, his presence commanding in a way that drew every gaze in the room, but his eyes never broke contact. Evette felt a chill run down her spine despite the warmth of the evening, freezing on the steps awaiting any sign that the smoldering look was meant for her and not another. When his gaze lasted a fraction of a second longer than was polite, Evette's cheeks heated.

"That's the one," her mother said, standing right behind. Her voice soaked in satisfaction. "I can see your future husband."

Her husband. The word felt foreign on her tongue, like it belonged to someone else's story. Was this to be her reality, marriage to a boy she's known forever? They were friends and ran in the same circles, but he had never looked at her as if she were the only person in the room.

"He's seen me a million times before now. Why is he looking at me like this now?"

"Never you mind, the why. He can't take his eyes off of you. He can't help it. I think someone must have given him a good slap upside the head."

"He's walking over here." Evette's eyes widened as Xander moved through the crowd with a commanding presence.

"May I have the first dance?" Xander's eyes smoldered as he offered his hand.

CHAPTER I
WHIRLWIND

The whirlwind began the night Xander first kissed her under the glow of lanterns at the summer debutante ball. Looking back, Evette realized that moment marked the start of a fairy tale she hadn't known she wanted. Cotillions, debutante balls, Polo matches, and Friday night dates quickly became the norm. She was always on Xander's arm, the picture of effortless grace, though she sometimes felt like she was playing a role in a carefully curated dream. Forever waiting to awake, to find reality was much harsher.

Even when school resumed their sophomore year, Xander made her feel like the center of his universe. Roses in her locker, hand-in-hand walks to class, and invitations to join his close knit group of friends solidified her place by his side. "You're the school's power couple," her best friend Mia had said with a grin one day. "It's like you two are royalty or something." Evette had laughed, but the title stuck. To everyone else, their relationship seemed perfect.

By the time graduation loomed, the world felt like it revolved around the future they were building together. They spent hours planning. Evette's acceptance to an East Coast school and Xander's to a West Coast one didn't faze them. "It's just three years," Xander had said, clasping her hands. "I'll have everything ready by the time you graduate. We'll be unstoppable." His certainty steadied her, and they parted with promises and plans.

Four years passed in a blur of phone calls, emails, and holiday reunions. Their commitment further solidified in Xander's grand proposal, and a beautiful diamond ring sparkling on her finger hours before she crossed the stage to receive her diploma. She had never been happier than she was in that moment with Xander at her side.

But returning to New Mexico after graduation introduced an unease she couldn't shake. Evette's plan had been straightforward: move back in with her parents, start work at her father's company, and plan her wedding. Instead, she arrived to find her belongings already transferred to the Hulston estate without a word of mention to her.

"It's tradition," Xander's mother, Lady Hulston, explained with a tight-lipped smile. "A future Hulston bride must learn to manage the household and uphold our standards."

Evette blinked. "Oh, I... I hadn't realized."

Xander took her hands, his expression pleading. "Just go along with it. It's only until the wedding, and this way we get to see each other every day. Please, Evie?"

She relented, though the arrangement unsettled her. Fourteen months passed in a haze of wedding planning, work at Cason Oil, and trying to acclimate to life under the Hulston's roof. On the surface, things were fine, but beneath the polished veneer, something felt off. The closer they got to the wedding day, the more distant and irritable Xander became.

Late nights at the office turned into overnight business trips. "It's just work," he'd say dismissively when she asked. When the nagging feeling in her gut wouldn't go away, she pressed further into the nature of the meetings. His temper flared over trivial questions replying that "it was none of her business" and "to stay in her lane, if she wanted the cushy lifestyle she was to inherit by marrying him." She'd had enough.

"I'm not doing this anymore," she said one night after a particularly bad argument that resulted in Xander throwing a crystal vase against the wall. Tears streamed down her face as she stood by the packed suitcase on her bed. Xander's face twisted in disbelief.

"Where the hell do you think you're going?"

"I am leaving. Dad called and I need to be in Montana in the morning." Evette swung the bag off the bed taking her engagement ring off her finger and placing it on the nightstand. "Just so you know, I will not be coming back when I return. At least not without some major changes around here."

"What are you talking about?" he demanded. "You can't just walk away!"

"Watch me," she said, her voice remaining steady despite the storm raging inside her.

The month-long business trip was a lifeline she needed to bring her head back above the water. It had given her space to think and evaluate if she really wanted this or if this was the game she had to play for family. She ignored his calls and messages, letting him stew in what she could possibly be doing without him.

On the day she returned, Xander met her with an overwhelming display of affections. Roses of every color, heartfelt apologies, and promises to do and be better along with her engagement ring. "I've been stressed," he admitted, his tone imploring. "The wedding, work, everything. It's not an excuse, but I'm trying. Let me make it up to you."

She hesitated, but the sincerity in his eyes gave her pause. "One last chance, Xander," she said, taking the ring back. "But I won't tolerate being disrespected again."

His relief was palpable. "I'll prove it to you. Let's go to Aspen for the weekend. Just us, I promise. No phones or work, just you and me in the cabin. A pre-honeymoon, to show you how much you mean to me."

Evette agreed, but as they planned the trip for literally two weeks before the wedding, that nagging feeling remained. Xander's apologies felt genuine, but could she trust him to change? The fairy tale life she'd been swept into now felt like a gilded cage, and she wasn't sure if she held the key to unlock it. She was firm in never being someone's trophy.

The sun was bright and blinding as it crossed over the New Mexico desert. September winds blew with great gusts turning the sand into dust devils, as Evette tried to work on the water wells in the less than stellar dry heat. Beads of sweat formed as her muscles screamed from the climb back up to the surface, she had collected enough samples to run back at the lab.

This was supposed to be a short work day for her, but as she sat on the edge of the well, Evette had noticed it was much later than she had intended on being in the field. Lost in her thoughts of the past two years along with the wedding being only ten days away, she begged for clarity, understanding, and for her life to finally move forward without dozens of people trying to make decisions for her.

As the dust devils chased one another across the open plain, Evette had to admit her fascination with how the elements seemed to have their own rules as they co-existed. She had studied for years to become a geologist, as both hers and her longtime boyfriend's fathers were Oilmen. While the families would have been happier if she had gone into the business boardroom side of things, Evette insisted on being a hands-on field hand.

Her brother, Larry Cason Jr., had more of a taste for the bright lights and attention received by being the face of the company. Evette was happy being in the shadows doing the research and keeping the company on the right side of the environmentalists. She viewed herself as making a difference from the inside instead of being one of those people screaming with picket signs.

Her mother cringed over the years of finishing school wasted on Evette. Betsy Cason hoped that once she settled down into the role of Mrs. Xander Hulston, she would be the proper young woman/ socialite she was raised to be. She was absolutely certain Xander would set her on the right course, as he would require a doting wife not a business partner.

As the phone rings in her pocket, Evette sighed as it could only be one of three people. Pulling out her phone, she frowned when it reads "Jamie Hulston"

"Hello." Evette tried to keep her warm inviting tone.

"Where the hell are you? You were supposed to meet us nearly 20 minutes ago."

Evette looks down at her watch seeing that it was nearly 1pm. "I'm in the field. Lost track of time."

"Well you have exactly 20 minutes to get here or so help me god girl you will wish like hell you had."

"Yes ma'am. I'm on my way."

Evette swiped her hands through her hair hoping once she married Xander these impromptu lunches would stop with her mother-in-law. After all, this was only the fifth meeting with the caterer and baker. None of her wants or suggestions had been taken into account up to this point, why was it so important for her to be there now? At this point, she was ready to throw her hands in the air, and suggest they elope to keep from going through this flashy fiasco.

Replacing the tank lid, she hopped into the company work truck with her bag. Evette was thankful she had remembered to grab her sundress before leaving the house that morning. She wouldn't have to hear her mother or mother-in-law's degrading comments of how she looked like a common "hood rat".

CHAPTER 2
THE PLAN

Pacing around the pompous looking office at Hulston Oil in his pressed three piece dark gray suit, Xander panicked. He had just gotten off the phone with his furious mother. Apparently, Evette hadn't shown up for the final tasting or viewing on time and he had to hear about it. She was also worried that Xander hadn't been doing enough to keep her happy to go through with the wedding. If this was what the next two weeks were going to be, he was going to have a full fledged meltdown. He was already distraught at what marrying Evette would mean for him.

The blonde haired blue eyed playboy was faced with a reality he never wanted, but when his brother's death caused him to be unceremoniously catapulted into the spotlight, what was he going to do? He couldn't walk away from the family money that funded his lavish behind the scenes lifestyle. Even when he was younger, Xander knew that it was loyalty to the family money not the family that kept him doing their bidding.

Xander was over the moon when Evette had packed her bag and left the house a month ago. He could finally move on and be the person he had always wanted to be, but when his mother had found out, all hell had broken loose. That was also when he was informed what was at stake for both him and the family if Evette refused to return. This is what prompted him to call and message her nonstop. While he didn't want her, it infuriated him to no end that someone else could gain what was, in his mind, rightfully his.

It had been Ethan who was supposed to be betrothed to Evette. It had been Ethan who was set to take over the company. It had been Ethan who was to stand as the golden child. Now, it was Xander that had to fill those obligations. While it had worked well up to this point, time was running out on his carefree lifestyle with the woman he actually loved. He didn't want to be tied down to the goody-two shoes Evette, when he had his wildcat in Nadia Morang, the heiress to the Morang mafia family.

Nadia had been his long-time companion, and while she knew about the family obligations to marry someone else, neither were too happy about the situation. They had both been racking their brains for years on how to get Xander out of marrying Evette without it looking like his fault. That way, to the family, he could openly pursue Nadia without anyone being the wiser. While that didn't work out well for them in their teenage years, they were older and the Hulston family had more dealings with the Morang family.

To Jamie Hulston, Nadia was the wrong kind of girl for her son, being from a mafia family. She was one step above a common thief in her book, and didn't have the right kind of breeding to be among the upper class. Hence the reason the two had kept their relationship under wraps for so many years. Stealing moments away during parties they both happened to be in attendance was their favorite game. The thrill of the chance of being caught in the coatroom.

"I don't know why you don't let me talk to my cousin, and have her completely taken out of the equation." Nadia sat in the soft leather wingback chair, watching the distress in her lover's eyes.

"This close to the wedding people will speculate that I had something to do with it. We aren't on the best terms right now and I'm holding on to this by a thread." Xander dragged his well-manicured hands through his hair.

"You don't want to live in a society like this, yet you don't want to do anything about it!" Nadia raised her voice, exasperated at the thought of him marrying another. "Family obligation be damned. You love me, not that bitch!"

"It's not like that and you know it." Xander shot daggers at her. He had been hearing the same words come out of her mouth since he was forced to drop to one knee by the family.

"Then what are you going to do about it? You should have let her walk away when she left you."

"I told you why I had to do what I did. According to the contract between the families, Evette wont receive the twelve million dollar inheritance until after she is married to me. Otherwise, she can't access it until she is twenty-five." Xander grabs the file off the desk and thrust it at Nadia.

"Do you think she knows? I mean not that it matters but you would think if she knew she would have pressed for the wedding to be sooner." Nadia wrinkled her nose at the legal paperwork in front of her.

"She doesn't. She has been very much kept in the dark. If she breaks off the engagement for any reason, or I am found at fault for her breaking it off, the Hulston family has to pay back the endowment. We also lose any further contracts with the Cason Oil group. From what I was told, that was twelve million dollars plus interest." Xander came to rest on the edge of his desk trying to change his tactic with Nadia. "If we are going to have the money to make a break for it out of both our families, we need this to go off without a hitch."

"What about an accident on the honeymoon? Would that work out to your advantage? I mean this world is a very unpredictable place." A sly smile spreads across her face.

"That's what I was thinking." Xander couldn't help but chuckle to think about all the things that could happen while they were in Barbados.

"Wait..." Nadia's hand hovered over a clause in the contract. "You have to be intimate with her." She pointed to the provisions on the paper. "A provision for continued active support from the Cason Group after the wedding will be null if parties are not either A. Both active in the company or B. Actively seeking procreation. The bastards put a consummation/ grandparents clause in here."

Xander had to get Larry Cason Sr. credit. When he had this contract drawn up, he wasn't playing. Mr. Cason had given Evette every little hole to weasel herself out of this marriage with little consideration for the Hulston family if it doesn't go through. But two could play at that game and Xander would do what he had to make them believe what he wanted.

"Not that the prude will allow me to touch her before marriage." Xander looked hard at the paper handed to him. "It shouldn't be too hard to fulfill their request, after."

"You're really going to sleep with her?" Nadia shrieked in disbelief.

"No, my love, but that doesn't mean I wont say that I did to collect. Plus it's a honeymoon, everyone should assume that the deed was done."

"Good because I don't think I could handle you touching her. No one can satiate your dark tastes but me." Nadia stood, running her hand from his belt up his pressed white shirt.

Xander's eyes darkened as the thought *I would have lived longer if it weren't for Ethan* crossed his mind. He would have his fortune, it didn't matter how he had to obtain it. No one was going to stop him from getting exactly what he wanted, but first he would have to get rid of Evette.

The thoughts of whether the contract would be void if she had gone missing played in his mind. What if she hit her head and got amnesia? Could he sell her off to the highest bidder, claiming she had gone missing? Would it be possible to play like she was still with him for a while but was very sick from the travels abroad? He didn't like the idea of killing her; for him it was much more amusing to watch the fear in her eyes as the toucher commenced.

19

As the scenarios played in his mind, he toyed with the straps on Nadia's dress. Aroused at the prospect of seeing Evette in the same positions he put Nadia, Xander let himself wonder if she would accept this side of him. This dominant primal side that begged to be let out at any and all cost. Would she run from him or would she embrace it as she had with everything else that was what she thought she knew? He would have to test that theory at least one time before he got rid of her. After all, what could be more exciting than having two women to fulfill his needs?

"To your knees," Xander boomed and Nadia was more than ready to oblige him.

CHAPTER 3
TRUST ME

By the time Xander had returned back to the family home that afternoon, he had his plan ready to set in motion. He believed that it would be as easy as taking candy from a baby, if he played his cards right. Nothing would stop him from being able to spend the rest of his life with his true love. They were so close to getting exactly what they deserved, but Xander had one little card up his sleeve that he didn't share with his beloved.

He had told Evette he had booked the trip to Aspen but he hadn't. He had other plans to see if she would truly accept the real him, as Nadia did. If she did then he would have to figure out how to handle both Evette and Nadia in his life. The real problem would be with stringing them both along until he had a better idea of what to do next.

Walking through the door to the house he had heard shouting coming from the kitchen, but it was hard to tell if it was his mother or the cook that was making the ruckus. He wanted to rush upstairs to see if Evette was home and put phase one of his plan into effect, but something told him he should figure out what the commotion was first. He was surprised to see Mrs. Morang, Mrs. Cason and his mother arguing back and forth.

Xander tried to make a quick escape before he had been seen, but he wasn't that lucky. His mother grabbed his arm as soon as he had entered the room, pulling him full fledge into the verbal altercation. "Tell them you have had nothing to do with that loose girl this instant."

"Watch your mouth about my daughter," Mrs. Morang screeched, pointing her finger into Mrs. Hulston's chest.

"Are you really going to dishonor my daughter in this fashion?" Mrs. Cason bellowed, giving Xander a look that could very well make him drop dead.

"Ladies, I have no idea what you are talking about." Xander did his best to think on his feet to what the actual meaning of this could be.

"So, that wasn't you I caught sneaking out of my driveway three nights ago? You're not the person my daughter goes and sees every day on her lunch break? Oh, and the reason that every good Italian man we set her up with refuses her after the first date." Mrs. Morang began pacing around the room like a wild animal. Xander could see where Nadia got it from but now was probably not the time to get turned on by her outburst.

"Ma'am, Nadia and I have been good friends since grade school. Nothing more. Now, yes that probably was me leaving your driveway two nights ago. But, it's not what you think. I was getting advice from my oldest and dearest friend on how to woo my bride-to-be. We had just had the first major fight of our relationship. Evette was due to come back into town that afternoon and I needed help with my apology." Xander applauded himself at giving just enough truth to make it believable. He had no idea that the truth would now have all three women turning on him at once like a pack of rabid dogs.

"What do you mean you two had a fight?" Mrs. Cason had intensified her gaze.

"What did you do to that sweet girl? You had better not lay a hand on her." Mrs. Morang growled.

"You told me that it was just a disagreement over wedding details," Mrs. Hulston spat, knowing she already knew but couldn't let the other two know that.

"First, I have never and will never lay a hand out of anger on anyone that doesn't deserve it. Secondly, it was wedding jitters and I lost my temper and raised my voice at her. While we were cooling off, she had gotten the call from Mr. Cason. She went to Montana for a month on business. Now if you don't mind I need to go and see how much damage control I have to do with my fiancée because of you three." Xander left the kitchen with the three women still bickering but at that point he didn't care.

When he had gotten to Evette's door, he found she locked herself in her room away from the rest of the family. Apparently, the afternoon had taken its toll with her being openly berated in front of everyone for being late, then returning home to find Mrs. Morang waiting for her to spill the beans about Xander's late nights with her daughter.

Xander was actually surprised she hadn't blown his phone up wanting answers. Was it too late? Did she believe the accusations that were being thrown around to beseech his honor? This was not going to bode well for his plans. As he had been told by his mother to put in more effort, but she was the one making it more difficult, what was the point?

He would remind himself to text Nadia about the encounter downstairs and tell her she has a spanking coming for it. They had a rule and it was either a lucky guess or Nadia had told her mother it was him.

Xander knew he would have to put those thoughts out of his mind for a moment as he leaned in to see if there was any movement inside the room. He could hear the light sobs but for him it was hard to tell if anything else was going on in the room. Xander decided to bite the bullet and knock.

"Go away." Evette's voice was strained.

"It's me."

"I don't want to see you."

"You're not even going to let me explain?" Xander heard stomping feet head towards the door.

If Evette could have ripped the door from the hinges to prove the anger and frustration she had felt, she would have. Standing before him disheveled, make-up running down her face, and molten hot glare evident that she had heard enough of the conversation before locking herself away in her room. "You think you can play me for a fool? Do you really think I'm that stupid?"

"My darling..." Xander began as Evette threw her hands up to stop him from entering the room.

"Don't my darling me. A mistress, Xander? A fucking MISTRESS?" Evette screamed at the top of her lungs. "How long has this been going on? How long have you been placating to my face and our families?" Evette's gaze could turn Xander to ash, and he rather enjoyed seeing the fire that captivated his attention.

"First of all, I don't have a mistress. Nadia Morang is a dear friend that was helping me in the pursuit of getting you back. Secondly, Mrs. Morang and my mother would have my balls on a silver platter if anything happened between Nadia and I. You must believe me this is all just a big misunderstanding," Xander desperately tried to explain his way out of this.

"Do you know how many times I have heard the just friends conversation from my friends for it to turn out to be more? It's the oldest excuse in the book." Evette, not being able to stand the sight of him, tried to slam the door in his face.

Xander stepped in, blocking her. Her look of defiance ignited something deep inside him that he was sure only Nadia could stir. *Maybe this could work* Xander thought as he reached out and ran his hand up her arm. She didn't pull away from him and that was all he needed to go on his attack. Sliding his hand up her back to the back of her neck, Xander pulled her to him, laying a kiss on her that left them both breathless.

"Now get your things together. We will leave for our weekend and leave all this behind." Xander gazed into her swimming crystal blue eyes.

"Wait, what about the fight going on downstairs?" Evette tried to put her mind on anything but the kiss.

"Fuck'em. You're all I care about."

"You mean it?"

"Of course I do." Xander's evil smile slipped across his lips but she didn't notice.

"I'll be ready in 10 minutes." Evette's heart was racing as she spoke. He had never kissed her like that.

"Okay. I'll meet you downstairs." Xander took one more look back at her as he closed the door and leaned his head against the frame. If it wasn't for the financial hit this would cause for the family, Xander would walk away now and figure out another way to fund his future with Nadia. For now, he would do his best to see if Evette would trust him enough to have his cake and eat it too.

It didn't take long before Evette came bustling down the stairs with her suitcase and carry on bag. She had fixed her make-up with the only remnants of her tears being the red rimmed outline of her puffy eyes. Xander wasn't completely heartless when it came to Evette, and it showed in the pang of guilt that radiated through his heart at the sight of trying to hold it together.

The arguing between the three women was still continuing in the kitchen as Xander reached out and took Evette's hand to lead her out the front door. He was thankful at that moment he hadn't put his car in the garage, as he was determined to get them out of there as quickly as possible. If she could overhear anything else those bickering wet hens had to say, it would foil his plans, and he simply didn't have the time to deal with that.

Opening Evette's door, Xander was disgusted with the turn of events. Why couldn't anything for once in his life go as he had planned?

25

Why did everything have to feel like a thrown together mop job? He was already going against his word to Nadia, but her mother had forced his hand in upsetting Evette. Xander wanted this played out correctly and now he was having to fly by the seat of his pants. Which was something he absolutely hated.

Xander understood two things would happen after that day. Either Evette would accept him and play her part in standing by him with the family, or phase two would have to be put in place leaving him a widower not long after he became a bridegroom. Since the only other option was to keep stringing both women along until another plan came to light, Xander was running out of time and in a lot of ways patience.

Pulling away from the house, Xander's expression was almost murderous. The flames in his eyes were something darker than the desire. Neither said a word as the palpable tension grew between them. The crushing silence sent uncomfortable waves of uncertainty crashing over, and while it thrilled Xander to see Evette squirm, she was heavily debating on jumping from a moving vehicle to end the torture.

When they pulled up in front of the Grand Ole Salon hotel, Evette looked at Xander with confusion plastered all over her face. To her knowledge, they were supposed to be headed to the airport for their Aspen getaway, not to a hotel, and a cheap looking one at that. Evette had never willingly traveled to this end of town, and had no idea why Xander would have brought her here.

"What is going on?" Evette finally broke the silence.

"Our flight isn't until 9. I wouldn't think you would want to spend five hours in the airport when we could freshen up and even get some sleep before the flight."

"That makes sense, but why here?" Evette looked at the rundown building questioning Xander's motives.

"This is the closest place to the airport. Everything else is on the other side of town." Xander had as many excuses as he needed to have her just where he wanted her. After all, if it was good enough for Nadia, then what was she complaining about? "It's really not that bad."

"Is it even safe for us to leave the car here?" The hair on the back of Evette's neck began to stand at attention as every fiber of her being was screaming to get out of there.

"Don't be scared. I just need you to come with me." Xander got out of the car and moved around to Evette's door, holding out his hand to help her out of the car.

It didn't go unnoticed; he only removed her luggage from the car, and Evette didn't remember seeing him put anything in the car before they had left. She didn't know if he had packed prior to leaving for the office that day, so it would be hard for her to know where his bags were. Deep down though, something didn't feel right and nothing was making any sense since she had returned back from Montana.

Xander's hot and cold demeanor gave her whiplash but she had no reason to believe he would put her in danger. With them only having one argument in their relationship, Evette was beginning to believe it was just that cold feet coupled with the stress from the merging of the companies. At this point, she believed she was looking for issues that were simply not there.

Evette's thoughts raced as they walked inside and through the broken-down lobby of the hotel with Xander pulling her rolling bag behind him. It should have been strange to her that they didn't stop at the desk to check in but if Xander had known of the delay in flight, he would have already had plans in place. While alarm bells went off through her body, Evette tried her best to give Xander the benefit of doubt, coming up with every logical conclusion.

As they got onto the elevator, Xander's reserved nature flipped. He wrapped his arm around her waist, pulling her closer to him. This shocked Evette, as she had never seen him show this kind of possessive nature toward anything or anyone. While it excited her to see this side of his personality, alarm bells rang in her head.

When the elevator stopped on the third floor, Xander practically shoved her out into the nearly empty hallway. Forcefully ushering her to a room at the end of the hall, Evette started to panic. He had never acted this way toward her and yet, he seemed to seamlessly transition into the aggressive person at her side. Was this a front to scare her over the previous interactions they had? Or had he always been this way without her really seeing the signs?

Stopping at the door, Xander pulled a key card from his back pocket. Evette noticed the room number on the door, as the 315 was barely hanging on by little finishing nails. The old green wallpaper cracked and seemed to be hanging on the walls by a thread. She thought the place looked more run down but definitely cheap in comparison to the places she would have normally stayed. Every little detail captured by her mind deepened the tone that something was very wrong about Xander bringing her here.

The inside of the room was no better, with dust nearly an inch thick covering every service. The bed spreads were also the same dark hunter green that seemed to be the theme of the hotel. The maroon shag carpet looked matted, sticky and stained. Evette's eyes went wide as she stood in the room as it looked like someone was already staying there.

Evette turned to Xander to ask what the hell was going on as he placed her bags next to the dresser. When she caught the overly toothy smile and his eyes as dark as spades, the lightbulb moment had clicked. There hadn't been a delayed flight, Xander wanted her alone somewhere no one would look for either of them. But somewhere if they were caught, it would tarnish their reputations.

"What do you think you're doing?" Evette said mustering whatever courage and strength she had in her body.

"I don't know what you mean." His voice had never sounded so cold and calculated.

"Why are we here?" Panic and fire grew in Evette's stomach as she gauged if she could get to the bathroom, which she hoped had a lock on the door.

"I told you there is a delay in the flight. I wanted some alone time with my soon-to-be wife away from prying eyes." Xander moved as if he was toying with her. Stepping within arms length of her, he ran his rough hands up her exposed arms.

Pulling away from his touch, "I don't know what you think is going to happen, but I have been very clear."

"I can't have a taste of what is to be mine?"

"No. I won't say it again. You know my stance on this." Evette squared up her shoulders and moved to get her bags to leave.

"You are mine!" Xander's temper snapped as she tried to leave the room. Grabbing her by her hair, he pulled her back screaming into her face. "How dare you disrespect me!"

Evette froze at that moment. Her hands went to his to attempt to release his grip on her hair. This action angered him, further tightening his grip and dragging her across the room to the bed. Evette clawed at his hands, arms, and clothes. She did anything that would allow her enough time to get away. Alas, that was not going to be the case here.

Xander unceremoniously dropped her by her hair onto the bed. His steely cold expression would haunt Evette after that moment. Removing his locked fingers from her hair, Xander tore at her clothes. Evette recoiled, bringing her knee up and catching him in the balls, but the force wasn't strong enough to stop him in the manic state. Instead, Xander's rage took over and he backhanded her so hard that she flipped off the bed, busting her head on the frame to the bathroom door. Evette was knocked unconscious from the impact.

Xander walked over to stand over her lifeless body. He would have what he wanted from her whether or not she would be a willing participant. At this time though, he was so disgusted by her actions to get away from him that he couldn't get it up if he tried. He could, however, make it so no man would ever want her.

A wicked gleam showed in his eyes, as he dragged her to the bed and tied each limb to the corners of the bed. It wasn't his best knotwork, but it would have to do. He dragged his hands over the exposed skin trying to decide how disfigured he would leave the precious Evette.

CHAPTER 4
THE ESCAPE

Some say the veil between life and death was as thin as a sheer fabric. Still being able to see but unable to touch the other side. This was the limbo Evette found herself in, certain she had crossed over. She was merely waiting for the hazy fog to lift, showing her the afterlife, when all of her senses came back to her one by one.

First, she felt the searing pain that seemed to engulf every fiber of her being like a wildfire. Next, the pressure from the swelling in her face along with her inability to properly open her left eye, not that she was trying to show any signs of being alert at the moment. Her arms were numb and being suspended overhead, and her legs had felt like dead weight as she tried to gently make them twitch to see if they had been broken.

Evette had no idea how long she had been unconscious, but knew it was long enough to withstand the beating of her life. The dark room smelt of blood and a scent she wasn't familiar with. While dread and panic began to set, Evette was hyper aware he was still in the room sitting at the end of the bed. Peaking through the only eye not currently swollen shut, she had seen the monster Xander had become.

She wondered if he had always been this way. Had he always wanted to hurt her? Did he really want her dead? Too many questions flooded her mind as she tried to keep herself as calm and still as possible. When his phone rang it almost caused her to jump, giving away that she was currently awake.

Xander looked down at the caller ID and quickly sent the call to voicemail. Then it rang again and again, each time being sent to voicemail. Finally on the fifth or sixth call, he answered, exasperated that whoever was on the other line wasn't getting the hint. Through the ringing in her ears she strained to listen in to get any information on what or why the hell this was happening to her.

"WHAT?" Xander snapped into the phone as he placed it on speaker.

"Where are you? You were supposed to be at my parents an hour ago," a high pitched female voice said.

"I got hung up with something, I'm sorry." Xander's tone softened as he looked between his watch and the bed where he had Evette tied up.

"I can stall for a few more minutes but you need to get here. Victor is in town and I wanted him to meet you," the voice shrilled.

"I understand my love but I'm currently in the middle of something."

"It better not be that bitch Evette. You promised me..." Her voice was cut off by Xander beginning to scream at her.

"Look here. I will do what I want, when I want. I promised you I wouldn't sleep with her and I haven't. So if you expect me to show up at this damn party, you will change that damn tone or so help me god I will leave you in the chains for a damn WEEK," he roared into the phone.

"Yes, sir." The woman's voice was meek with just a hint of playing into his ego.

"That's better." Xander's lips curled up into a smug smile. "Nadia, let everyone know I'll be there in half an hour. I got stuck in traffic. I will run by the house, shower quickly, and put on my suit." Xander looked at the dry blood under his fingernails with disgust. He would have to have more control if he was going to allow himself to keep playing these games. Xander snickered at the thought *at least someone else would have to clean up the mess this time.*

"Are you going to spend the night? I have something important to tell you." Nadia's voice dripped sensuously.

"I'll see what I can do. You know we are leaving for Aspen tomorrow." Xander wandered around the room looking for his effects.

"What time's the flight again? I still have to pack."

"9am." Xander huffed as he checked his pocket for the room key. "You told me you packed already. You want time suspended in the chains don't you?"

"Whatever you think is best, Sir." Nadia's voice went low and seductive, making Evette want to puke more from the exchange between the two than the blinding pain racing through her body.

Xander hung up the phone after her remarks. He left the room locking the door as he strolled out. Evette didn't know how he could leave so casually, as if he didn't just beat her within an inch of her life. As if he didn't just have a full blown erotic conversation with the woman he had declared was "just a friend" earlier that afternoon. Too many questions came flooding back to Evette's mind like a title wave taking down a ship. She tried to steady her ragged breathing.

As the time ticked on in the room, Evette forced her one good eye open. She wasn't ready to process what she had to see at that moment. Her legs were spread wide as they were tied to the posts of the queen size bed. From the harsh orange light from the lamp on the dresser, she could see her black, blue, and purple bruises. Rope burns on her ankles appeared to look like she struggled in the restraints even with her being unconscious.

The mirror over the dresser showed the rest of the room's filth along with a full view of her reflection on display. While it broke her more to physically see herself like this, she made herself look for nothing else than to see if there might be any visible ways to escape. As the tears fell down her cheeks, Evette allowed herself to think one last time why Xander had done this to her. What had she done to him that would invoke such an action to leave her broken, humiliated, and at the brink of death?

Closing her eyes, Evette tried hard to push through the electric shock of her numb limbs regaining circulation. She willed herself to move her arms and legs through the sharp tingles. Realizing she had just enough give in the ropes to pull herself up, she painfully twisted her hands to grab onto the rope to pull up. It took several gut-wrenching tries before she was able to achieve her goal, but through streams of tears, loss of breath, and a racing heart, Evette was finally in a better position to be able to free herself.

She strained to turn her neck to look at the restraints. While this was a serious matter, Evette couldn't keep herself from laughing, looking at the sloppy knots. For a man that prided himself as an expert rock climber, Xander didn't do that great of a job with this. The tie offs at the top of the headboard looked solid. The double knots around her wrists were sturdy enough to hold her in place but sloppy enough she could potentially free her hands without causing more damage. Evette mustered all the strength she could and willed her right arm forward with a downward thrust.

The knot closest to her wrist tightened and bit hard into the flesh, but the one above it opened enough for her to use her teeth. With this one gone the rope had about four more inches of play. Relieved that she had a little more motion in her arm, Evette clung to the spark of hope of her freedom. Diligently, she worked on the knot at her wrist. After crying, cursing, and the salty sweat burning every open wound, Evette finally felt her right arm fall limp next to her. A surge of adrenaline forced her to quickly work the numbness out of her fingers before she made short work of freeing her other hand.

She lay there for a moment hyper aware of her surroundings. Every footstep, elevator ding, or knock on another door sent a wave of panic through her. She dreaded the moment she would hear his card key unlock the door. Evette knew she couldn't be there when he decided to show back up. It was the not knowing if or when Xander was going to raise his snakelike head that had her fighting through the stabbing and burning sensations to free her legs.

Once she was free, Evette fought the stiffness in her body to curl up into a ball. Her sobs were deafening as she felt every wound inflicted on her. The ringing in her ears made all the cuts and bruises to her face throb in agony. The sharp stabbing pain sent her stomach into a lurch making her want to throw up. With what strength she had left, Evette dragged herself off the bed and toward what she hoped was the bathroom.

As the bright white lights hummed to life, Evette squinted, trying to focus. Between the nausea and seeing what had been done to her in the mirror, Evette's body wracked as she emptied what was left of the contents of her stomach into the toilet. The damage to her face had been worse than she had observed through the mirror in the other room. The harsh orange light hid more than she was prepared to acknowledge. It also didn't help that she stood there in next to nothing. Her clothes looked to have been ripped from her body except for her bra and panties.

Only one clear thought seemed to flash in her mind. If he was capable of doing this to her now, what would it be like if she actually married him? She couldn't/wouldn't let this happen to her again. Taking what appeared to be a clean hand towel from the rack above the toilet, Evette prepared a warm compress to clean up the dried blood on her face. Her hands shook as the warm water made its way to the cuts and abrasions on her hands and forearms. She winced, wringing out the rag and beginning to dab it onto her face.

A buzzing noise caught her off guard, causing her eye to go wide, and her to freeze in place staring into the mirror. She hoped and prayed that he hadn't returned without her being able to hear the door unlock or open. Evette reached up to angle the bathroom mirror to the bedroom mirror. Hoping that the old trick she had used as a child would be enough to see into the other room. Breathing a sigh of relief when no one was lurking around, Evette noticed a metal baseball bat that seemed to have been left behind leaning against the footboard.

While most of the injuries looked to have been done by Xander's hands and fists, Evette wondered if he had used the bat or was that his grand finale? Another wave of nausea hit her at the thought, only this time nothing came out as the dry heaves did further damage to her ribs.

Evette tried to piece Xander's thought process together while she regained some sort of composure. When the realization hit her like a ton of bricks, what was left of the bile in her stomach rose into her throat. He either didn't expect her to make it through the night, or had every intention of returning to end what he had started. The purpose behind his actions were no longer important to her. What difference would it make if the end result was her death?

Not being able to bear her reflection any longer, Evette hobbled out of the bathroom and back to the bed. As soon as she sat down, she clung to the bat. She would at least have a way to defend herself if he returned. Looking around the room, her eyes fell on the source of the buzzing noise. A small weak smile spread across her lips, as she saw he had not taken her suitcase or her purse when he exited the room.

Hope bloomed in her chest as she launched herself at her belongings. She breathed a sigh of relief when she noticed not one thing was missing. Her plan formed quickly from there with only one major thing driving her forward. She had to make it through the night without being seen, noticed, and most importantly alive. No matter what it took, Evette would be safe.

Rummaging through her suitcase to find something loose to wear, her phone went off again. Digging it out of her purse, her heart dropped at the hundreds of missed calls and voicemails. Most were from Xander, probably setting up his alibi if she had succumbed to her injuries. She had underestimated his need for control over every situation and vowed to never make that mistake again.

The messages that stood out the most though were from her mother and his mother. Both half telling her it was her duty to forgive him and stand by him over the Nadia scandal, and half berating her for not answering her phone, calling her childish for running away from the house. Did they honestly not know she had left with Xander? Her work truck was sitting in the garage. How did they think she would be able to leave the house without a car?

It was the messages from her father's phone that were the real kick to the gut. Some were about work meetings and the test results from the well she had collected earlier that day. The others, which sounded completely out of character for him, followed the same line of "how could you do this to the family?" Not "where are you, are you safe, or why haven't you answered your phone?" But a "how could you do this to the family?"

God knows what he had told them when he returned back to the house without her. What lies he had spun to keep his head out of the noose. She had no idea what would happen if she managed to find a way to show back up at her family home busted up and bruised. Would they believe her version of events or Xander's? Would they do the unthinkable and hand her back over to him. Telling her this was her fault and she would have to deal with the consequences of her actions for the sake of family.

As the anger and resentment grew, Evette knew the only person she could trust was herself. Hell, she couldn't even chance reaching out to her brother. Evette sighed, dropping her phone back into her purse. It was obvious she would have to lay low for a while. She remembered what her grandfather used to tell her from the old westerns he would religiously watch. "You need to lay low, you head for Mexico."

Evette slowly pulled herself off the dirty carpet. Her first order of business was to change out of what was left of the torn rags and into something clean and warm. Evette had no clue if her body was cold due to shock or the fact Xander had set the air in the room at 50 degrees. Unfortunately, it really didn't matter as Xander had been the cause of it all.

She was thankful she had packed her oversized hoodie and sweats. The thought of the fleece lining hugging around her injured body gave her a sense of warmth and security. As she dressed, Evette prayed the clothes would be loose enough not to stick to the open wounds causing further damage later. Biting the inside of her cheek, trying to keep herself from screaming from the potentially dislocated shoulder, Evette pulled the hoodie over her head, and the inside caught on something. Pulling her head through, she looked down on her hand. The blood-stained ring stared back at her, almost mirroring everything she had been through in that room. Rage filled, Evette pulled the ring from her hand and slung it across the room.

Resting on the bed, she remembered the heels she had left the house in. As she searched the floor for them, Evette played through the possible reactions Xander would have finding her gone. Her mind played out his panic and rage with maybe a hint of relief. He couldn't take her life, and that would be his downfall. She would see he paid the price for what he had done to her but for now, she had to live long enough to see that come to fruition.

Abandoning the search, Evette grabbed the sneakers from her bag. While she was struggling to put them on, panic set in once more. How was she going to leave? Racking her brain on any possible option that wouldn't give her away, the light bulb went off. Her car was still at the off site office, as she had driven her work truck to lunch that day. All she had to do was figure out a way to her car. Evette zipped up her suitcase and grabbed the bat, knowing it was now or never.

The ding of the elevator had her hand hovering over the doorknob. Her breath hitched in her throat as the footsteps headed closer to her. She backed herself against the wall behind the door and raised the bat to defend herself. Evette tried to slow her breathing as her heart pounded in her ears. As the footsteps went past her room, she heard another door open and shut. Taking no chances, she counted to three and ran from the room with her belongings.

The hallway was dimly lit and empty. Evette steadied herself as she walked toward the stairwell. She had debated on taking the elevator, but thought against it. If Xander happened to be in the lobby, her goose would be cooked, and she was pretty sure he wouldn't care if there happened to be witnesses. At least, not from this side of town.

The burning pain that seemed to radiate from every fiber of her being subsided for a moment as the adrenaline spiked. She practically flew down the first two flights of stairs, but when she rounded the corner for the last flight, she collided with a janitor's cart knocking every bit of the wind out of her. Stumbling down a few stairs, Evette dropped the bat and caught herself on the railing. The loud clanging from the metal on metal echoed up the stairwell.

"Oh I'm so sorry. I didn't see you there." An older man rushed to check on her.

"It's fine. I'm fine. Should have been looking where I was going," Evette choked out her response as all the pain surged back.

"Oh no, Miss." As the man reached her Evette tried to pull up her hood but it was too late. He had seen she'd been badly beaten. "Who did this to you?"

"It's a long story. One I don't care to tell right now." She grit her teeth, trying to breath through the pain.

"Ma'am, we need to call the police. Whoever did this, needs to be charged." He came to stand in front of her surveying the damage to her face.

"Unfortunately, he has money. It'll be all too easy for him to get away with this." Evette looked into the man's warm brown eyes. "I just need to get out of here before he comes back."

"Ma'am I have an office right off the stairwell door to the left. Go there and lock the door behind you. I'm off in about thirty minutes." The man's eyes were kind even if his face was stern.

"Thank you," she told him as he helped her down the last few steps.

Evette had done as she was instructed and waited for the old man in the Janitor's office. She didn't know why but she had a reassuring feeling she could trust him. Maybe it was the anger that was evident on his face at what had been done to her, or the lack of peppering questions of how she found herself in this situation, either way, the man had offered her safety and that was enough for now.

True to his word, the man came back to his office nearly thirty minutes later. He was holding a sandwich and a cold compress for her face. Evette flinched away when he tried to doctor her, but eventually succumbed to the gesture. The cool compress against the heat of the already swollen eye made the tears flow uncontrollably.

"Oh none of that now." The old man petted her hair trying to calm her. "I know you have been through a lot. It's going to be okay. We will figure this out."

"Nothing is ever going to be okay again." Evette sobbed, coming to the same realization she had when she woke up in this terrible nightmare.

"It might not look like it now but mark my words, you survived, and you will continue to do so." the man knelt down in front of her.

"How can you be so sure?" Evette's pleading eyes begged for answers only the universe had.

"Because I was once in your shoes." The man cleared his throat. "Well sort of. I was a medic in the Army. One night out on patrol, I got jumped. I fought tooth and nail but there were more of them than there were me. The guys that were supposed to watch my back let it happen to prove something. I don't know what, but when the smoke cleared, I looked as bad if not worse than you do. Here I am 50 years later." The man shrugged at the story.

"My name is Evette."

"Nice to meet you. I'm Jack, but everyone calls me Jackie." He offered her a small smile. "Now, how do we get you out of this little pickle?"

They had sat in the office for nearly an hour while Evette gained a little strength. Jackie hadn't forced her to tell him what had happened, and she was grateful for that. He did, however, tell her stories of growing up in a small town in Texas and being in the Military. He gave some much needed advice on how to avoid being found, and what her next steps should be.

He smiled when she told him her car was an old 1990s model. As he put it, those cars didn't have a tracking system and she could disappear like smoke through a keyhole if she really wanted to. He told her if anyone came looking for a missing woman, he would make sure to send them in the wrong direction with an evil glint in his eye. Jackie had also agreed to drive her to get her car, and follow her out of town in case anything happened.

After they had left the hotel, Evette remained vigilant of her surroundings. She was constantly looking over her shoulder waiting for Xander or someone else to jump out and grab her. She held onto the bat as the only life line she currently had until she was safely in Jackie's old truck. While Jackie had taken her bags and placed them in the bed, Evette fidgeted in the seat.

"Are you alright?" Jackie could understand her being scared but she looked like she was going to combust at any moment.

"Sorry, it's just that I get very nervous when someone else is driving."

"In light of what has happened, I would call you crazy if you weren't. Now, which way am I headed?" Jackie offered her a reassuring smile as they drove out of the parking lot.

Thankfully, it had only been a twenty minute ride to the site. Evette hadn't realized she was so close to her car and her freedom. It wasn't until she had seen the turn off to the Cason Groups digging site that she let herself breathe a sigh of relief. She hoped Xander hadn't known where her car was and gotten to it first.

While Jackie did cut his eyes toward her when she instructed him to turn, he never said a word as he drove. He figured the worst that could happen was being held up for his truck and having to walk back into the town on his bum knee. Hell for him that would be a welcomed adventure. It had been a minute since he had a good shake down, he mused to himself.

Evette had a smile spread from ear to ear as they approached the gate. Her bright blue Corsica sat there welcoming the dawn of a new day. She instructed Jackie to pull over so the building's cameras didn't pick him or the truck up. She painfully hopped down from the truck, using the bat more like a cane now, and hobbled over to the fence. She kept her hood up, so she wouldn't be recognized if they rolled the cameras back.

Since the opener was in the work truck, Evette had to get creative. She ended up using the bat to pry the gate open enough to fit through but not enough to damage it. If she hadn't had to do it a dozen or more times in her life, Evette might have been more worried about the fit, but alas she knew exactly what she was doing.

Once she got to the other side, Evette did a quick walk around making sure her car hadn't been touched. Relieved everything was as she had left it, she made her way to the driver's seat and pulled the keys from the sun visor. As the beauty came to life, she wasted no time in getting out of there. She had been lucky up to this point, and hoped her luck would not soon run out.

Jackie had followed her down to the gas station at the turn off. He made sure that her car had gotten filled up before he sent her on her way. Jackie had instructed her not to get out of the car, while he walked in and paid in cash so they couldn't track her by the credit card transaction. If all the years in the Military had taught him anything, it was how to get around hiding in plain sight.

Once her car was filled, he walked over to her window. "You remember what I told you. They could be watching your movements. Pay for as many things as you can in cash. Please be careful." Jackie bent down and gently gave her a hug. "Oh and get rid of that cell phone as soon as possible. They might not be able to track your car but they can that phone."

"Thank you." Evette's voice was small.

"I lost a daughter once because of an asshole like this. I won't see another woman lose her life on my watch. You take care of yourself, ya hear." Jackie had tears pricking the back of his eyes. He took one last look at her before he walked back to his truck.

"Wait, what was her name?" Evette called out the window.

"Piper," he called over his shoulder as he climbed back into his truck and drove away.

Evette wouldn't let the tears fall as she pointed her car north. She would do as Jackie had told her and gather as much cash as she could. Thankfully, the banks didn't open for several hours and by the time anyone had seen the transactions, she would be headed in the opposite direction.

Evette thought it would be nice to see if she could find that small town where Jackie had grown up. Maybe it was still the picturesque place he had described, and she could lay low for a little bit until she could plan her next move. She didn't like flying by the seat of her pants but now she found herself doing just that.

No one told her that running away would feel like this. Terrifying, exhilarating, and freeing all at the same time. She had never felt like this even when she had left for college. Her path was now unknown without any real structure or expectations. Evette was sure the families, if not Xander, himself, would eventually come looking for her. After all, she was a loose end he would eventually have to tie up.

It had been three days since she had left New Mexico with nearly thirty thousand dollars drained out of six different accounts. She had driven day and night, only stopping a few hours here and there for rest and food. The more distance she had put between her and the other life, the better her clarity, giving her room to breathe. Her anxiety, though, gave her panic attacks if anyone even looked like someone she may or may not know.

Evette was still unrecognizable. Even after three days, her face was swollen beyond recognition. Yellow, purple, and bluish hues painted her body from head to toe. Evette was also certain she had at least one broken rib on her right side. Although everything in her screamed for her to seek medical attention, it would only be a matter of time before someone called the cops and they reached out to her family. She would deal with the pain, but that seemed to be all she could handle.

When she had finally found the town Jackie had told her about, she was happy. A little nowhere place between her and the border. They wouldn't come looking for her here, not when everything she had done pointed out she had gone north. They would chase their tails for a little while, and she would relish in knowing she would never be found. Her only regret at the time was her not switching her car, though she had been sure none of them knew her tag number.

Blowing into town happened to be the easy part. Finding a place to stay deemed to be a little more tricky. It wasn't until she had found a little diner on the edge of town that her wish had come true. Sitting in the quiet booth, Evette contemplated what her next move would be.

"Hard day?" a brunette woman, who looked to be in her late thirties early forties, asked not looking up from her notepad.

"You could say that." Evette squirmed trying to get comfortable pain evident in her voice.

Evette's tone caught her off guard, making her look up. She gasped, "Honey, what happened to you?"

"Would you believe the other guy looks worse?" Evette tried to crack a joke.

"Does he?"

"Nope," she painfully giggled.

"Oh lord. What can I get you?"

"Cup of coffee and some information."

"What do you need to know, honey?"

"Where can a woman hide in a small town like this?"

CHAPTER 5
EYES THAT NEVER LIE

The motel the waitress had directed Evette to wasn't anything special but it was at least clean with multiple locks on the doors. Ralphy, the owner, seemed to like things quiet, and that's what she needed more than anything. He didn't ask questions either; he just took the money and handed her the room key.

The first night, Evette didn't sleep at all. She sat on the end of the queen size bed clutching the metal bat to her chest, staring at the door. The curtains were pulled tight, but she could still see shadows of people walking past her room. Every noise made her so jumpy, she couldn't even bear to have the T.V. on. For her, even the silence was too loud.

The rhythmic ticking of the old clock that hung on the green wallpapered walls seemed to soothe her, putting her into a trance. As her eyes grew heavy and her body began to relax, the clock gently rang out, startling her back to the room and the reality she found herself in. When the clock struck midnight, Evette saw more shadows move across the wall and loud voices she couldn't quite make out. Though she was sure she'd locked all the doors, Evette began to shake. She had been absolutely certain she had not only been found, but Ralphy had told whoever had come to collect her which room she was actually in.

Evette didn't know if she had the strength to fight off another attack. She rose from the bed as quietly as possible and made a run for the bathroom, hiding in the tub. Her plan was simple and slightly irrational. If someone had entered her room and seen she wasn't there, they might tear the place apart but leave when they found nothing but her bag. If they happened into the bathroom and pulled back the curtain, she would hit whomever hard with the bat and make a run for her car. Hoping to get as far away as she possibly could.

Evette didn't know what time she had finally passed out. Her concern was more of the mind numbing pain that was her broken body curled into a ball holding the bat in the bathtub. Tears fell like a waterfall as she attempted to stretch her locked body. The only thought that played in her mind, *Was this really to be my life now?*

Three times now, she'd almost died, and no one had noticed or cared. She had not succumbed to her injuries. Though with the surge of pain that electrified her body, Evette was beginning to believe she would be better off if she had. The world would be better off without her in it, and she knew at least one or even more people that would be overjoyed at the news. After all, she was pretty sure she was worth more dead than alive. What other reason would Xander have to almost kill her?

Coaxing herself out of the tub, Evette strained every fiber of her sanity. It took several moments before she could stand steady on her feet before she settled herself in front of the sink. Looking into the mirror, Evette didn't recognize the woman staring back at her. It was more than the bruises, the swollen eyes, and disheveled hair. Evette looked hollow. A robot going through the motions with only the fear and pain to prove she was human.

"I'm not giving up on you," she squeaked at the woman in the mirror. "This isn't over for us yet. He might of broken us, but he doesn't get to win. Not now, not fucking ever."

A stoic resolve settled on her as she grabbed a wash rag, and gently tried to wash the dried blood away. She was determined to do what she could to stay as far away from Xander Hulston and anyone in New Mexico. She didn't care if she had to change her appearance and fly under the radar. She would do the one thing he wasn't banking on her doing. LIVE.

Sitting on the side of his king size bed, Nicky Valence held his head in his hands, thankful for the black out curtains on his windows. His head pounded from the drunken stupor he endured the night before. He didn't remember how he had gotten talked into bar hopping by his second in command, but Dom seemed to be not only motivated but also very persistent. He had only gone to keep his buddy out of trouble. Or at least that's what he would tell himself.

In all actuality, Nicky had more important things on his mind than booze and women. Even though he seemed to find himself waist deep in both, he was grateful this morning he hadn't woken up with a stranger in his bed. Nicky had actually hoped that the night's events would have produced more information on the new woman in town.

Rhonda, a waitress down at the diner, had called Nicky a few days prior over a matter he needed to be aware of. Since the Valence family basically ran the town, she didn't want anyone thinking the diner had allowed something like this to happen. Everyone knew who the muscle was and what would happen if anyone caused a brawl. They kept everything quiet and running smoothly, just the way Don Valence liked it.

Nicky had found it odd that no one seemed to have any information on this woman. They had a vague description, and she looked like she had gone a couple rounds with someone's fists. Nicky understood Rhonda's concern as they hadn't had many drifters roll through over the years. Especially not ones that looked like they were on the run.

Rhonda had told him she was very skittish and kept to herself when she came to get something to eat. She had directed the woman over to the motel, and called Ralphy to let him know she was coming. Thankfully, his cousin not only respected his guests' privacy, but also preferred to be paid in cash. Above all, he had a soft spot for women that had the courage to get themselves out of life threatening situations.

Nicky had seen her in passing, but hadn't paid much attention to her. She had always worn an oversized hoodie with the hood up to hide her face. Since that seemed to be the style with most of the teenagers, Nicky didn't think twice. When he saw her at the market that Thursday, it was her crystal blue eyes that had drawn his attention. Something about her made him want to know more about her story, putting him on the hunt for her routine.

There had been reports of a woman showing up at a few of the bars in town. She always kept to herself, and barely said two words if she wasn't ordering a drink. Nicky knew right away this was how he would get close enough to her to talk. Hence the reason he allowed himself to get talked into the massive hangover he had that morning. The only place they hadn't stopped at on Dom's quest to drink his way through town was the Dustbowl Bar and Grill. Which meant he either had overlooked her presence at one of the other bars, she had been at the one bar they hadn't gone to, or she hadn't gone out at all last night. Nicky would have to switch up his tactics if they happened to go out that evening.

Knock... Knock... Knock... Nicky glared at the door, hoping if he didn't say anything whoever was on the other side would go away.

"I know you're in there." Dom's voice was way too cheerful for someone who drank two fifths of Jack the night before.

"Go the hell away." Nicky's voice made his own head split.

"I have food and a bloody mary." Dom attempted a singsong voice. Nicky half heartedly admitted defeat walking to the door. "There's my boss."

"Go to hell." Nicky grabbed the drink and the breakfast burrito that was offered.

"Oh someone got up on the wrong side of the bed, or is it the lack of someone else in it that has you grumbling today?" Dom knew all the right buttons to push to gain the middle finger reaction.

"What has you so damn chipper this morning?" Nicky took a healthy gulp of the drink.

"Besides the blonde that already crawled out of my bed? I have news on the mystery woman you are so keen to speak to." Dom bounced on the balls of his feet like a happy toddler.

"What makes you think I want to talk to her?" Nicky said, making his way into the kitchen, which was entirely too bright.

"You can play a lot of people, brother, but alas I am not one of them. I know the reason you let me jump from bar to bar, and it wasn't because you needed a night out." Dom poked the bear awaiting his reaction. "What is it about this chick that has you in such a tizzy?"

Resting on the kitchen island, Nicky let out a heavy sigh, "I don't know. I honestly don't have a damn clue why I need to know about her. It's just something in my gut that is telling me she is in some sort of trouble."

"You know you can't save them all." Dom's face fell with the realization of why Nicky was doing this.

"I don't know what you're talking about." His voice went low as his eyes went dark.

"She isn't Gia." Dom's voice went flat.

Nicky rounded on him. "I told you a thousand times, nothing I do has anything to do with her. Now, what have you found out?"

"Personally, I think this might be something you need to see with your own two eyes."

A solemness had fallen over the men, spoiling at least one of their moods before leaving for the bar. Nicky was trying hard not to think about Gia or the fact he failed to save her. But when his hands were tied by the family and the law, all he had left was the guilt. It ate at him like a cancer he couldn't treat or remove.

The dark cloudy sky mirrored the turmoil that brewed within Nicky's mind and body. As they were leaving the house, the rain fell in misty sheets and the gusting winds blew cold. Both seemed to cut through the men like a knife, seeping into their bones. Dom accepted it was just that time of the year. Nicky, on the other hand, debated on aborting the mission, staying home to drink himself into oblivion.

He didn't know if it was Dom's smug attitude, about not giving him any information, or his pride, but he needed to know more. Nicky couldn't stand any man that thought he could put his hands on a woman, and if it was within his power, whoever had done this would be dealt with in the most creative way possible. He couldn't save the world but it would never stop him from trying.

Nicky had allowed Dom to drive to the bar. Citing, if he wasn't going to do his job, he could at least be useful to him. In reality, Nicky didn't trust himself to not make a run for the border. There was something about going to see this mystery woman that put him on edge. Maybe it was nothing, but with all the reports he had received, she was on the run from someone or something. It was his duty, as his grandfather's enforcer, to find out which.

Pulling up outside the newly remodeled Dustbowl Bar and Grill, the rain fell harder with a clap of thunder off in the distance. Climbing out of the old truck, Nicky's murderous expression mirrored the strengthening storm. Flipping up his hood to cover his already drenched hair, Nicky turned to look out over the open desert. It had been a while since rain had come through like this and the desert desperately needed a good soaking rain to keep it from burning. In the mood he found himself in, Nicky didn't care in the least if everything went up in flames. Hoping whatever rose from the ashes would be better than the world he currently found himself. Rain washed away while fire cauterized the wound.

Dom climbed out of the truck and looked around at the full parking lot, hoping that the crowd wouldn't have deterred the mystery guest from showing up. Making his way toward the door, he smiled at the poster plastered on the side of the building for a live band that night. It wasn't often bands came rolling through town but the bar took full advantage of it when they did. This would normally draw crowds from two to three towns away, and from the looks of it, this night was no different. The smile spread into a grin when he caught sight of one car backed into a spot, a car without Texas tags.

When the bouncer saw the two men approach, he nodded and held open the door. The sounds that came bellowing out of the building told the men that this might be a little more difficult than they intended. After all, no one liked having a conversation if they had to shout over a screaming guitar. On the other hand, it might make it easier for Nicky to get close to her. There was only one way to know for sure. Walking past the bouncer and through the set of saloon swinging doors, they found themself among a sea of bodies.

Most of the locals, who recognized the two men when they came in, split like the Red Sea. Nicky quickly took the path to the bar, while scanning the room. He was happy to see Val was bartending that night. Nicky knew if there was any information to be had, Val would be quick to share. It also didn't help that Val had basically raised him until he was a teenager.

"There's my boys." Her booming voice warmed even Nicky's cold heart. "What will it be tonight?"

"Jack and Coke," Dom shouted, moving from behind Nicky to take the only available stool.

"Do you think your liver will handle it?" Val shot back, starting to make the drink.

"What's that supposed to mean?" Dom feigned shock and surprise.

"I heard about the bar crawl last night, boy. You know nothing gets around here without me knowing about it." Val slid the drink over to him. "Starting a tab or pay as you go?"

"Tab." Dom grabbed up the drink and swigged half down in one gulp.

Val shook her head at him, knowing he was going to be a handful if he kept drinking like that on her watch. "What do you need, Nicky?"

"Rum and Coke...." His voice tailed off, looking around the room. "And some information."

"On what exactly?" Val kept her hands busy making the drink for him.

"The new woman in town." His voice went low so only she could hear him.

"You mean the one at the other end of the bar?" Val slid the drink to him.

Nicky looked up to see a semi well dressed woman in a graphic hoodie with the hood pulled up over her head. "That'd be the one."

"She's sipping 1990 Vintage Highland Park Limited, which is keeping most of the assholes away. The few that wander up to her get shut down quickly without her even looking up from her glass."

"She ever take the hood off?"

"Not really. The other night she did when one guy wouldn't leave her alone, but it went right back on after he had seen her face." Val's voice tightened. "I don't know who hurt her, but whoever did, needs to be taken out behind the woodshed."

Nicky knew exactly what Val ment. She didn't mince words and that was one of the things Nicky loved about her. Well, that and her momma bear mentality. Val was one of those old southern women that would "bless your heart" in more than one way. He hoped tonight she wouldn't be going momma bear on him over the young woman.

"How many has she had?" Nicky was looking for a way to strike up a conversation.

"First one of the night is in her hand." Val looked down at the end of the bar. "And she is looking a little low."

"Start my tab. Even if I can't get her to talk to me, she won't pay for another drink tonight."

Val smiled at Nicky's words, and tilted her head for him to move it along.

It took him several minutes to make it from one side of the bar to the other. Between the drones of people trying to get a drink and retreating back to the tables, Nicky had been bumped into nearly five times and almost dropped his drink once. All his resolve was being tested and he was trying to save it for a brooding young lady.

There were three stools next to her when he finally found himself close enough. Her scent had been more intoxicating than the drink in his hand, which caught him off guard. His mind began to swirl with where he would like that scent to be, but had to quickly shut himself down. Of all the times for his libido to start stirring, now was not the time.

She sensed him behind her, as he was standing there far too long to not want something. "Whatever you're going to ask, the answer is No!"

Nicky settled himself down on the stool two away from her. "How do you know I'm going to ask anything?"

"Because you're not the first to venture to this side of the bar tonight, and I suspect you won't be the last." She grabbed her glass and gulped down the rest of the amber liquid, signaling for another.

"Why don't you let me buy you another drink?" Nicky scooted over closer to her.

"Look man, I am in no mood to get drunk, roofied, or whatever else you might have up your sleeve. I merely want to drown my sorrows in peace." She looked up slightly but still wouldn't make eye contact.

"It looks like you're in trouble, and I can help."

"What makes you think I want or need your help?" The anger in her voice seemed to stab right into Nicky's heart.

"I've been checking you out. New in town, paying cash for everything, keeping to yourself. Now, that leads me to believe two things." Nicky paused for a moment as Val placed another drink down in front of them. "Thanks Val." Nicky smiled and turned his attention back to the young woman. "Now, as I was saying. This leads me to two things. You're on the run and you don't want to be found. But you give yourself away."

"How so?" She turned to him this time letting him see more of her face.

"Not many people around here can afford top shelf whiskey, let alone drink it."

Evette hadn't taken into account that her habits could give her away. The anger as well as the naiveness caused the tears to prick her eyes. She didn't know if this was her sign to leave or not but she took it as such. Standing from the stool, Evette reached into her pocket to throw some money up on the bar.

"Where do you think you're going?" Nicky spun on his stool to face her.

"Back to my room, and then down the road tomorrow." Evette's voice was raw with emotion.

"When will you stop running?" Nicky reached out and grabbed her wrist before she had time to jump into the sea of people.

"That is not an appropriate question to ask a lady you've just met." Evette glared daggers at him, but had to admit this stranger was the man of her dreams. She couldn't believe it, and certainly wouldn't allow herself to jump into another red flag relationship after what she had already been through. Even if his slicked-back jet black hair begged for her to touch it, his warm chocolate brown eyes disarmed her, and his strong capable hands kept her rooted to spot.

"It might not be an appropriate question, but it's my question nonetheless." Nicky couldn't let her leave, not like this anyway. She was emotional and he feared she would do something more rash than just leaving town.

"It's one I don't have to answer. Not to you or anyone." She tried to pull her wrist from his grasp but Nicky tightened it, sending shivers she had never experienced before down to her core.

"Your name then." Nicky was grasping at any and all straws to get her to stay at the bar with him.

"If I gave you my name, what would you do with it? Run back and try to find where I really came from?" She reached up, pulling down the hood, hoping he would be like the last.

Nicky's eyes went as dark as a sky with no moon, which pitched Evette's stomach once again. "I would make sure, if anyone came looking for you, they wouldn't have a tongue to speak your name."

"Evette. Evette Cason." Her voice was small barely above a whisper in the loud bar.

"Now was that so hard?" He loosened his grip but didn't dare let her go.

"Look you might think I'm being paranoid, but the truth is I'm worth a lot more dead than alive. Or at least that's what a certain someone seemed to think."

"He's the one that did that to your face?" Nicky's voice was smoldering.

"Wasn't just my face." Her voice was cold as she yanked her wrist from his grip.

Nicky caught her hand, reaching for the sleeve. Evette tried to stop him, but he had already pulled it up, seeing the restraint marks. His grip tightened on her hand. It was worse than he had imagined. She hadn't just been beaten, she had been tortured.

"Where is the bastard?" Nicky had an ominous look in his eyes.

56

"A long way away from here and me." Tears welled in her eyes as she tried to push down all the emotions. "So, I suppose you want to ask me how I escaped." Evette climbed back on to the stool, putting her hood back in place.

After several hours and what seemed like a whole bottle of tequila, Evette had opened up about every single thing about her life up to that day. She was very careful not to mention Xander's name or the Hulston family at all. Evette had kept it to the facts and the bare minimum at that. She didn't know if she could trust anyone, but if Nicky was just going to be someone she happened upon in passing, what harm would there be?

It didn't take long before Dom had joined them on the other side of the bar. He had kept his distance as long as he possibly could, but he was nosey and there had already been a slight altercation from where he had been sitting. It didn't take him long to catch up on the details, which promoted him to start asking questions. "You had time to call the police. Why didn't you? I mean, we wouldn't have but that's us. You look like the kind of girl that the cops would come for."

"Probably because both his and my family have money. Things like this look bad in the press." Evette threw back another shot, and through a raspy voice, "It didn't matter who was going to bury it, it was just going to get buried. Scandals aren't becoming of two oil tycoons like Larry Cason and John Hulston."

"Why would you want to put yourself through something like that?" Nicky was trying to keep her talking while the drinks were flowing.

"You act like I had a choice. I was brought up in that world. The perfect little Debutant went to college to become a geologist to work at her father's company. I was going to marry the man not only my family approved of but thought loved me. Then I find out 10 fucking days before my wedding to that asshole, he's been fucking around on me since day one. Can you fucking believe this shit?"

57

"Okay... Okay... So, what made him flip the script?" Dom leaned in wanting to know the answer just as much if not more than Nicky at this point.

"I told him no. I was raised, not until marriage. No one is going to buy the cow if they get the milk for free, my mother would say." Evette drunkenly mimicked her mother. "He knew my stance on it, as he had tried several times. He brought me to this nasty ass hotel room out on the edge of town by the airport under the guise of our flight being delayed and this was closer to the airport. He made a move and when I told him no, this wasn't happening -BAM... I went ass over tea cups over the bed and hit my head against the wall."

"That's some shit." Dom looked at Nicky flabbergasted by the story.

"I know right. Hey ma'am can I get another drink please." Evette's words slurred, politely calling Val over.

"Honey, I think you have had enough. I can get you water or even a coke but I'm sorry darling I have to cut you off." Val looked at her sympathetically but glared a murderous look at the two men that sat there. She should have cut her off when she had noticed the boys had stopped drinking as quickly as she was. "Y'all should be ashamed of yourselves."

"Oh, don't be mad at them," Evette pleaded. "I could of said no."

"Honey, I think you should go home and get some rest." Val patted her hand. "I'll call you a cab."

"No need Val. I'll get her home alright." Nicky spoke up. "I messed up. I'll fix it."

The look on her face spoke volumes, and Nicky had no intention of getting his ass handed to him by a 5'6" Italian woman. All she had to do was call his grandfather, and Nicky had no intention of dealing with that old man either. He would be on his best behavior even if it killed him.

"How am I supposed to get my car back to my room?" Evette cocked an eyebrow at Nicky.

"You're not going back to the motel. You're coming back to my house." Nicky said so matter of factly.

"I'm not sleeping with you." She crossed her arms in defiance.

"Good. I don't sleep with drunk women." Nicky fired back causing coke to come out of Dom's nose.

"Why are you being so infuriating?" She looked at him with a childish pout on her face, arms still crossed as she leaned into him.

"Because I can't let you walk away without knowing you'll be okay. So, I'm going to take you home, get you fixed up, and figure it out from there. You can pout at me all you want, but I'm your best option, and you already know that." Nicky prayed he could invoke that kind of reaction out of her, when she was sober. "Dom will drive your car back. You'll ride in the truck with me."

Evette stood to protest, getting ready to jab her finger into his well muscled chest. Unfortunately, the world started spinning, the clouds rolled in, and she fainted into Nicky's waiting arms. She played right into his hand, and he was more than happy about it. Picking her up bridal style, Nicky carried her to the truck calling over his shoulder to Dom to pay their tabs. She had a fire still in her and Nicky welcomed the challenge in bringing the flames back to life.

CHAPTER 6
RISING FROM THE ASHES

It had been weeks since Evette had met Nicky and Dom in the Dustbowl Bar and Grill. She cringed remembering that night along with the first time she had ever tasted tequila. The hangover the next morning had her praying to the porcelain gods for death as the two men joked about her doing better than they did their first time. This didn't comfort her. In fact it made her feel like crawling into a deep dark hole never to be seen again.

She had no idea what she was doing that night. She didn't even understand how she ended up spilling her guts little by little until she had thrown caution to the wind. Evette had sworn to herself she would never drink like that again. All she wanted to do was drown her pain and attempt to figure out what her next steps would be, alas that was not what she had gotten that night.

Evette still didn't know who she could trust or if the same thing that Xander had done would happen again. Needless to say, she was weary of every man that crossed her path, but somehow Nicky and Dom were different. They had kept watch over her safety and wellbeing with Nicky staying true to his word of being on his best behavior. Her life had been turned upside down by Xander and now finding herself hidden on the Valence family estate made her whole world spin out of orbit.

Waiting to figure out what the next steps would be for Evette, both men gathered any and all information on not only who she actually was but also the family she was due to marry into. Nicky had a hard time equating the prim and proper little princess on paper to the spitfire in front of him. He had seen his fair share of young women going wild once they had slipped the bonds of their controlling families. Evette didn't seem to fit that mold, though. More of a gilded bird finally released from their cage.

While neither wanted to rush her recovery or her decision on what would be next for her, time was passing faster than both men could control. They knew it was only a matter of time before Don Valence would make the discovery, and start asking questions about the woman that seemed to be shacked up with them. Not wanting her reputation compromised in anyone's eyes, they needed to come up with a course of action quickly.

When Evette had emerged from her room, she still seemed a little confused about her whereabouts. The bruises had faded and according to the family doctor, the broken ribs and cheekbone were healing better than he had hoped for a woman that fled with those kinds of injuries. It hurt Nicky greatly hearing every detail from the doctor. He wanted to find the bastard that did this to her and teach them the proper way to treat a woman. Xander Hulston would pay with his life for the damage he caused.

Nicky was impressed she hadn't given the time old excuse of falling down the stairs or walking into a door. She had been up front about how it had happened with little to no persuasion for information. It was only with the alcohol she had given the nitty gritty details. The only bit of information she hadn't given up right away was the name of the asshole that had laid his hands on her. A few drinks later, Evette had given up the last name. Which led the men into a deep dive for information.

Nicky had understood why she had been apprehensive to give up that tidbit of information, but to him, it felt to be much more than her not knowing him well enough. The look of panic in her eyes when he had grabbed her wrist spoke volumes, but the words were too distorted to understand their meaning.

She was afraid of being returned to him. Nicky couldn't blame her for that. Even the thought of someone telling him where she was or was headed, had Evette pacing the floors of her room not sleeping for long each night. When she would sleep, the nightmares had her screaming herself and them awake. The questions that seemed to plague both Nicky and Dom's minds, were more of how to help her. The two felt ill equipped to handle the situation, but wouldn't give up on her.

It was the laughter radiating from the kitchen that drew Evette from her room. She loved the relaxed nature of their mornings, and wished she could understand their dynamics better. Looking at the two men, she had realized something very important, and made her long for what they had.

She had never truly had friends. Even now with her being gone nearly a month, no one was looking for her. No one cared if she lived or died, but these two men had opened their home and lives to a complete stranger. It probably helped that she was female, but Evette would like to think it was more. If anyone had crossed their path in the same condition as she was in, they would help.

Evette stood in the doorway for a few minutes watching the men banter back and forth. For the first time in a long time, she felt at peace. Evette had contemplated if this was what a family truly was. She had grown up in a very sheltered environment compared to the chaos she found herself in now, and wondered if this was always the way it was supposed to be.

Her bright smile drew the men's attention from their animated conversation. Dom had jumped up from the table offering his seat to Evette, as Nicky went to the counter to make her a cup of coffee. "Cream and sugar?"

"Yes, please." Evette eased herself down into the chair offered. While the wounds had healed, the small pricks of pain still remained, reminding her she was still alive.

"I'm sorry if we woke you up." Dom tried to show concern through the giggles he still had rolling out.

"No, I was already awake."

"How are you feeling this morning?" Nicky handed her the mug, searching her face for any clues. "The bruises are healing nicely. Thankfully, the cut on your face won't leave a scar." Nicky said, running his knuckles so feather light over her cheek, sending shivers through her body.

Evette hadn't felt that buzz of electricity before, not even with Xander. It had been so long, she couldn't remember if Ethan had stirred that kind of reaction from her. It pained her to think of Ethan and what his thoughts would be on the current situation if he was still here. How different her life would have been had he not died that night?

Pulling her attention back to the table, Evette looked at the two men who now flanked her at the breakfast table. "So, what was so funny?"

"Kris decided he had had enough of Mark putting things in his morning coffee. So he decided to get even and well lets just say the prank went spectacularly horribly wrong." Dom couldn't stop laughing as he gave the gist of the conversation.

"What had he done?" Evette sipped from her mug, settling in to hear the gossip.

"Kris? Well, he took it upon himself to add something extra to the creamer only Mark uses in the house, and now Mark can't get five feet from the bathroom without having to change his clothes."

"Oh my god." Evette gasped. "How long has this been going on?"

"I don't know. Nicky, it has been about six or seven months?"

"Maybe even longer. The guys will call a truce for a bit then bam here we go again." Nicky laughed at all the pranks the two had pulled on each other over the years.

"Boys..." Evette rolled her eyes thinking of all the times her brother's friends had done the exact same thing to him and the one time to her by accident.

Evette had sat quietly as the two chatted back and forth. She tried to keep up with the conversation but not knowing any of the people involved, she had little input she could give. She hadn't noticed that Nicky was staring at her intently watching her every move, while Dom went off on another train of thought. It all felt too surreal and almost normal to be sitting here like this was any other day.

"So, Evette." Nicky began not breaking eye contact. "What's the next step for you?"

"I don't know what you mean. There was honestly never any plan other than putting as much distance as I could between me and New Mexico. My grandfather used to say if you need to lay low, you head for Mexico. He was a big westerns kind of man. So, I headed south." Evette absently played with the mug in her hands.

"Well, the way I see it you have two choices. Or at least two that will keep you safe."

"And those are?" Evette placed the mug down on the table, looking directly at Nicky. His intense eyes were telling a story, she didn't understand just yet.

"We can let you heal up some more. I can get into contact with a few associates that will change your identity. We set you up in a safe house far from here, probably on the east coast. Then rebuild your life, living happily ever after under our protection."

"Option 2?" Evette's heart sank at the thought of him not wanting her around.

"Option 2 is you stay here with us. We still change your identity and you work for me. I can tell you have some talents that would be of great use to the family. You're obviously educated, debutant level manners, and with a little training you could be much more." Nicky leaned in dangerously close.

"What's in it for you?" Evette crossed her arms and looked intrigued by the offer.

"Well..." Nicky side eyed Dom. "I have a grandfather that has it in his head that I need to settle down. You would play my decoy, while becoming part of my crew."

"What would come with playing decoy?" Evette's face hardened.

"Since no one knows who you are and where you came from, other than a few people that I have under my control, it really should be relatively easy. After all, I travel quite a bit for work."

"What about those that have already seen me? People are going to talk and I'm sure word gets around faster here than in high society." Evette worried it was out of the frying pan and into the fire with this plan.

"Ralphy, the owner of the motel, is my cousin. His father, Ralph, is from my grandfather's third marriage. He's given a living but is kept FAR from the family business. He's a good guy but not ruthless enough. While he is the eyes and ears of the town, he understands the meaning of privacy and wouldn't dare go against me. Val, on the other hand, took care of us when we were kids. She has a momma bear mentality that would cause even the Don to shake in his designer suits. Needless to say, no one would say a word. Plus, you look completely different from the first few days you spent in town. Most wouldn't even make the connection."

Evette sat back for a moment evaluating her options. On one hand, she dreaded the thought of walking away from Dom and Nicky. They had shown her kindness and protected her. On the other hand, Evette had no idea how to live a life, where she hadn't been told every step of what she was going to do for the rest of it. She was terrified of the unknown that both options gave her, but with option B, she had two men that would protect her at any and all cost, or so she hoped.

"Do you really think anyone is going to believe we are together? And what happens when people find out the truth? This could get very messy very quickly. On top of the fact, my family and or ex could be looking for me. A public relationship could expose both of us quickly." Evette pointed out some of the kinks in the plan.

"You let me handle that one. Are you in or out?" Nicky's piercing gaze couldn't read the turmoil that was brewing within her mind.

After several minutes of silence, Evette finally said, "In."

"The key to hiding your identity is well documented online", or at least that is what Nicky had told Evette when they started down this rabbit hole. He had explained every facet of her new identity and personality. From where she had come from to her family being long gone, no detail would be left to chance and no question unanswered if asked. Nicky had been thorough, and for good reason. Don Valence could spot someone trying to pull the wool over his eyes from a mile away.

Convincing the old man was going to be the hard part. He didn't like women working in this area of expertise, and for good reason. Even on tame days or contracts, things could go sideways quickly, leaving someone holding the bag, and others mourning the loss of a fallen brother. On the rare occasion situations spilled over into everyday family life and someone got hurt, Don Valence took it upon himself to ruthlessly handle the offender. Nicky had to skirt the line between keeping the Don in the dark about his movements, and still keeping up appearances.

It didn't take long before the three were gathered around the table looking at all the documents that would give Evette a new lease on life.

"You need a new name." Nicky looked up from filling out the last of the paperwork.

"We could just call her Evie or Eva. It would keep with her original name and make it easier for the transition." Dom leaned over Nicky's shoulder.

"No, it's too close. Someone from the outside might still catch on to it." Nicky looked to Evette for a decision.

"Piper," she blurted out, thinking about Jackie and remembering the patch on his shirt. "Piper Johnson."

"Talk about way left field." Dom snorted. "I like it."

"Okay. Welcome to the family, Piper," Nicky snorted.

"Happy to be here." She smiled, walking over to the counter to pour her another cup of coffee.

"Okay, now that's settled. We have one more problem that needs to be handled." Nicky side eyed Dom, while filling out the rest of the papers.

"What's that?" Piper looked at him with a bit of confusion, wondering what detail they had left out.

"Your car. It's going to have to make a disappearing act to be found or straight up sold. Either way it needs to be far away from here and you." Nicky sat back in his chair. They had left the car at the motel as a decoy on the off chance anyone came through looking for her. Ralphy had been slipped a couple of extra bucks for the extra work and information.

"Bring me the title out of the glovebox. I'll sign it and you can do what you think is best with it." Piper sighed heavily. That car was the first thing she had bought herself that set her apart from her family. She understood that small detail would give her away, but she didn't have to like it.

67

Nicky nodded. It wasn't going to be an easy transition. He could see that from a mile away. It didn't take any time at all before he had finished everything up, and left to drop off the papers. While he was gone, Dom and Piper had unexpected visitors. Two tall, older men dressed in tailored suits had shown up at the house, looking none too happy about being there.

"Kendrick. Manny. What do I owe the pleasure?" Dom's voice was polite but had lost its usual chipperness.

"Where's Nicky? The Don would like a word with him," Manny had said looking around the living room, spotting Piper sitting at the kitchen table. "Keeping pets now?"

"Pets?" Dom looked confused until he followed his line of sight. "That's no pet. That's Piper Johnson, from Montana Springs. You know the Graves family, Montana Springs."

The two men looked at each other confused. They hadn't been told they were receiving outside visitors from another family.

"What is she doing here then?" Kendrick popped off more skeptical than his partner.

"Nicky picked her up from the airport this morning. Damn, guys don't you talk to each other? Piper was coming into town to handle an exchange. She is supposed to be staying here for a few days." Dom was great at thinking on his feet. While most of Piper's backstory had already been worked out, these details weren't. Though, they hadn't planned on being found out this soon either.

"Why doesn't the Don know anything about this?" Kendrick leaned in a little harder with the questioning.

"I don't know, maybe it slipped his mind to tell you. Either which way, Ms. Johnson doesn't like her morning coffee interrupted. And I think I'm more scared of her than I am of you two." Dom laid it on thick praying he was at least sounding believable.

"Really? Why's that?" Manny spoke up looking at the long legged woman sitting in a tank top and shorts, sipping her coffee.

"Piper is their peacekeeper. She handles the big jobs quietly, leaving the customer satisfied and no witnesses to complain."

"She looks like a stiff breeze would blow her over." Kendrick chuckled.

"Yeah, she does, and that is where she has you over a barrel. Trust me men, that wildcat is just fine sipping her coffee, not bothering a soul." Dom put his hands up playing along with the web of lies he was spinning.

Before the men could open their mouths to make another comment, Manny's phone went off. He had a "your goose is cooked" smile cross his lips and he answered the phone. "Well I guess we will see if you're lying. Yes, boss."

"Did you go to my grandson's house?"

"Yes, Sir. We are currently standing in his living room talking to his flunky." Manny said with a gleam in his eyes. He had never liked Dom, even when he was little.

"Manual! I have told you a thousand times to address Dom with respect. Do we need to have another conversation about it?"

"No, Sir."

"Very good. Now, the reason for this call. A representative of the Graves family is supposed to be arriving shortly. Her name is Piper Johnson. Make sure things are ready for her arrival."

"Sir, she is already here."

"What do you mean, she is already here?" Don Valence's voice strained through the speaker.

"Nicky picked her up from the airport this morning, Don Valence," Dom raised his voice to be heard.

"So, she is there with you?"

"Yes, sir. She is drinking her coffee and relaxing. Nicky had to run an errand in town and will be back shortly. He left me in charge to keep her entertained." Dom eternally smirked and sighed.

Thankfully, Don Graves had agreed to help Nicky out weeks ago. Dom and Nicky did a search and rescue off the books a few months prior, and now they had to cash in the favor that came with it. Hopefully, the little white lie wouldn't come back and bite them in the ass. While their plan had a lot of moving parts, it was staying one or two steps ahead of the old man that would prove whether or not they could pull it all off. They had covered as many bases as they possibly could in a short amount of time.

"Oh well. I suppose we should have a small dinner then. I would like to see the woman that Don Graves speaks so highly of. After all, anyone that can get my grandson out of bed that early in the morning is one to have an audience with," Don Valence spoke with a hint of curiosity in his voice. "I'll send Nicky the details. See you all tonight."

"Great, now we have to go make arrangements with the cook," Kendrick grimaced.

"You don't think the Don isn't already calling her into his office for that?" Manny said, still glaring at Dom. "I don't know what you two think you're pulling here, but I will get to the bottom of this." The two exchanged a look before leaving the house.

As the door closed, Dom let out a shaky breath and proceeded to pull out his phone. Typing out a quick "the vultures are circling" text, Dom looked back at Piper. She had a ruthless nature that was starting to emerge, but her training had just begun. Thankfully, she already had quite a bit of the pleasantries down, being raised in a high society family. Dom worried it wouldn't be enough to keep certain things under wraps.

It had been nearly an hour of Dom pacing the living room before Nicky had returned. All the documents had been put in order. Piper had a birth certificate, a filed social security number, and drivers license. All they needed now was to get through the evening without anyone actually figuring anything out.

Piper sat nervously on the couch as the two men had gone over each and every stage of the plan. They had given her a list of information she had to memorize in a few hours. Everything from the work she had done for Don Graves to her back story. They grilled her for hours leaving nothing to chance.

It wasn't long before Piper had her fill of the men dictating to her over every perceived wrong answer and started firing back. "Dear fucking god. I am doing my best."

"Your best isn't going to be good enough. This has to be perfect." Nicky fired back again after Piper had messed up a small detail. "One wrong answer, one thing out of place, and my grandfather will know."

Piper glared at him. It wasn't that she didn't know what was at stake here. Hell, her life was the one that was on the line. "I don't have a dress for dinner," she blurted out, hoping to get the men off her back.

"In that whole suitcase, you don't have one dress?" Dom looked at the woman in front of him confused.

"Oh I have one dress. But remember I was supposed to be on a trip to Aspen. Not having my whole world turned upside down, beaten within an inch of my life, going on the run, and changing who the hell I am because some jackass thought I would be more beneficial dead than alive. So excuse me if I didn't think to pack a damn evening dress," Piper's crystal eyes shimmered with pain and disgust.

"Oh, I get it. You're trying to weasel your way out of having to practice." Nicky's lips twitched as he had seen what she was trying to do.

"I'm not trying to get out of anything. I am merely trying to play into the image I have inherited. Now, if you want me to show up in a simple cotton dress, and blow the damn cover out of the water, be my fucking guest." Piper hauled herself off the couch and walked to her room, slamming the door.

"You definitely know how to push her buttons," Dom half heartedly laughed, dropping himself down onto the couch.

"Don will do worse. She needs to be prepared." Nicky ran his hands through his hair exasperated by Piper and the situation. He knew it was only a matter of time before someone got curious on why he was staying away from the main house and came looking for him. He thought they had more time to transition Piper into the life. Now everyone was getting a crash course.

"She is right, though. If she shows up in anything less than the perfect dress, everyone is going to know she doesn't belong." Dom looked at the flustered Nicky.

"That's what has me aggravated. She already knows." Nicky knew how high society worked and the cut throat environment it could be. He had been forced to mingle with enough of the men on his grandfather's behalf.

"She's smarter than you're giving her credit for."

"There's just something..." Nicky clenched his hands together.

"That makes you lash out irrationally?" Dom chuckled. "You two are either going to kill each other or end up together. Jury is out on which, but should be interesting to watch."

"None of that. She is going to level us up in the Don's crews. Someone with a diplomatic head for business. Someone that's going to be the whole package." Nicky's voice sounded commanding, as his eyes told a different story.

Dom knew that look in his eyes as he cocked his eyebrow at Nicky. "So, are you going to get her dress or am I?"

"Call Val. Tell her we have an emergency. I'll be there in ten minutes." Nicky turned on his heels, leaving the house for the second time.

CHAPTER 7
SHOWTIME

It had been nearly three hours since Nicky had said a word to Piper, and she had been fuming. How dare he look down his nose at her like that. She wasn't some floozy he rescued off the street. Piper had the upbringing of royalty, or at least high society's version of such. She had been raised to be a proper young lady, and she knew how to conduct herself. Everything else was details, and that was one of many things she was good at, keeping the details straight.

She had been pacing the room in just a towel trying to decide what she would wear that night. She had no formal wear with her, not even one of the pants suits she was made to wear when she happened into the office. Dinner was in less than an hour and Piper was already exasperated by everything. She was so distracted she hadn't heard the knock or the door open. What did catch her attention was the clearing of someone's throat. Piper turned slowly to see Nicky standing in the doorway with an amused look on his face.

"H-how long have you been standing there? Don't you knock?"

"I did. Several times to be exact." Nicky was taking in the full site of her long lush curls hanging wet and loose down her back.

"You didn't answer my question. How long have you been standing there?" she repeated, anger, flushing her skin, turning her tan body almost pink.

"Long enough to know you mutter to yourself when you are frustrated." Nicky smirked, holding out a bag.

Piper walked over to him in defiance. She wouldn't let him see that his perfectly crafted features did anything for her. Even though she was dying inside to have those hands brush her skin at least once. She took the bag and looked inside. "What's this?"

"Your dress for dinner. You were right. If you're going to make the impression we need, you can't come to dinner wearing just anything."

Piper pulled a slinky silk black cocktail dress from the bag and gasped. "Give me one good reason why I should wear this dress."

"Because as one of my employees, you're getting paid too. Now hurry up, we leave in thirty minutes." Nicky's eyes had a wicked gleam in them as he backed out of the room and closed the door.

She had groaned seeing how little fabric she held in her hand. Piper had never worn something so revealing and it made her more than a little self conscious. Closing her eyes, Piper tried to steel her nerves. She had chosen this path for her life, and now it was time to make good on it.

After some shimmying, jumping, and praying, Piper carefully pulled the skin tight dress up over her curves. She cursed Nicky's name for getting her something that made her look more like a hooker than an associate of a Mafia family. Piper didn't believe she was going to be believable. She was sure this was a test that she wasn't going to pass.

Piper walked out of her room shoulders back. As she entered the living room, she saw the two men sitting on the couch discussing her. Piper stood there for a few minutes taking in the conversations with her arms crossed. When they finally realized she was standing behind the couch, both jumped to their feet looking like two children that got caught with their hands in the cookie jar.

"That's what you picked for her to wear?" Dom choked seeing the second skin that was supposed to be a dress.

"Isn't it a little late to be asking that question?" he asked, turning towards the door. "We've already crossed the line." Nicky refused to make eye contact with either Dom or Piper as they headed out the door.

The ten minute ride across the compound felt like an eternity to Piper. She had no idea what kind of viper's nest she was getting ready to walk into. In all actuality, she was beginning to believe that Nicky wanted it that way. They had drilled her on all her information but gave her very little to go on when it came to Don Valence and the rest of the family. She would have to wing it and unfortunately, she wasn't great at winging it.

Pulling up outside the massive three story mansion, Piper's stomach pitched and her face hardened. It was show time. Two men that were waiting for them at the bottom of the stone steps opened their doors. Other well dressed men, she could only assume were Don Valence's, rushed down the stone steps to greet the group. Toward the back of the crowd, she had seen a slightly older man that looked a lot like Nicky.

"Son, so happy to have you grace us with your presence." His condensing tone put Piper on high alert.

"Grandfather asked and here I am." Nicky retorted, keeping his tone even. "May I introduce Piper Johnson of the Montana Graves family." Nicky placed his hand in the small of her back. "Piper, this is my father, D'Angelo Valence Jr.."

"Oh my dear, welcome to our humble neck of the woods." Valence Jr.. bowed, taking her hand and kissing the back of it. This made Piper's skin crawl.

"Yes, thank you for having me." Piper cut her eyes toward Nicky. "Dom and Nicky have been more than accommodating for my stay."

"I'm sure they have." Valence Jr..'s eyes started to turn dark but lightened when he tried to take her hand and escort her into the house. "This way my dear, I'm sure Don Valence would love to make your acquaintance". Nicky had relinquished his hold on Piper but stayed close. He knew what his father was capable of and would try hard not to subject her to him for long.

Walking down the hallway to the formal dining room, Piper had noticed this wasn't going to be some simple family dinner. The corridors were lined with men in suits and women in lavish evening dresses. Don Valence had held a party in her honor. Piper knew how to work a room, but very rarely allowed herself to be the center of attention. Especially, when that attention came with a room of people she had no idea how to interact with.

All eyes were on her and the group of men that followed. Piper cursed Nicky's name again for picking out such a ridiculous dress. Her skin flushed but she wouldn't show anything was wrong. She would merely blame it on being around so many new people, when her job was meant for her to stay in the shadows. Piper had a plan, whether it would work or not was entirely debatable at that moment.

"Ah Ms. Johnson. Thank you so much for gracing us with your presence." An older man approached taking Piper's hand. "I am Don D'Angelo Valence."

"Good evening, Sir. Thank you for inviting me to your lovely home." Piper put on her best smile.

"So, polite." Don Valence looked over at his grandson. "And commanding."

"Commanding?" Piper arched her brow.

"Well only a woman as commanding as yourself could not only get my grandson here on time but also have him dressed appropriately." A smile played on the Don's lips while Nicky scowled.

"I am always dressed appropriately." Nicky scoffed.

"Yes but neither you nor Dom are ever on time." The scold was evident in his voice. "Now, Ms. Johnson, let me get you a drink."

Nicky watched as Piper was ushered away with his grandfather. He cut his eyes over to Dom, who seemed to have his attention focused elsewhere. When Nicky looked in the direction of Dom's gaze, his heart sank and his whole body tensed. Roxie, a young woman who was the daughter of an associate, entered the room wearing a show stopping sparkling red mini dress with a waist length black mink shawl.

Both men cringed as they tried to escape into conversations of nearby groups. This didn't deter Roxie, as she had grown accustomed to getting her own way, and what she wanted. The target of her current desire was Nicky. While he placated her for nearly a month a few years prior, Roxie had it stuck in her head that Nicky belonged to her. She would be his other half in matters of the family.

"Long time no see, Nicky." Her voice was sultry sweet. "What has kept you away so long?"

"Don Valence has had me working hard. Afraid there is no time for socializing." Nicky's tone was clipped.

"Not too busy to be seen bar hopping with Dom." Roxie fluttered her eyelashes.

"That was still business. Either which way..." Nicky trailed off as Piper was being escorted back by Don Valence.

"Nicky, make sure our guest enjoys herself." Don Valence kissed the back of Piper's hand. "And don't forget I need a word with you, tomorrow."

"Yes, Grandfather." Nicky shook his hand before turning back to the group.

"Who is this?" Roxie's voice went viperous.

"This is..." Dom started to introduce Piper, before she held up her hand to introduce herself.

"I'm Piper Johnson. You are?" Piper honed in on the woman's tone and didn't appreciate it.

"Roxie VanClear. Nicky's significant other." Roxie puffed her well endowed chest out.

"That's funny..." Piper snickered. "In all the years of working with Nicky, I've never heard of you. Must not be that significant."

"Roxie, how many times must I tell you we have never been each other's significant anything. Now will you please stop, you're embarrassing me and yourself this evening." Nicky took Piper's arm and nodded for Dom to follow them.

Roxie was fuming at the open refusal. She had never been turned down before or in such a public way. Staring after the three as they moved through the crowd, Roxie vowed to make them pay for the now pitying looks she was receiving. After all, she was a VanClear and would not stand for such disrespect.

Nicky ignored the death glares from the other side of the room. His mission with this party was to make sure Piper had a good time but also to introduce her to as many of their associates as possible. If he could fold her into the family seamlessly enough that no one really questioned her presence, Nicky would have one of the biggest hurdles accomplished.

Formally asking her to stay and work for him wouldn't look out of place and Piper would be accepted and protected. Everything fell into place better than he could have dreamed. All eyes were on her and she never faltered or hesitated. Even when Valence Jr.. tried to make a move on her later in the evening, Piper had put him in his place quickly and privately.

Toward the end of the night Don Valence had asked for a meeting with the three, and while Nicky was sure their gooses were cooked, he played it off seamlessly. He would never openly defy his grandfather, but Nicky knew when to dig in his heels. Within the short time of knowing the woman at his side, he knew there was something special about her.

As the three were escorted into the large office, the hair rose on the back of Piper's neck.

"Ah, thank you for meeting with me before you head out." Don Valence leaned back in his chair.

"Not a problem, Don. What is this about?" Nicky settled in behind Piper hands protectively on the back of the chair.

"Ms. Johnson or should I call you Ms. Evette Cason." Don sat forward with his hands gripping a file on his desk.

"Ms. Johnson." Piper straightened her back even though all of the air had been sucked out of the room.

"Ms. Johnson it is. Do you three want to tell me what's really going on here?" Don Valence's smile faltered, sending cold shivers down everyone's spine.

"I am the heiress for the Cason Oil family. While we were expanding our operations I met Don Graves. I had a certain peacemaker mentality he liked. Which led me to be brought in on certain jobs. I was engaged to Xander Hultson of the Hultson Oil company, we had problems before my last run to Montana." Piper's body stiffened "When I returned home from the last job for both my father and Don Graves, Xander tried to make up with me. For the sake of the wedding and families, I was inclined to do so. Needless to say, that didn't go well. He got the jump on me and left me for dead, tied to a bed."

"Why didn't your family or even Don Graves do something about the heinous act?" Don Valence twisted the file into his hand.

"Mine and his family blamed me for walking out on him, when I found out about his mistress. Nadia Morang of the Morang family. Don Graves, I'm sure would have had him killed and everyone would have been pointing the figures at me. So, I did the only thing I knew to do. I ran."

"Nicky found you in the bar, figured out who you were, and took care of you?" Don Valence's eyes softened.

"Yes. He reached out to Don Graves and told him where I was, since I had no way to contact him."

"Don Graves is a good man. Takes good care of his people. Don Morang on the other hand likes to play big shots and doesn't maintain his own house. That daughter of his is a piece of work. I can see why you chose the path you did. But what do we do now?"

Nicky cleared his throat and addressed his grandfather. "I would like for her to remain here on my crew. Don Graves would like to remain in contact if he needs her but this would be her home base."

"So this file..." Don Valence walked over to the lit fireplace, and threw it in. "Alrighty then, You two have a goodnight. Ms. Johnson, it's been a pleasure meeting you and now, having you aboard. Nicky can I have a word in private please."

Piper and Dom quickly stood and left the room. She looked back at Nicky for a moment and he shot her a reassuring smile. She had done great. Better than either man would have liked to admit at the time. She had given just enough information on both sides of the story.

"Talk about being able to think on your feet," Dom said, escorting her back into the dining room.

"Not the first or the last time." Piper smirked as she saw Roxie draped over another man's arm. "Shameless. I guess it really doesn't matter where you were raised."

"What do you mean?" Dom's brows furrowed.

"Whether it's one version of high society or another, there is a lush in every one. Begging for any man's attention, money, and power." Piper cringed. "She does understand that's not a way to make a man like Nicky jealous right?"

"Not entirely sure but don't entirely care either. Nicky is pretty good about keeping that loon at bay for the most part." Dom snickered and cleared his throat, as he had seen Nicky walking up the hallway. "All good? That was quick."

"Yeah, I'll explain later. Let's get out of here." Nicky chuckled, embarrassment evident on his face.

As the three were leaving, Piper accidentally bumped into Roxie causing her to spill the red wine down the front of her dress and the mink shall she still had draped over her arms. "Oh beg my pardon, didn't see you there."

"You bitch. You'll pay for that," Roxie screeched.

"Send me the cleaning bill." Piper dabbed at the growing stain. "Oh, I don't know if that will come out."

"You better hope it does. This is my favorite dress."

"Again, so sorry. Well we must be going now." Piper turned on her heels toward the men that were standing there bemused by the situation.

"Was that entirely necessary?" Nicky's voice was low, as he tried to keep it together.

"It was an accident." Piper batted her eyes at him.

"I bet it was." Dom chimed in.

The three returned back to the house without any further incident. Piper was glad she could finally shimmy out of the dress and back into something more comfortable. Dom wanted to change and head into town. It was Saturday night and he was sure he could find something more interesting than staying in for the night. Nicky, on the other hand, refused to go bar hopping again, even when Dom begged. Piper had assured the men she would be fine at the house alone, but Nicky decided to use this as his excuse not to go.

When Piper emerged from her room, the house was quiet except for the faint sound of Italian opera music coming from the den. She walked over and stood in the doorway watching Nicky look out over the desert through the sliding glass doors. He had a drink in his hand, hair disheveled, and his tie hanging loosely around his neck. She wondered if he wanted to be left alone or was the door being open a sign for her to enter.

After several moments she finally spoke, "Didn't want to go to town with Dom?"

"Why drink in a loud ass bar, when I can drink here in peace?" Nicky didn't turn to look at her, but she had seen the way his muscles flexed under his dress shirt.

"Very true. I mean the only reason to drink in a bar is to get lost in the crowd." Piper said, inching her way across the room.

"Didn't work so well for you," Nicky retorted, bringing the amber liquid to his lips.

"Not as well as I would have liked but it did the job, at least for a little while." Piper was inches from him wanting to run her hands over his back.

"You keep telling yourself that Princess. You might believe it one day." Nicky put the glass down and swiftly turned standing nose to nose with Piper. "Did you want something?"

"I was just... I was just..." Piper stumbled over her words, smelling the smokey scent of his cologne.

"You just what, Princess." Nicky reached out, running his hands over her exposed upper arms.

"I just wanted to make sure you were okay. You know I can take care of myself if you wanted to go out." Piper's voice was barely a whisper but with little conviction.

"What if I wanted to stay here with you? What if I wanted a quiet evening alone with you?" Nicky's voice was low and sultry.

Piper hadn't realized she had been backing up from him as he advanced until her back was against the wall. "Nicky..." Her voice was just above a whisper.

"Nico..." Nicky grabbed her wrists in one hand, placing them above her head. He ran his other hand up the bare skin now exposed by the position she was in. "Do you want me to stop?"

"No." Her voice was breathless, while her eyes never left his.

"Could you be happy here with me?" Nicky asked trailing kisses up her neck from her collar bone.

"Yes." The answer came out more as a moan. She would do anything for the man in front of her. He had saved her life by giving her the choice of who she wanted to be.

"You belong with me, to me. As I do to you." Nicky kissed her hard, fueling it with all the heat, power, and frustration he had felt in that moment.

When they broke apart breathless, Nicky scooped her up and marched toward his room. He needed her beside him, under him, and any way she would allow him to be with her. This would complicate the working relationship a bit but he didn't give a shit. She would be his, even if only for the night.

CHAPTER 8
PROVING WORTH

It had been a long first month of Piper being within the folds of the Valence family, and the whirlwind of events that seemed to follow were nothing more than spectacular chaos. No one had questioned Nicky's decision to ask Piper to stay but more than a few had their own suspicions on why. They were more than convinced something was going on behind the scenes, though Nicky and Piper openly denied it.

Some of the more traditional men, including Don Valence, had a hard time trusting that a woman could handle the high stress of the job. Even if her reputation from Don Graves preceded her. Don Valence had been skeptical at best, even though he opened his family to her. Most didn't want to work with her but wouldn't dare outright say it. They knew crossing Nicky, even if Don Valence openly didn't approve, was a death warrant no one wanted to deal with.

Even when Don Valence put Nicky's crew on a job that needed a more delicate hand than a "shoot first ask later" tactic, Piper had come through with flying colors. She had even renegotiated a peace treaty that had been broken by one of Valence's men. Piper proved to be useful for the family. As there were many jobs they would have had to hand off to other families, because they didn't have anyone with that level of tact. Now, Don Valence was up to his ears in contracts.

The requests ranged from cut and dry search and rescues to transports of various items. Don Valence had even started collecting contracts from women who just needed enough proof to end their toxic relationships. Word had spread faster than anyone could have predicted. Piper and the men were "making offers" and/or catching the bastards red handed with another woman or man, as one of the situations turned out to be.

She was good at what she did and never had a complaint. She was quick, efficient, and could charm her way out of any real trouble. With Nicky and Dom there, no one suspected her or them. That's what gave them the advantage to the majority of the marks. She wasn't afraid to get her hands dirty, and Don Valence took notice of that right away. It did also help that Piper could keep Nicky in line better than Dom ever could.

While the family business was moving along nicely, there was just one person that couldn't stand Piper. It was disheartening for Roxie to have to hear about every little thing Nicky's crew had done or the latest place Nicky and Piper had traveled to. The rumor mill had been working overtime and it was all about them. Roxie was no longer receiving favor from anyone.

As she had been shot down by Nicky at every turn, Roxie tried to distract herself with other male attention. Most wouldn't give her the time of day and those that would, got sick of hearing about Nicky Valence, which would leave Roxie furtherly obsessing over Nicky. She had never seen Nicky so hung up over a woman before, and figured it would be a passing adventure for him. When days turned into weeks and now a month into Piper's stay, Roxie was perturbed. She had stood by far too long being overlooked by him, and she wasn't going to stand for it any longer.

This is what caused her to take drastic steps to ensure he knew who he was turning down. Roxie started out small with threatening letters to Piper to try to scare her away. She would start each one the same way: "Dear reader, I wish I could tell you that it ends well for you." making them more and more menacing as they went along. When all that seemed to do was piss Nicky off, Roxie had to go into her bag of tricks and try another tactic.

Roxie started letting rumors spread, and spread they did. Everything from Piper being a spy from another family to an undercover cop. Roxie's personal favorite: Piper was a call girl that was trying to get her hooks into Nicky to get herself off the streets. Every scenario ended with Piper ruining the family and poisoning it from the inside, and Roxie trying to shine light on the situation. Before they knew it they had a brewing war on their hands, painting Roxie as the damsel in distress from both sides with Piper as the culprit.

While Don Valence squashed most of the rumors with little issue, some of the information had reached Dom before the rest. He took it upon himself to gather information instead of running back to Nicky and Piper with the potential problem. Dom's philosophy was simple: don't cry wolf if there doesn't seem to be at least a big dog in the area. Whether that big dog is a wolf determines in which way the situation gets handled. Dom's first stop would be the security office. He needed to know what the cameras could or couldn't see.

As the CCTV footage advanced frame by mind numbing frame, Eilo was about to disappear for a coffee run, when he saw Dom approach on the cameras. "Well this can't be good," he muttered under his breath.

Eilo was shaking his head when Dom walked into the command building. Silently pleading to whoever might be listening, Dom had lost his car again and needed to know where he had left it. Which wasn't as rare as one might think. He had a bad habit of leaving things around while he was intoxicated and needed help locating it once he was sober if Nicky wasn't with him.

"Hey, Eilo, I need your help with something?" Dom's face had that certain look that spoke volumes to the situation. This would not be a "I lost my car again" thing.

"Could we get arrested for this? Or is Don Valence going to have me black bagged?" Eilo looked annoyed. This was a fact finding mission, and Eilo knew whatever Dom had come hunting for would definitely be worth the trouble in the end.

"Where's your sense of adventure? I mean no, nothing like that..." Dom trailed off looking at the monitors. He had thrown himself in front of the monitors when he had seen Nicky walk by one of the cameras with Piper stealing a kiss.

"What the hell are you doing man?" Elio looked around his arm seeing Nicky locked up with Piper. "You know they have been doing that a lot lately." Eilo was amused.

"You know it wouldn't be in your best interest to tell anyone what you've seen." Dom towered over the younger man.

"I value my head staying attached to my neck." Eilo snicked. "Plus, it is none of my business who Nicky chooses to have in his bed."

"I don't believe it's gone that far." Dom cleared his throat. "But you're right it's none of yours or my business."

While the two men stared each other down, the screens flickered to another part of the compound. The movement in the normally vacant library had caught the men off guard. They watched as Roxie moved from behind one of the paintings and back behind another across the room. The men stared baffled at the screens.

"Where does that go?" Dom looked harder pointing at the screen where Roxie had just been.

"I have no clue. I didn't even know the house was set up that way." Eilo arched an eyebrow at Dom. "Did you know?"

"The main house has many secrets. Most designed by the OG Don himself. I'm sure Don Valence doesn't even remember all the passages his father put in." Dom's eyes watched the camera's closely. "I'm going in. Text me when she reappears."

"Will do." Eilo sat back in front of the monitors watching carefully. How had he worked for this family for three years and not known about the passages? This was going to end up being a long shift and Eilo knew it wasn't going to be good.

It didn't take long for Dom to make it from the security office, to the main house and down into the library. What did take him a few minutes was figuring out which painting Roxie had disappeared behind. There were three possible choices but only two that were close enough together that could allow her to appear and then poof. After a phone call to Eilo, he had his answer.

Venturing down the dark corridor, Dom had to pull his phone out of his pocket to use it as a flashlight. He could hear footsteps a good distance ahead of him, but couldn't tell if they were walking toward or away from him. Dom lowered his light and picked up his pace. He stopped short when he heard voices coming from the other side of a nearby painting. He leaned in to hear Roxie's voice and a male's voice he didn't recognize.

"You were meant to be watching him!" Roxie shrieked.

"What's the point of all this?" he muttered. "We're running out of time, and nothing's changed."

"The point is for me to end up with Nicky and you to be brought into the family. Once we have control over Nicky, we control the Valence family." Roxie's voice was heaving with disdain.

"If Dom or Piper figure it out we are dead. I don't feel like dying over this."

"I'm not asking for your permission." She gritted her teeth, pacing. "I'm doing this with or without you."

"This isn't just about you. It's about what's best for all of us." The man raised his voice slamming his hand on something hard.

"I am doing what is best for all of us. For our family to be forever linked to the Valence's, we would be untouchable. No one would dare go against us. My father might be fine just being an associate, but we need something more permanent."

"I hope you're right. Who did you talk into the attack? Joey and Marcus' crew, they are 150 strong."

"Do I want to know what you told them to get them to stand with you?"

"Nothing much... Just that bitch disrespected and threatened me."

"But she didn't… You don't think they will figure that out?"

"Joey is so in love with me, I could tell him the sky was purple and he would believe me with no questions asked. Marcus wants to be with Tracy so bad, he's not thinking straight. Now if someone slipped some information about making their dreams come true, and they believed it, that's on them, not me."

"You did a bad thing for a good reason, I hope it doesn't come back to bite us in the ass."

"It won't, you'll see. Now, we have to go. Fireworks will be going off in a few hours."

Dom stood there flabbergasted. He had to get out of there before he was discovered. He ran up the corridor without looking back. He was grateful it was a long hallway and even in the dark he could make his way with little effort. This allowed him not to have the flashlight on his phone active. When he made it through the painting and into the library, his phone had started ringing off the hook. It was Eilo.

"Yeah, what do you got?" Dom said, trying to control his breathing, as he had racked his brain on how he had not seen through Roxie's scheming ways?

"She came out into the billiard room. She was in there with someone I have never seen before. I know he's not one of ours. I'm running a face scan now. What do you want me to do with the information?"

"Is there any sound on that camera?"

"Unfortunately, no. Let me guess you had no signal in the passageway?"

"Nope but I heard everything. I was hoping I would have something to back me up."

"You got me, brother."

"Good to know. Do we have anything going on in a few hours?" Dom went back to what Roxie had said.

"There is supposed to be a sit down between Don Valence and a few of VanClear's crews, why?"

"Joey and Marcus?" Dom prayed he said no.

"How did you know? Wait, I don't want to know how you knew that." Eilo rubbed his temples.

"It's happening today. Put all men on alert. Keep it discrete. We don't need them to know, we know why they're really here."

"Will do. What about Don Valence?"

"I'll handle that with Nicky." Dom's voice went silent as he heard footsteps headed toward the library. "Hold on, I got some sketchy shit to do. Will be in touch within the hour." Dom hung up the phone and sprinted outside the library and toward the kitchen.

Standing inside the doorway, Dom watched Roxie stick her head out and look both ways before exiting the library. Dom kept a close eye on her as she exited the front door. Dom picked up his phone, shooting a 911 text to Nicky and Piper. He told them to stop sucking faces and get their asses to the main house now.

Within ten minutes, the three were standing in Don Valence's office. Dom was spilling his guts on what he had heard and the fact Roxie had been seen walking in and out of the "special" corridors. Don Valence was fuming, but knew just because they had the information, it didn't mean anything would come of it. They would have to wait, regardless if they wanted to. Tipping off the crews would cause another plan to be put in place, and they might not find out about the next one.

"I don't have a license to kill. I only have a learners permit." Piper cracked a joke hoping to lighten the mood.

"License or not, you know how to handle one of these don't you?" Don Valence had handed her a 9mm handgun.

"I prefer to use my words, but when push comes to shove, yes, I am a good shot." Piper took the gun, checking the clip, and chambering a round.

"Good girl. You need to stay with Nicky. Things start getting out of hand, you leave. After all, they are here for you."

"I can handle myself. If they are here to take me on then they are going to get a fight."

"Please don't argue. You need to leave when we tell you to, you aren't safe here if we can't protect you." Nicky reached out grabbing Piper's wrist. "I can't lose part of my crew."

"I promise, if things get real I'll run." Piper agreed but she had other ideas on how to handle this situation. Examples needed to be made, so no other would test her again.

The next few hours had everyone on edge. To distract everyone, Don Valence had instructed Nicky to show Piper upstairs and a few places in which she could hide if things got bad. He also instructed Piper to pick out a room in the main house, as she would have the same accommodations as Nicky and Dom did. While all of this should have been reassuring to Piper, her stomach stayed in a lurch over the upcoming events.

"You know it's going to be okay right? Things like this happen more often than you can imagine. Grandfather won't let it get too far." Nicky's reassurance fell on deaf ears.

"All I know is people keep trying to kill me, and I'm getting a little sick and tired of it." Piper walked through another of the second floor rooms with an on suite bathroom.

"Well then you might have wanted to take option A. Little late for that now though." Nicky snickered leaning against the post for the bed.

"Are we ever going to have a serious conversation?" Piper folded her arms looking at him.

"We are having one right now. But sure, what would you like to talk about?" Nicky's eyes darkened.

"What happened the other night, or the stolen moments when no one is looking?" Piper's voice had a hint of annoyance as she had tried

91

to brooch this topic with him many times with nothing more than sarcasm. "What am I exactly to you?"

"You're part of my crew. You have my back and I have yours. Everything else is just details." Nicky shrugged off expectations and hoped she would do the same. "We are what we are. Nothing more or less."

Piper's heart sank in her chest and before she could fire back a response, a loud commotion could be heard from down stairs. Nicky grabbed Piper's arm pulling her behind a painting in the room. They quietly hurried down the stairwell that led them into the library. Piper had the gun at the ready as they crept across the library and toward the main hallway.

Shots were fired and they both knew there was no time. They had to make it to Don Valence's office. Nicky had another bright idea of heading off to another secret passageway that would get them closer to the office. It just so happened it was the same one Dom had been down earlier. They ran as fast as they could in the muted light.

Nicky had gone through the first painting they had come to, and instructed Piper to go to the next one. Even though she had kept running, she heard Nicky cuss and more gun fire. No man left behind for her. As soon as Piper popped out in what looked like a steam room, she had doubled back for Nicky.

Looking down the hallway to make sure it was clear, she saw a man standing there holding Nicky at gunpoint. Nicky to his credit was trying to talk the man down but it wasn't going in his favor. Piper crept silently up the hallway, getting in good position behind the man. She placed her gun to his temple and told him to drop it. The man didn't take her seriously until he had heard the hammer go back. That's when he dropped the gun and Piper escorted him like a human shield down the hallway to where the bulk of the commotion was happening.

She called out letting everyone know to drop their weapons or the man she was escorting would get a bullet in the back of the head. She had even started counting, when the man in front of her told everyone to stand down. She proceeded to walk the men into Don Valence's office and made them get on their knees. The attack was over in seconds.

"Well, my dear, what do we have here?" Don Valence looked at the men with a wicked gleam in his eye.

"A gift of my undying loyalty, Don Valence."

"Good girl. You may leave now. Nicky, take her out of here she doesn't need to see this." He rose from his chair flanked by ten of his men.

"May I, first." Piper looked at the man who had Nicky at gunpoint, put the gun to his head, and pulled the trigger. "I wouldn't want anyone to think that I'm merely some damsel in distress. Good day to you, Don." Piper turned to walk out of the room flanked by Nicky and Dom.

"Piper, what the fuck were you thinking?" Nicky grabbed her arm and spun her around to look at him.

"I just saved your life back there. You could be a little more grateful." Piper's voice was cold and calculating.

Nicky had never seen anyone pull the trigger for the first time and not hesitate. A switch had flipped in her and Nicky didn't know whether to be scared or impressed. As the two men exchanged a look, Nicky had let go of Piper's arm. It was better for him to stay on her good side.

"Now if we are quit through, I believe we were discussing dinner plans, and I can't go out covered in blood. So, I'm going back to the house and getting ready. 7pm should be fine for a reservation." Piper turned on her heels and walked out the front door like this was any normal afternoon.

"You do realize we have a hellcat on our hands right?" Dom stood there slack jawed. He had never seen anyone, let alone a woman, talk to Nicky like that.

"You see that too huh?" Nicky watched after her in amazement.

"I see much more than that." Dom snickered.

"It's business."

"Business and pleasure..."

CHAPTER 9
MEXICO

The sun was setting in Cancun when Nicky, Piper, and about four others had gotten off a six hour private flight. They hadn't planned on going to Mexico. Nicky and Piper were earmarked to be in Italy for two weeks to pay tribute to Nicky's great-grandfather for his birthday, but when someone goes on the run with nearly eight million dollars of Don Valence's money, plans reverted quickly.

Neither Nicky nor Piper were happy about the development but when push came to shove they didn't have a choice in the matter. Don Valence didn't trust anyone else to go on this pick up. He needed this rat brought back alive, and there weren't too many on staff that he trusted to complete the task. After all, he was still trying to make his way through the list of suspects that had contact with this swindler, so all could stand before him and pay the price for screwing him over.

Nicky had a bad feeling about Edgar Canon from the moment he laid eyes on him. Don Valence had brought him in at the recommendation from another family to deal with the finance side after Ralph finally took retirement. While Nicky never trusted him, Don Valence swore things would run smoothly and with some updated practice that so many of the other families were already reaping the benefits of.

While things went well for the first year or two, Nicky and most of the others had noticed things were starting to get sketchy. Don Valence was starting to believe the once trusted muscle were skimming off the top and some were severely dealt with on Edgar's word. Valence Jr..

kept his nose out of it while Nicky did a lot of digging to figure out the truth. It took Piper and him two years to come up with enough evidence to even get a sit down with Don Valence for him to calmly hear them out. By that time, Edgar had skipped town.

Nearly a month later, word had gotten around about a big time roller in Cancun matching up with Edgar's description. Seemed like someone that would have been smart to lay low was racking up debts all over Mexico using Don Valence's name just before skipping town to the next location. They had him located currently in a pretty pricey resort. Seems that Edgar had a taste for gambling and fancied himself a card shark. When he got caught counting cards at the last resort, he nearly got his hands broken but left town before the family down there had got their hands on him.

"You know this isn't what I had in mind when I said I needed to get out of town for a bit." Piper pushed her sunglasses up her nose getting in the BMW.

"At this point I would rather be driving a Maserati down the coast in Sicily, but at least we aren't chasing our tails. We know where he is and should be able to wrap this up quickly." Nicky grumbled climbing in next to Piper.

"Yes, it should be quick. I don't see him coming without kicking up a fuss." Piper said under her breath.

"I know Papa wants him to be delivered alive. I'm hoping with whom he sent with us he will get what he's asked for."

"Dom maybe will play by the rules but the other two might have other plans as they were part of the wrath when this all started." Piper looked over at Nicky to see him taking in the scenery as they drove through town.

Piper knew Valence Sr. had put quite a bit of pressure on Nicky to bring Edgar back to face the music, and she wasn't happy about seeing Nicky used as some sort of pawn in the old man's game. To her, Valence Jr.. should have been the one to finally get his hands dirty, but he had gotten out of it due to a technical issue. Those "technical issues" involved a beautiful blonde that had just been sent to another of the families in Texas along with a very large bottle of scotch to drown his sorrows when this one turned him down for his age.

While Piper should respect Nicky's father, she couldn't stand the man that lived his life either pretending to be a socialite, headlong in the next scheme to weasel himself to the top of the family, or ass deep in whatever expensive liquor the old man kept around the house. There were many reasons Valence Sr. took Nicky after his mother died, and unfortunately, these weren't even the tip of the iceberg. Piper wasn't sure if she ever wanted to know the whole story, but she knew regardless she would be what Nicky needed.

As they approached the large villa, Nicky sighed. They were supposed to be staying at the hotel but last minute plans had changed and Don Valence didn't want Edgar spooked if he happened to run across them in the casino. They had to be cold and calculating, staking him out for a few days so they could make the best plan in which to snatch and grab.

It was okay, none of the men had noticed this was going to take longer than promised. Hell, what did they care, they were in Mexico with half naked women parading around without a care in the world. Nicky and Piper's worry is whether they could keep them on task long enough to grab Edgar and get the hell out of town without them adding to the population.

"We are keeping it tight around here until Edgar is in hand. This isn't a vacation," Nicky barked, seeing every man with them drooling over the eye candy.

"Isn't that going to take a few days? I mean mixing a little business with pleasure isn't always a bad thing," Carl said, shooting a look over to Nicky.

"You heard the boss. No grab ass'n until the rat is in hand." Dom spoke up before Nicky had a chance to respond.

There had been some talk around the house and family for years over Nicky and Piper's closeness. It was very much a don't ask don't tell situation, and depending on who brought it up how much Nicky was going to react. He could go from zero to someone picking themselves off the floor in two seconds flat. Piper always played it off as they were friends, comrades, or partners in crime. She played it closer to the vest than most and while most speculated on why they always made it where no one could prove anything.

"Carl, if you and the others plan on having all the parts you left with returned back to the states attached, I'd stick to the job." Piper's voice was barely over a whisper but the threat was clear.

"Yes, ma'am," they all clearly said, shuffling bags into the villa and getting their room assignments.

"Sometimes I wonder if they are more scared of you or me?" Nicky smirked, grabbing the last of their bags out of the trunk.

"A healthy dose of fear is never a bad thing. As I am your right hand, the fear of me is also the fear of you," Piper said, running her hand over the dagger strapped to her thigh.

"I guess I should be lucky you didn't pull that during the flight."

"You should be lucky I got on the plane."

"You know it's faster than driving."

"And you know why I don't fly. Now we are going to play the circle jerk game or are we going to get ready to catch a rat?" Piper glared at him proving her point.

"Well go get showered. We leave for dinner in thirty."

Snatching up her bags, Piper strutted into the house to start phase one of this thrown together plan. Nicky couldn't help but admire the woman she had become, and with little help from him, he had to admit. She was a spitfire if he had ever seen one but it was the stone cold rage that pushed her forward that Nicky tried to chip at little by little. She would never let her guard down even when it was just them. Which had saved his life a few times, even if he didn't want to admit that one.

"When are you going to tell her?" Dom said, taking a cigar from his pocket and offering it to him.

"Tell her what?" Nicky's forlong look was gone and now he was snapped back to the reality of the situation they had found themselves in.

"Come on Nicky. Don't play stupid with me. We have been thick as thieves since we were kids."

"I honestly don't know what you're talking about Dom. Piper and I are just partners, and not romantic ones either," Nicky said, feeling that pang in his chest that he had felt since the day he had seen her in that bar.

"You're kidding yourself man. But hey I get it. Don Valence wouldn't be happy with the choice. Even if it is none of his old ass business," Dom said, throwing the rest of the cigar down and stomping it out with his boot. "Don't wait. Forever is a long time to spend alone." Dom threw his bag over his shoulder and proceeded to walk into the house.

Nicky wasn't as clueless as he made others believe he was, but he couldn't risk Piper's life. Well more than he already did. She chose to stay after she was healed up. She chose to train and become part of his world. He had told himself for years it was because she didn't want to go back, not that she couldn't ever go back. Nicky feared the day she would choose to leave but for now he didn't have to worry about that.

Nicky had the men staked out at several different hotels to garner information about Edgar. Since he didn't just play in the hotel he was staying at, it made more sense for them to spread out and track his movements. They wouldn't grab him unless they had a clear shot not to be noticed. Nicky and Piper's job was to be seen and find out as much information as they could about the resort he was staying at.

It was nearly three days of headhunting before Edgar had slipped up. Every night, Nicky and Piper would go to the tables gambling for a few hours acting like tourists. For the first few nights they sat side by side at the tables, but as they caught the attention of Edgar, Nicky removed himself to watch Piper work her magic. Edgar, who seemed too drunk to notice who they were, started flirting with Piper almost immediately after Nicky went a few tables over to play Blackjack. She played that to her advantage. After all, they only needed to know which room was his to do a snatch and grab.

Edgar thought he was playing big shot betting double or nothing on a double king river. Piper called and knowingly lost. They played a few more hands before Edgar got cocky enough to slip his hand over onto Piper's thigh. "You know if you lose this time you're going to have to come up with something a little more than money."

"I always pay my debts." Piper batted her eyelashes at Edgar.

"I bet you do." Edgar licked his lips looking at Piper in a short flowy lace skirt and matching poet shirt.

When the last card flipped over, Piper knew it was show time, as she feigned disappointment at the turn of her luck. Looking over at Edgar, she had to fake shock that she had lost for the fifth time in a row. Racking his winnings into the black velvet bag laying next to him, he grabbed Piper by the wrist, "I think I know how you have survived this long by yourself? But I think it's time for you to show me what I have won."

Piper didn't act surprised at his words. Though she knew she would have to take a long shower to get the smell of the cheap tequila off of her. She giggled to herself that if they could just get him near an open flame he would take care of the job himself. He surely smelled flammable.

As he dragged her to the elevators to go upstairs, Piper started dropping random items to make sure Nicky could follow her path. She knew he would have already been on the phone with the guys letting them know Edgar had taken the bait. It was up to her now to keep him within arms reach until the guys came and claimed him. She was thankful this would be her last night in Mexico.

Edgar had his hands all over her as they entered the elevator alone. She playfully pushed him away knowing she would only have to play along for a little while longer. The boys would either bust down the door within minutes of their arrival, or be standing outside the elevator as they got to the floor. Either way Piper's patience for being the bait was wearing thin as the drunk Edgar began to take liberties that most men would get stabbed for. She knew the stipulations to being paid for this job teetered on him being brought back alive. With the way he was touching her, Piper wanted to put this man down like the vile vermin he was.

By the time they had reached the 23rd floor, Piper had accidentally kneed him in the balls three times and elbowed him in the face twice. He was unsteady on his feet as they exited and headed down the hall toward his "high roller" suite. She offered herself to lean on as she took the key card from his pocket letting them into the room.

What Piper had seen when she entered the room made her want to vomit. The room was trashed with so many bottles and rotten food containers you would think there had been a frat party there for a week with no maid service. They would definitely have to slip the cleaning crew a huge tip for dealing with this horrendous mess. As she dropped him in the middle of the living room, she heard screams coming from the bedroom.

Pulling her gun from her purse, Piper eased open the door to find a young woman tied to the bed. Putting a finger to her mouth, she cleared the room until she had determined she was the only one in there. She untied the woman, checking her out from head to toe to make sure she had not been harmed.

"What's your name?"

"Isabella," she cried, rubbing feeling back into her wrists.

"I'm Piper. I'm going to get you out of here."

"How he's going to be back any minute?" Her eyes darted about the room.

"Because he's passed out on the floor and well lets just say I have some friends that are going to be coming to take care of him." Piper reached into her purse handing the woman a large stack of money. "Take this and run."

The woman didn't think twice, as Piper walked her to the door. She knew the fear in the woman's eyes all too well when she looked back at her stepping on to the elevator. Edgar would pay the price for what he had done the same way she hoped Xander would pay for all he had done to her. For now, Piper had to put the past aside and deal with the present.

She waited for nearly twenty minutes when she finally picked up her phone to figure out where the guys were to pick up this trash.

"Where the hell are you?" Piper screeched into the phone when Nicky picked up.

"What floor?" Nicky barked.

"23 penthouse 3"

"Be right there."

Piper had slammed the phone down and found a sturdy enough chair to hoist Edgar's body into. She even used the ropes that he had tied the woman up with as a lovely little touch. He would soon know what it was like to be helpless and beg for his life, knowing that the end result would be Valence Sr. using him for fertilizer for his roses. There was no way out of this one and Piper wasn't sure if Edgar had caught on to that as of yet.

The knock on the door startled her as it almost sounded like the police and not five men here to collect Edgar. Piper looked through the peephole and sighed. Thank god the cavalry had finally arrived so they might be able to get the damn show on the road. Opening the door Nicky had busted in first followed by Dom, Carl and the others. Nicky had rushed to see if she had been hurt, while the four swept the penthouse from top to bottom.

"I'm fine. There is no one else here. But we are going to have to leave a rather large tip for the maid services. Edgar was nasty," Piper said, trying to get Nicky to stop.

"Where is he?"

"Drunk, slightly unconscious, tied to a chair," Piper told him in her usual sarcastic tone.

"Let's get him and get the hell out of here." Nicky's hand lingered a little too long on her arm as he made his way out of the foyer and into the massive living room.

"Damn Piper. Think you could leave us a little something to do next time." Carl complained as it wasn't often since she joined the crew that he had anything to really do.

"Technically he did most of it to himself. I just proved a point that a man should never put his hands unless welcomed on a lady." She feigned innocence as the others busted out laughing. Nicky stood there with a fire in his eyes that Piper didn't understand.

"And since she has done all the work, I say you four can take him back to the villa and lock him up. We leave out bright and early." Nicky said, staring daggers at the men that stood before him.

"You heard the boss," Dom said, shaking his head. He knew Nicky had panicked when he had lost her at the elevator and had no idea what floor they had gone to. Dom and the others had been searching the floors for any sign of her when Nicky had texted and told them the 23rd floor. He wished that Nicky would be honest not only with himself but with Piper.

It had been hours since they had gotten back to the Villa with Edgar in hand. Nicky had tried for two hours to get ahold of the pilot to no avail, and when he finally reached the co-pilot he had found out they both had been drinking. He told them to sober up and call Dom when they knew a take off time. Unfortunately, Nicky knew it would be sometime the next day before they could deliver the package back to Don Valence.

While the rest of the guys were to stay on guard duty, Nicky decided to make the best out of a less than ideal situation of having to spend one more night in Mexico. He was grateful that Dom backed him up on keeping Carl and the others at the house. The last thing anyone needed was three Italian men chasing tails all around Mexico, leaving gifts that wouldn't appear until long after they were gone. Don Valence would also have their heads if by chance Edgar disappeared in their pursuits, and Nicky couldn't have that.

Walking down the hall toward Piper's room, he had hoped she would accompany him out that night to a little spot he loved to visit when he happened to be in town. He would give her the well deserved night out that he had been promising her for longer than he cared to remember. Unfortunately, something like this had always come up and here they were off to do his grandfather's bidding, but when he could find little moments like these where he could steal her away from everything, he took them with no questions asked.

Knocking on her door, Nicky prayed that the day hadn't been too much on her, and she would go and have a drink with him.

"Carl, I already told you to fuck off," Piper screeched, throwing the door open to reveal Nicky fuming for some odd reason. "Sorry. Carl was just here ten minutes ago, and I thought he was back for round two."

"Do I need to have a word with him?" Nicky was already planning a way for him to be left in Mexico hogtied naked to a cactus.

"No, I handled it. I don't know why he seemed to think I was going to help him out after all the sly comments he's been making. He also seems to think by his passes not being reciprocated that I belong to someone else. Explaining to that asshole that I belong to myself and no other doesn't seem to be sinking in." Piper fumed, wrapped in a towel taking clothes out of her suitcase.

"I'll have him dealt with once we get back home. His mouth is overloading his ass. But in other news, the pilots have to sober up before we can head back."

Piper hung her head hoping that they would be on their way to Italy, not waiting for two men to sober up so they could get back to Texas. "So it's going to be tomorrow?"

"Yep, but there is one bright side."

"And what would that be?" Piper flipped her hair out of her face from being bent over the bed.

"There is a little place around the corner. Good food, music, and a stunning view of the water."

"Fine, but you're buying." Piper's playful smile played on her lips.

It was a beautiful outdoor spot that overlooked the beach. Even more glorious than he had remembered, though it had been more than five years since he had set foot there. As the sunset over the water, Nicky couldn't think of a better place to be or a more perfect person to be sharing that moment with. Piper was strong, beautiful, and had an attitude that would put most grown men to shame. When they were alone together, they were just two people enjoying each other's company.

They ate and talked about what was hopefully next when they got back home. They were pretty sure the Italy trip was off, but Don

Valence always had something up his sleeve to keep them on the move. Piper seemed to always be in a perpetual state of motion, but when it was just her and Nicky time seemed to stand still. As if they were trapped, for however long they were allowed, in their little bubble.

Staring off into the orange and pink fading lights, one margarita turned into two, which turned into three, and as the drinks kept flowing so did the conversations. Hopes, dreams, and futures of what ifs proceeded to be spoken out loud as if they might somehow come true. The way thieves would steal precious gems, they were stealing the thoughts of times that couldn't be.

Before anyone knew what was going on Nicky and Piper had found themselves on the dance floor spinning around like there was no one else in the world. As Nicky went in for one of those famous dips, he had almost gone too far which would have landed both of them on the hard wooden dance floor. He recovered and when they came back together Nicky had softly kissed her on her neck. Piper's already over-stimulated system begged for him to do it again, though she would never admit it.

When she had suggested they get tattoos so they would always remember that night, Nicky took her to the first shop he could think of to make it so. She didn't know if it was the alcohol talking or the fact he was the only thing not spinning, but after the tattoos, she begged him to touch her, to look at her like she was a woman and not just the person that had his back. Nicky was more than willing to oblige her every whim that night or any other. Therefore when he asked her to spend the night with him in his bed, she figured what could be the harm in obliging him.

When Dom came knocking the next morning, heads were pounding and the sun was too bright to be peering through the windows. Piper, hearing the pounding on the door, had to jump up and run into the closet to keep from being seen.

"Hey Boss. The pilots called. We can be wheels up in thirty." His gruff voice cut through the hangover.

"Fine. Tell everyone to be ready to leave out of here in twenty." Nicky moved to a sitting position. As he flexed his arms back and ran his hands through his hair, he revealed a glimpse of something that wasn't there yesterday.

"Will do. By the way, did Piper come home with you last night?" Dom smirked with a knowing look in his eyes. The answer was clear as he could see her silhouette in the shadows on the floor along with the remanence of yet another night the two would never talk about.

"Yeah she came home with me last night." Cutting his eyes toward the closet. "Is she not in her room getting ready to leave? Maybe she went around the corner for coffee. You know she can't function without it," Nicky said, smirking at the fact he was openly staring at her luscious body trying to hide in the nearly empty closet.

"Nope not in her room, but I'll keep an eye out for her." Dom chuckled trying to look anywhere but where Nicky had his eyes trained.

"Yeah, I'm sure she will turn up before we are due to leave. Go make sure everyone else is good to go. I want nothing left to chance getting Edgar back to Don Valence." Nicky nodded with a sly grin spreading across his face.

Dom left the room holding the secret he had known all along. This wasn't the first time he had almost caught them in bed together, and if they wanted to play the same old game of nothing happened, who was he to say anything. He hoped Nicky would come to his senses about her before time ran out for the both of them.

Piper poked her head out of the closet once she had heard the door close behind Dom. That had been a too close for comfort call, and secretly she was glad it had been Dom to come knocking that early in the morning and not one of the others. They already had a long flight back to deliver Edgar and she didn't need the whispers from the other men.

Walking over to Nicky, who now had his feet on the floor, she stood in front of him running her hands through his wavy hair. He laid his head on her stomach and ran his hands up the back of her legs. A single tear, she would never let him see, escaped her eyes before she tore away from his grasp. She walked across the room gathering clothes when the sting of her fresh tattoo caught her attention.

Piper didn't remember much of their drunken escapades, but the fact she still couldn't find her bra said volumes of what had happened the night before. They had sworn to each other this was the last time. To the ache in both their hearts, they would never speak of the promises they had made to each other under the star littered sky. A pack was always made that nothing would ever change between them. While that wasn't the first night they had found solace in each other's arms it was certainly the most memorable one.

Nicky would have a lasting reminder of the spade on his inner left arm, and a visible reminder of the same spade on Piper's left shoulder blade.

CHAPTER 10
NO GOOD DEED

The screeching of tires as the motorcycle had come to a halt outside the Valence family homestead, Piper let down the kickstand and unseated the powerful beast. She had been riding for days, coming clear across the country hopping from one job to the next pick up until she had found herself back at the only home she had known in the last decade.

Piper only stopped to rest or when she thought someone was hot on her trail. She had a knack for being overly cautious, which kept the assignments coming. Some would only work with the family if Piper was handling the job; this caused a little more animosity than was actually needed but it wasn't her problem. She kept her team, especially Nicky, alive by playing by certain rules.

The motorcycle was her last pick up on her way back from New York. A graduation gift for one of the grandchildren she assumed, but it wasn't her business to ask. Nicky had taken off in the old Cadillac with Dom. They were due to drop it off in Oklahoma. Piper knew Nicky relished in the fact the next pick up would be a Hellcat. Dom was picking up a 67' Camaro. So it was safe to say they would beat her back by nearly two days. Everything was a race to them, and Piper didn't pay them any attention. When she saw that spark in Nicky's eye, she knew the game was on.

There was no sign of either of them upon her return, Piper had just assumed they were probably out or hadn't heard her pull up. It wasn't uncommon for Nicky to wait for her to come into the house before bragging about him beating her back. Dom, on the other hand, would only appear if he didn't have a hot date waiting for him, when he got back into town.

"Hey, Piper. Think you could of come in any faster?" Kris hated the dust she had kicked up from the gravel road.

"I could have but didn't want to lay the bike down by accident. Don't think the Old Man would pay me for damaged goods." Piper smirked, taking the helmet off and placing it on the handlebars.

"Speaking of the Old Man, he's in his office waiting for you." Mark was now the one with a grin on his face, which normally meant trouble for Piper.

"Can't catch a break huh? Well, no rest for the wary," Piper remarked knowing that was never ideal for her to be summoned within minutes of her arrival back at the Valence family homestead.

Walking up the stone steps and into the foyer, Piper became hyper aware that something was awry. If Nicky was home, he hadn't come bounding down the stairs to gloat about beating her back, and Dom hadn't found his way out of wherever he happened to be hiding. In fact the whole house was eerily quiet. Not even the other guards, who would normally be playing poker in the parlor, were anywhere to be seen. Piper's skin began to crawl at what this could mean. While she wasn't one to back down from a challenge, she was also trying to remember if her pistol had the safety still on.

Squaring up her shoulders, Piper strolled military style down the long corridor toward one of the three offices. Maybe it was the last contract or the fact she felt like she was marching to her doom. Piper couldn't shake the feeling she wasn't about to like what was going to come next for her. As she drew closer, Kendrick and Manny stood tall outside Valence Sr.'s office.

They refused to make eye contact and Piper had even picked up a hint of what looked like disgust on their normally easy going demeanor. What had happened since she left a week prior that she was now not privy to knowing? Piper kept her facial expression cold as stone, as she stood there waiting to be either let in or announced. Manny gave her a small wink and smirk before cutting his eyes toward Kendrick. Opening the heavy oak door, the two had stepped to the side letting her pass into the office.

"Ms. Johnson," Valence Sr. boasted, coming from behind his old Victorian desk and kissing her on both cheeks.

"Don Valence," Piper warmly greeted looking around the room to see if they were alone.

"How was your trip?" Valence Sr. inquired sitting in one of the overstuffed chairs and gesturing for Piper to do the same.

"It was fine. I believe Ralphy Jr.. will be pleased with his present. I know I was." Piper eased into cracking jokes as she always had with him.

"I'm sure he will." Valence Sr. shifted in his seat looking straight at Piper. "But the reason I sent you to New York?"

"It was handled. I'm not going to lie... it got messy. Wasn't my intention but..." Piper shrugged knowing he would understand. No doubt that it had caused trouble back this way and now he was going to have to clean up a bigger mess than she went up there to contain.

"Was it found?" His voice grew darker and Piper understood what he was asking.

Reaching into her boots, Piper had pulled out two small burlap bags and handed it over to Valence Sr. "It's all there. The papers, money and the diamonds."

"That's my good girl." His smile spread as he had opened up the small bag revealing what she had been sent for.

"Here are the receipts on the first and second pick-ups and drop offs." Piper took the paperwork out of the inside jacket pocket and handed it to him.

"Very good. Your money will be transferred by the end of business day. But unfortunately you're not going to get to rest. I have another contract for you."

"Oh come on, you promised me. I haven't had a vacation in over a year." Piper scoffed. *What was the point of making money if you never get the time in which to spend it.* "Why can't one of the guys handle it?"

"Because it has your name on it." He grabbed the file that was sitting on his desk and handed it to Piper.

Evette Cason in bold letters stared back at her. Only three people in this house knew her real name or as she referred to it, her dead name. After twelve years, why hadn't they let the search for her be over? Why couldn't they accept she was gone and there was nothing anyone could do to bring her back? She wondered why she hadn't faked her death and this file would be moot.

"She's gone," Piper sneered, throwing the file up on the edge of the desk refusing to even open it.

"Well it's time for her to be found. This contract has quite a few moving parts." The wicked grin he normally reserved for the victims that were brought before him spread across his lips. "Apparently there was a broken betrothal, and the Cason family needs this set right. Just so happens that the Hulston family has two contracts out. Guess they didn't know playing the competition against one another is a no-no. But either way both families have paid handsomely to bring you to them in three days time to marry Xander Hulston."

Piper's jaw hit the floor. First, why was this so important? Second, why couldn't he do what he had already done and that was to tell them he couldn't help. This wasn't the first time that they had come to any of the Families looking for help to locate her. Unfortunately, it wouldn't be the last. Piper remembered a few years back when they got news. At the time the bounty wasn't high enough for Piper to be worried about anyone collecting. Now two or more families jockeyed for the 100,000 dollar price tag that had been placed on her head.

A sense of dread washed over Piper. *Were they really going to sell her out for the sake of the money? Could they really be that heartless after everything she had done for the Valence family?* Questions flooded her mind faster than she could even react in the moment. Piper had not even noticed they were no longer alone in the room.

"Don, you asked to meet with us?" Kris's voice was now a little more shaky than his usual cold and calculated demeanor. Mark stood there as stiff as stone refusing to look at Piper.

"In a moment boys. I have to finish up with Ms. Johnson first." Valence Sr. waved them out of the room.

"So, is that it? You're just going to hand me over?" Piper finally spit out like venom on her tongue.

"Yes and No." Valence Sr. reached for the discarded cigar on his desk. "Seems Mr. Xander has done some shady deals with the Morang Family. As we both know the Morang Family has a loose cannon on their staff, who has made friends with Xander Hulston. Hence the reason, your contract hasn't come up in several years."

"Let me guess, Victor VanGuard?" Piper dropped her head into her hands. She had had dealing with Victor in the past, and the last had ended with Nicky having to talk her down from ending his life.

"Right. Victor has gone rogue. He has a 150K contract to see that you will never be found alive, let alone make it to the altar."

"So, let me get this straight. I am not only being handed over to the man that nearly killed me but I am also bait to lure out the biggest loose cannon west of the Mississippi?" Piper stared at the floor exasperated.

"We bring Victor to the Morang Family and there is a half a million dollar payday. You stay married to Xander for 5 years..."

"6 months"

"4 years"

"A year max" Piper's eyes bore crystal blue holes into Valence Sr.

"How about we will see what happens?" Valence Sr. grinned, blowing the cigar smoke through his missing teeth. "Let's put it this way. Your family is interested in making sure their darling Evette is returned safe and sound. Your father doesn't seem to be in the best of health and is ready to sign over everything to you. There will be no prenup between you and Xander, and even if there was, you know that boy can't keep it in his pants. Within a year or two he will have access to the Hulston money and you walk away with half. Plus, this doesn't mean you can't keep working for us, it just means we will have to be more careful about how long you stay away from your doting husband."

"I don't have a choice, do I?" Piper sat back in the leather office chair knowing the answer before he had said a word.

"Not this time, but at least it does come with a hefty wedding gift for you."

CHAPTER II
THE COST OF LOYALTY

Running wide open down the dust-covered road, Piper noticed there was only an hour until sunset. She was angry at the turn of events that had led her to this moment in her life. For the first time in a long time, something besides Nicky and Dom, had her blood pressure boiling over. Time was ticking by faster than she would have liked, but it wouldn't stop the mission at hand. She knew what was at stake here as she shifted the gears in the old 61' Impala that Valence Sr. had insisted she took with her. A knot of fear forming in her stomach with every mile she drove. A knot Piper knew all too well.

Valence Sr. wasn't lying when he promised her a hefty gift for completing this contract. Within twelve hours of her leaving, nearly a hundred thousand dollars had appeared into her account. She had been paid handsomely to complete this job, there was no doubt about that, but there was something more on the line here, her reputation.

She would not let her reputation be ruined because of something as trivial as fear. Two hundred and forty-nine completed contracts and with any luck this would be her last one for a while. At least that's what she would tell herself every time. Piper wasn't sure she could walk away from the life, or if they would let her. She knew for a fact that Nicky wouldn't, and Valence Sr. had made too much off her skills to turn her loose now. Though this contract would teeter on whether that was true or not.

Pulling off for gas at the first exit she had seen in what seemed like hours, Piper contemplated calling the whole thing off and disappearing into the great beyond which was the New Mexico desert. She could fuel up and head north to the Bonneville Salt Flats, getting lost for a few months until things blew over. The only problem with that would be the price on her head when she resurfaced. Not that there wasn't already one on her now.

She never had second thoughts about a mission before this one, but as each mile drew her closer to the location, Piper's stomach began to tie up in knots. It never crossed her mind in the past decade whether or not she was doing the right thing. After all, she enjoyed living her life in the "morally gray" territory others only dreamed of. This was different. This was her willingly walking back into the lion's den, without so much as a chair for protection.

Deciding this was no time to grow a conscience, Piper filled up her car to make the last leg of the journey. According to her phone, she had less than forty-five minutes until she made it to the hotel. With the lack of traffic and police on the road, she would make it in less than thirty. Unfortunately, Piper knew this road like the back of her hand. Every cut-off, off-road, and hidden passage between where she now stood and Nowhere, New Mexico. Pointing the Impala toward the open road, Piper had let her mind wonder ever so slightly to cement the task at hand.

She never thought it would be possible for her past and present to cross paths, not like this anyway. The memories of that night still wreaked havoc at the corners of her mind. She had been badly beaten, broken, and bruised, but she overcame it. But the one person that stood by her through it all, was now M.I.A. Valence Sr. had sent him off on another job with Dom, and Piper was left to deal with this shit alone.

While she had cut contact with everything and everyone, now she was being pulled back due to her connections. Family connections that is. It would never get as far as the job entailed; Piper wouldn't allow it. Thinking about it made her skin crawl. Her self-respect, dignity, and even her own mental capacity screamed to get it done and disappear without a trace. This was the reason she second guessed everything.

She didn't know if she had the resolve to face that slimy bastard without putting a bullet between his eyes.

Screaming loudly at the void that was the setting sun, Piper gripped the steering wheel, violently shaking it within her hands. There was no way out of this, she was damn well certain of that, but the bigger slap in the face was she had no idea what Nicky's role would be in the job. Not a soul had said what the plan was or how it was to play out. The only thing she had known was Kris and Mark would be running back up for her, and Piper believed that was scarier than jumping into a tank full of hungry sharks on her period.

Pulling into the cracked asphalt parking lot of the Grand Ole Saloon hotel, Piper noticed how much this place had been turned more into a tourist attraction than the rundown roach motel she had remembered it as. Her audible groan over the now overly rustic building caught the attention of a few people walking past, and she scolded herself for even bringing the slightest bit of attention toward her.

It was fitting to have the meeting in the last place she had been seen in this godforsaken town. No doubt that Valence Sr. had been the one to make the arrangements and find humor in irony. Piper hadn't though and as she had grabbed her bag out of the back seat of the land yacht, she set her mind to the task at hand.

Piper walked with a heavy step across the old wooden porch, and pulled on the dark batwing door made to look like the traditional saloon doors. Her full bodied frame shuddered at the memories she kept tucked away. Fixing her external mask, Piper walked into the grand lobby to check-in.

"Good Evening Madam, checking in?" the polite young man boasted from behind the counter.

"Yes, Evette Cason." Piper said, taking out her ID from what seemed like a lifetime ago. There were very few reasons why she would keep her original licences up to date. Piper supposed she always knew this would eventually come to pass, even if this was the last thing she had ever really wanted.

"Ah, yes Ms. Cason. We have been expecting you. Your party has already checked in." He beamed at her. "They left this here." Handing her a piece of folded paper.

Piper had the drill memorized like the back of her hand and wouldn't open the note until she was secured into the elevator or her room. The man behind the counter looked let down by this action but Piper wasn't bothered by it. She couldn't understand why most if not all clerks were this level of nosy. She smiled at the young man as he handed her the keys and pointed the way to the elevators. Piper began to wonder if he was even old enough to remember the horrible things that this place was known for.

"Hey, one more thing." Piper knew it was a long shot.

"Yes, ma'am?" The man looked at her questioningly.

"Does Jackie still work here?"

"Who ma'am?"

"He was the overnight janitor?"

"I'm sorry. I don't think we have anyone here by that name."

"Okay, thank you." Piper knew it was a long shot, but she had hoped maybe there was a chance.

Strolling over to wait for the next elevator, she kept an eye over both shoulders. Something didn't feel right to her. It was as if she was being watched but there was no one in the hallway. Piper knew whoever Valence Sr. sent would have cleared the area and made sure to keep an eye on it until her arrival. This was also the reason Piper had to come alone. She wouldn't risk blowing the cover and the contract.

Once the elevator finally arrived, Piper darted in finding security in the emptiness. Taking the first easy breath since she had crossed into town, she opened the note. "Something Old, Something New, Something Borrowed, Something Blue." in the mocking handwriting of none other than Valence Sr. She growled in anger and frustration slamming her fist into the elevator wall. Piper knew she was the bait. He didn't have to rub her nose in it.

An arranged marriage to the bastard that had laid hands on her a decade ago was the only way for her family to save face. When she had fled that night, three things had come to pass. The Cason and Hulston families had fallen out of favor with the elite. Once the top tier of the powerful, now left to ruins and disgraced by their daughter's broken betrothal and Xander's open affairs. Then Piper's disappearance into thin air made the families look like they were hiding something, which caused the families to be viewed under a microscope. Her reappearing act would set things right among those that trusted and respected her, especially in the family business.

The job put both issues to rest. The Cason family would have their missing daughter and the honor restored. The Hulston family would finally have the only male settled down and with any luck a legitimate heir to the Hulston fortune. When it was all said and done, Piper would walk away the heiress to both family fortunes. Watching them all crumble to the ground would just be a bonus for her. Her vengeance would be swift and clean and her escape cleaner than the last. Xander Hulston had made his bed, now it was time for him to rot in it.

The fact she had to entertain being married to him for a year made her stomach churn. They would be lucky if she waited til the ink dried before he met his untimely demise, but Piper had to remind herself there was more than one way to skin a cat. If Valence Sr. stayed good to his word then the next year would fly by a little more entertaining than she imagined. If he didn't, Piper hoped that Nicky would step in and come for her.

Piper tried to steady her nerves before the elevator made it to the third floor. As the doors opened, she squared up her shoulders and swung her duffel bag up on her back. Moving toward her room with the same stealthy grace as she always had, Piper still couldn't shake the feeling she was either being watched or followed. It wasn't until she rounded the corner she had seen Kris and Mark waiting outside her room. No doubt that they would have slipped the desk attendant money to be made aware of her arrival.

"Hello, Boys. Waiting long?" Piper gave her best sarcastic smile.

"You're late," Kris said, holding a garment bag over his shoulder.

"Traffic," Piper said using her usual excuse.

"Did a tumbleweed cross in front of you?" Mark said a little less amused than the smile that seemed to spread across Piper's face.

"Something like that." Piper snickered, looking at the hallway to see if she could see cameras. "Let's get inside, you never know who is watching."

Relenting to the fact she was right, the men stood to the side to let her open the door. As the three shuffled into the themed bridal suite, Mark turned on the light to reveal the grossly decorated room illuminated in harsh red and white lights. Piper rolled her eyes at the Mr. and Mrs. decor with rose petals draped over every surface. She shook her head, staring daggers at her companions in warning not to say a word unless they wanted her wrath unleashed on them.

"Where's the dress?" Piper said, exasperated by the situation.

"Here," Kris said, slinging the bag off his shoulder and handing it over.

Piper knew she had a limited amount of time before she had to be presented by the two "hunters". There was no time for her to properly freshen up, but she would take the time to wash off the road grime from traveling for the last few days. If this was her last taste of true freedom, she would take whatever she had been afforded. Taking the bag, she retreated into the bathroom slamming the door to show her distaste for the situation.

She could have been there in less than a day, maybe a day and a half if she had taken the plane the guys had come out on, but Piper didn't like to fly. There were always too many people and a chance she could either be recognized or picked up by security for a number of other reasons. Piper had done her best to never be recognized or put herself in those kinds of situations. She knew her family had paid a pretty penny for her not only to be found but also to be brought back alive, and ten years is a long time not to be found. She had hoped like so many others they believed she was just gone.

As she was half way through her volcanic waterfall, she had heard a commotion from the other room. While she tried to tone out what would undoubtedly be the two arguing over the remote for the T.V., their ever rising tone became too much for her to ignore. Instead of screaming through the bathroom door, Piper climbed out of the shower, wrapping a towel around herself, and emerged from the bathroom ready to take their heads from their shoulders. All she wanted was a few minutes of peace, denied to her by the situation that she had currently found herself.

As the argument grew to an alarming level, the "call the front desk" kind of level, Piper pulled the door to the bathroom open with such force it rattled the hinges. Stomping into the room, she had seen the two on their phones screaming at whoever was on the other end. Piper had stopped short when she saw both Kris and Mark checking their weapons, readying themselves for a fight.

"What do you mean he escaped the compound?" Mark hissed to the man on the other end of the line.

"No, he doesn't know what is going on. He was never supposed to." Kris screamed.

"You better find him before he ruins everything." Mark slammed his phone down on the table letting out a frustrating growl. Kris quickly followed suit.

She had never witnessed these two react in this manner before today, as it wouldn't be wise for the bodyguards to be freaking out like hysterical newbies. If it had been any of the others, Piper would have been on edge. She knew she had to keep her head regardless of what the situation was. Nothing could be left to chance if the Valence family was to get this contract handled correctly. Hence the reason these two had been her escort. Even though it disturbed her about Nicky's absence in this matter, Piper had no choice but to go with it, as it was her head that was currently being hunted.

As her anger grew, Piper's patients began to get thinner. When she realized the men had not taken notice of her standing there fuming, she picked up and slammed one of the Mr. & Mrs. statues on the table. The two went dead silent and simultaneously turned to look at the drenched raven haired woman. The color drained from their faces at the prospect of her knowing exactly what was really going on. They had been sworn to secrecy before leaving the old man's office, and unfortunately, the anonymity looked to be running out by the second.

"Do I want to know what the hell is going on?" Piper said, standing in a large puddle of water that seemed to be creeping across the carpet.

The two remained quiet for a moment, contemplating what to say next. They couldn't tell her under any circumstances what had been entrusted to them, and if she did know, well let's just say they wouldn't be making it out of New Mexico in one piece. It wouldn't matter if they were only carrying out orders, Piper would have them ripped apart piece by piece.

It was already bad enough this was all done behind Nicky's back, and the men would have hell to pay once they got back to the house. If Piper knew the real details of this assignment, and the fact Nicky knew nothing about it, there would be an explosion no one was ready to see.

Trying to think on their feet, Kris and Mark mentally knew only one of them could speak. Only then, they would know which way to spin the version of events to Piper.

"We don't have all night, Gentleman." Piper's voice came out smooth as silk, as rage began to smolder. Anticipation grew heavy in the room.

"Nicky has left the compound," Kris finally blurred out, letting out just enough truth that it should be a little bit believable.

"And..." Piper crossed her arms and pressed firmly for more information.

"He's headed this way." Mark looked terrified but followed suit with the breadcrumbs of information.

"Is that supposed to scare me?" Piper stood there confused as to why these men looked like they had seen the grim reaper instead of getting the news that their boss, who was late to the party, was finally on his way. If anything, she was relieved he had finally resurfaced.

"It's truly nothing for you to worry about." Kris shot a look over to Mark for back up.

"Nicky was supposed to be out of town for the next month. Hence the reason he isn't here. When he got back yesterday evening, he inquired about the whereabouts of the three of us. He isn't too happy that we had left without him." Mark hoped he sounded believable as Piper could pick up on any loose string in the hem of a story.

"You know what? We don't have time for this. He's late and that's not our problem. The show must go on or Valence Sr. is going to have a coronary." Piper's eyes narrowed at the two men in front of her. "Now you two have a job to do. Make sure this room is properly ready or so help me god I will show you what the other end of your manhood looks like." Piper turned on her heels retreating back into the bathroom slamming the door.

Once the music started blaring out of the bathroom, the two men sighed in relief. Neither would dare to set her off in the danger she would make good on her threat. They had personally seen what she had been capable of doing if the mood had fancied her, and the last thing they needed was their blood all over the decor.

Kris could tell Piper wasn't herself. While she always appeared to be on edge, this was different, and he couldn't put his finger on it. She would have jumped at the chance to torture information out of someone, but she had taken their explanation with no questions asked. She had even drawn her own conclusion without so much as a second thought. They had felt guilty for what they were doing, but unfortunately, there was nothing that could be done.

A million dollar price tag was more than any of them had seen in some time. It was a shame it landed on Piper's head and maybe this would workout in everyone's favor. Maybe Nicky would finally move on with his life.

CHAPTER 12
SILENCE

As the three of them approached Piper's old family home, the moon started to rise in the desert sky. While the panic rose in her body, Piper had to keep her demeanor one of a broken child instead of the fierce right hand of one of the most feared men in the south. She wondered where Nicky was, and if he would get there in time to get her out of this particular mess. It wasn't that Piper couldn't handle this herself, but knowing backup was on the way, did make this a little easier to maneuver.

She had not laid eyes on this old house in nearly twelve years. Thinking about how her family just handed her over to the Hulston family two years before Xander and her wedding didn't seem fishy at the time. It wasn't long after though things had shifted and the man she thought she loved became violent.

Driving up what seemed like a newly paved drive, Piper was surprised nothing had changed. It was as if the entire property had frozen in time. The landscape waited for life to be breathed back into it, even though it looked as pristine as the day she left. Certain things she had taken such pride in adding to outer aesthetics begged to be released from whatever curse that had been placed on it in her absence.

As Piper gazed up at the dark, brooding building perched on the hill in the first glimmers of moonlight, the word "tradition" echoed through her mind. Countless memories, both pleasant and unpleasant, came rushing back. Bile rose in her throat. She had done everything within her control to push this place into the depths of her memory, but now she had no choice but to face the music. Even if it were only for the mission at hand, Piper had to play her part.

As the last events and conversations played over and over in Piper's mind, it was what transpired in Valence Sr.'s office days before that she couldn't seem to shake. She knew there was more going on than she was privy to in the moment, and Kris and Mark's behavior cemented her suspicions. They had always been a little off to say the least but they were keeping something more from her. Unfortunately, she didn't have time to be the bloody bride.

"It's Showtime." Mark looked back from the front passenger seat knocking Piper back into reality.

"I'm guessing I can't get a once more around the block." Piper's dry humor caught the men off guard.

Something had changed in her from the hotel to pulling up at the mansion. Her stone cold expression plastered across her face looked almost stoic. It was as if all emotion had drained from her body and she had engaged autopilot. Even under the cream sparkle of the tulle vail, Piper looked like she had not even a glimmer of hope. This was not the woman they had come to know and even fear from time to time. She looked broken.

Kris and Mark exchanged a quick, unrelenting glance. They knew what they had to do and if one thing went awry they would be the ones paying with their lives. Don Valence had given explicit instructions for them not only to deliver her but to witness the marriage. Unfortunately, they were starting to feel guilty about the spot they were putting Piper in. They knew more than they were allowed to say and it was eating them alive. Not enough for them to lose their lives over but enough to remind them they hadn't been to confession in a while.

Getting out of the car, they stared at each other over the top. "If we both stick to the story, they won't be able to prove anything."

"For our sake, you better be right this time," Kris shot back, opening the car door and offering his hand to Piper.

The billowy white satin ball gown seemed to swallow her. The long sleeved heavy lace cloak had covered everything the dress or veil didn't. Piper had been buried under what looked like a mountain of fabric. Her appearance was one more of an overly frosted cupcake than a bride. While her annoyance had been clear when she fought to get into the car with the dress, now she moved with grace and poise never faltering a step. The men didn't know whether to be impressed or terrified at the switch in her personality.

Piper had known when she opened the dress bag that Valence Sr. had not only picked out the dress but decided to take a little more liberty than was needed. Bright white, not off white, not even cream. He had a sense of humor Piper would give him that but this was far beyond the reach of a joke. Even the bright blue garter had been purchased. Piper swore if she survived this she would smack that smug smile right off his face and send that cigar flying from his mouth. For now, she had to play the fragile, contrite daughter and willing bride.

There hadn't been a planned backstory to where she had been for the last decade or even how the Valence family had found her. All three would have to fly by the seat of their pants navigating this situation. Piper had reserved to stay quiet until it was time for her not to. It was easier that way. She could watch her surroundings and be able to figure out if there happened to be an extra guest.

Walking up the stone steps, Piper was flanked by Kris and Mark. Before they could get to the door, two of the older cousins had opened the double doors to see who was approaching. A superior contemptuous expression adorning their tight little faces. When they had caught sight of their golden child cousin being escorted home to face her judgment, they moved to the side mocking her as she passed. Piper kept her eye's casted down as she was led to the doorway of the grand hall.

When Betsy Cason caught sight of her daughter, she quickly removed herself from the group of women she had been conversing with and walked over to the door. Her eyes were narrowed, scanning every inch of her face to confirm indeed it was Evette. When she noticed that each of her cousins had an arm, Betsy stared daggers at them to unhand her quickly. The Cason family would not appear to look like animals in front of the Hulston family.

"Follow me." Betsy quickly moved across the hall where a Bridal suite had been made up for her daughter. Gritting her teeth, Piper followed the group into the room.

Once inside, Betsy took a good long look at the men that seemed to surround Evette. She waved her hand before saying, "You can go wait with the rest of the guests."

The two younger men had taken their elders' warning and scurried out of the room. Mark and Kris on the other hand hadn't moved a muscle flanking either side of Piper.

"I'm sorry ma'am but that's not going to be possible," Kris spoke with as much respect as he could muster.

"Excuse me?" Betsy's eyes narrowed.

"We have strict orders ma'am. She isn't allowed out of our sight until we see the marriage license signed," Mark piped up.

"And since we have not confirmed who you are, we have no idea whether you will help her escape." A hint of amusement played in Kris' voice.

Piper would have rolled her eyes if she could have. These two were getting entirely too much enjoyment at her expense and she was seething over it. Once she was free of this situation, she would make sure they would end up on the worse assignments for the next three years. If she didn't handle the disrespect personally.

"The ceremony doesn't start for at least another thirty minutes or so. Wouldn't you rather go and enjoy some refreshments? I hardly believe her mother would be a danger to her." Betsy put on her brightest smile to put the two men at ease.

"I'm sorry ma'am rules are rules." Kris shrugged.

"I just want a quick word with my daughter. I mean it is her wedding day. Don't I have the right as her mother to be able to do that?"

"Ma'am it wouldn't matter if you were God, himself. We have orders and on top of that we haven't been paid yet. You're already pushing your luck being this close to her before the ceremony," Mark growled proving his point by grabbing Piper's arm pulling her closer to him.

"Unhand the merchandise before you damage it you damn mongrel." Betsy's tone changed as her eyes glinted with an unspoken promise of what she could be capable of doing.

When Mark gripped tighter on Piper's arm refusing to let her go, Betsy swung up and attempted to connect with Mark's cheek. He caught her wrist and forced her back making her stumble falling to the floor with a loud thud. The dressing table had been turned over in the process causing the room to erupt into chaos.

Kris took Piper's other arm and moved her in front of him like a shield as Mark stood in front of the two. The whole situation had turned quickly, and the men had no idea whether they should enact plan B or see if this was going to resolve itself. Unfortunately for them, Piper was going to be of no use either way as she was resolved into standing there like a well placed porcelain doll. They understood she couldn't give up her cover but why now of all times she was compelled to actually stick to the plan?

The commotion in the room didn't go unnoticed, as shouting could be heard from beyond the door. When two dark haired gentlemen dressed in tuxedos busted through the door, Mark and Kris thought their gooses were cooked. Pulling their weapons from under their jackets, the men put Piper to their backs. She had to be protected at all costs. After all, coming home without the million dollar payout would result in their lives no longer being of this world.

"What the hell is going on in here?" Mr. Cason said, looking from his wife on the floor to the two men that had guns drawn.

"They attacked me." Betsy pointed at the two men.

"What is the meaning of this?" Mr. Cason said, coming to stand between his wife and the others.

"She tried to assault my partner, after being told we wouldn't leave the room. One gentle shove later and well you see she landed on her ass," Kris retorted, never taking his attention off the second man or the fact that the door was still open.

"We don't have time for this," he hissed at Betsy. "Are you trying to sabotage the union? So much is riding on this and you want to make it all about you."

"But Larry?" Betsy sniveled, picking herself up off the ground. Her dress was covered in various make-ups and perfumes, leaving her in a tattered mess.

"Not another word. Go up-stairs this minute and change your dress. The ceremony will begin in less than twenty minutes." He glared at her, shooting a warning to not defy him. "As for your two gentlemen, I am very sorry that our hospitality has been less than accommodating. Please forgive us, and as a token of sincerity," Mr. Cason took a black bag from the man standing behind him, handing it to Mark.

"It's all here, right? No need to count it?" Mark noticed the weight of the bag. It was definitely all there, but he was still going to give him shit about it.

"Yes, Sir. I wouldn't dare try to swindle the Valence family." There was a shakiness to Larry Cason's voice that the two relished in. Even Piper was beaming on the inside, cursing at the fact she couldn't show it.

"Good. Now let's get the show on the road." Kris remarked waiting for the two men to back out of the room. When they didn't, Kris became a little uneasy.

130

"Isn't there something you're supposed to be doing right now?" Mark looked more annoyed with the fact he had pulled his weapon but didn't get to use it.

"Oh we thought once we handed over the case, our deal was completed," The man from behind Mr. Cason had remarked.

"Well, you thought wrong." Kris glared tilting his head ever so slightly. "it doesn't work that way. We have to witness the signing of the license. Then we can be on our way. Otherwise..." Kris steps to one side, reaching back to grab Piper's arm hard, yanking her forward. "She comes back with us and Don Valence can do what he wishes with the returned merchandise, and the fee." As if on cue, Mark held up the bag as if to give the full picture.

"That's not what we agreed upon with Don Valence." Mr. Cason's eyes grew dark but knew there was little he could do. Kris and Mark were holding all the cards.

"Well our orders were simple: deliver the Bride, pick up the money, and make sure we witness the union as proof for when we return back to Don Valence." Kris glared at the men hoping they would make a move.

Piper silently prayed that this would be it. Her way out of this whole mess. She was certain that her father and his men wouldn't back down, which would cause a shoot out and she would escape back to the hotel. This whole ugly mess would be put to rest along with her betrothal to Xander Hulston.

It was a good thing she hadn't formally bet on it, as Mr. Cason nodded his head, saying through gritted teeth. "Leave them."

Once the door closed, they could hear raised voices but nothing the three could make out. Kris and Mark exchanged glances hoping it was some family drama and not a surprise guest. After all, no one knew the exact location of Nicky and the last thing they needed was him busting in to steal the bride away.

"Your family is nuts." Kris said, finally loosening the grip he had on Piper's arm.

"You haven't seen anything yet." Piper's voice came out barely audible.

Mark and Kris exchanged a worried glance between them. They honestly didn't know what would be worse, Piper finding out the real arrangements Don Valence made or knowing that this had been the old man's end game since he had found out her true identity. They had been put in this precarious spot but seeing the hardened expression of Piper, they had wondered if this was truly the right thing to do.

When the knock came at the door, Kris and Mark exchanged looks before they called out to the person on the other side. "What is it?"

"It's time." the male voice called back.

"Well, here goes nothing." Piper said her voice was stone cold with the resolve she was barely holding onto.

As Mark reached for the doorknob his hand shook, "I am sorry it had to go down like this."

"It's the nature of the beast. We don't have to like it but we do have to follow orders." Piper offered both men a small smile before they exited the room,

The room erupted in gasp as she walked into view flanked on either side by the two men dressed in black. The Cason family had gathered on one side of the room and the Hulston were on the other as Piper moved defiantly down the aisle with her head held high. Nothing would stop her from completing this part of her mission even if this went against everything she wanted.

Looking at the slightly older playboy in front of her, Piper wondered how she ever had feelings for this bastard. All the rage she felt the night he tried to break her came back in a flood of fury that simmered just below the surface. Wondering if it would be poor taste to cut his throat at the altar, Piper merely took his hand and nodded for the men to take their seats.

"I've been waiting a long time for you, and this time you won't get away from me." Xander's words were both a threat and a promise, as no one but Piper knew what had transpired between them over a decade prior.

"We will see which one of us are left standing when the smoke clears this time." Piper's voice was as low and threatening as ever as she took his hand and walked toward the family priest.

From any onlooker, it was a beautifully orchestrated ceremony that went off without any real problems. The families had handled every facet of the gathering from the ceremony to the reception. Even the food and music had been carefully selected more than likely drawing off the original plans for the day from twelve years prior. Piper inwardly cringed over the popups display but to the crowd of former family and friends she still had to play the timid remorseful Evette.

The first dance was something that Piper dreaded more than standing at the altar and signing the marriage license in front of the priest. With all eyes on them, Xander led her around the floor as if they were a couple still in love instead of one that despised the others' very existence. The worst part of the whole ordeal was the song that had been chosen. It had been their song since she was sixteen and the very sound of it made her want to be violently ill.

Piper didn't know how she was going to keep up this facade when his touch physically repulsed her. She stiffened when he dipped her in the last turn and brought her back up for what he thought would be a kiss. She turned her head at the last moment, having it land on her cheek. She reminded herself to scrub everywhere he dared lay a hand later. His smug grin plastered on his face. Piper would be more than happy to knock off but with the room full of people, she had to restrain herself.

Once the dance was over, everyone joined them on the dance floor. Piper tried to retreat back to her seat, when her father took her hand to have his dance with her. She could tell he was trying so hard to keep his conformity, but with the situation at hand certain decorum had to be addressed. He had opened his mouth several times to say something, but the words seemed to fail him. This had her wondering, if he had missed her at all or was this just a missing piece of a now completed puzzle?

When that dance ended, her father-in-law was the next to take the honor. As the hours ticked on, Piper was passed between every male relative on both sides of the family for their turn to dance with the bride. It hadn't gone unnoticed that Xander wasn't made to go through the same predicament. In fact she couldn't remember how many dances she had gone through before she had lost sight of her now husband. As the last dance with one of the cousins had ended, they were looking around for Xander to cut the cake.

"I'll go look for him." Piper's tone was one of exhaustion and exasperations.

Leaving the ballroom, Piper began to search everywhere for Xander. She ascended the stairs to see if he was hiding in one of the old offices, as he had when they were teenagers. The fond memory of the two sneaking in and out trying to elude her mother, sent a fire through her chest that she had no time to address. Piper didn't want to admit to herself that all the good memories were shams, even if she knew otherwise. She had no idea why it hurt her more than it did then. Even seeing her childhood room, still as she had left it, had feelings stirring that she was not ready to deal with. After all, what does one say to a shrine of the happy life that turned out to be anything but.

Realizing he wasn't anywhere to be found, Piper thought he might be in the study. When she was about halfway down stairs a familiar smell and sounds caught her attention. Piper's steps were quiet and deliberate as she followed the musk of sex and the muffled moans of the thralls of pleasure, leading her to the coat room by the front door. Piper tried to keep her composure when she pulled open the door to reveal Xander wrapped in what she could only presume was his lover's arms with her straddling his lap. Xander and Nadia froze.

"We are cutting the cake. You might want to pull up your pants or should I let out a scream and end this all now?" Piper's words were sharp as well honed steel.

"I'll be there when I'm finished here." Xander held Nadia closer to him.

Piper reached in and picked Nadia up by the hair, and dragged her out the front door, dropping her on her ass. Red rimmed eyes looked back at Xander as Piper's restraint was being held by a thread. "You follow her and there will not be a license to turn in tomorrow. Now get your ass together and come cut the fucking cake. Then you can do whatever you see fit."

CHAPTER 13
COVER UP... NOT SO COVERED

A week had passed since the wedding day of Piper and Xander and things had become unbearably tense between the two. There was always going to be animosity but this went further. Piper couldn't get over the fact she had caught Xander hiding in the coat room with whom she could only assume was his lover. The worst part of the whole ordeal was recognizing the woman that Xander had been accused of having an affair with over a decade ago. Piper would have known Nadia Morang anywhere.

The blatant disregard for her and the fact they had just said their vows not even an hour prior boiled her blood for some unknown reason. This was a ruse for all intensive purposes, but Piper was feeling more of a sense of betrayal than a mission that needed to be completed. Coming to terms with the evidence from his past indiscretions, had Piper's blood boiling over. She hated when her emotions got brought into a situation instead of being the cold and calculated killer she had become over the last decade. For her it was as if all the old wounds had reopened to confirm everything she had already known, but wouldn't dare acknowledge.

When they had moved into the marriage home that was a wedding gift from her parents, Piper had thrown herself into making the cold sterile place comfortable, as this was now to be her cover. What bothered her more was not Xander's behavior, that was predictable at the very least, but the fact that it had been a week and not a word from Nicky or the Valence family.

Unfortunately with all the "newlywed" events and the expectation of a "honeymoon", Piper hadn't had time to look at her phone. When she would find a moment to herself, someone would pull her into something else. She would go back to the house most times alone and be exhausted from keeping her mask up for so long. She would pass out hoping to wake up from this horrible dream.

As the days ticked on, memories kept playing over and over in her mind. From the way Kris and Mark acted at the hotel to even Mark's apology before she left the bridal room. Nothing was adding up, and the worst part of it all she would never truly know why. Piper had to play her part until death do they part, or at least until she had enough evidence to bring to the Cason/Hulston family to end this sham of a marriage. She hoped it wouldn't take too long as she had a life to get back to.

Word had gotten around quickly that Evette Cason had returned, and she had finally married Xander Hulston. Nadia Morang was less than impressed by the nuptials as she was due to be the next Mrs. Xander Hulston. Looking at the wedding announcement in the Sunday paper, made her want to rip that bitch's hair out. How dare she take what was rightfully hers.

Nadia didn't believe that Evette had appeared out of thin air. After all, it had been less than a week when Xander and Nadia had announced not only their engagement but also the fact she was three months pregnant with Xander's third child. The Hulston family refused to allow the marriage after the first or the second child, but Nadia was certain that the third would force everyone's hand. It drove her crazy that Xander wouldn't marry her without his family's support. It wasn't that long ago they had planned for their escape from both their worlds, and now here she sat carrying another Hulston heir without so much as a diamond on her hand.

Her appearance at the wedding had again been Xander's idea. Though it didn't take much twisting of her arm to go along with it. She had even taken it upon herself to pick the most form fitting crimson red dress to wear to the ceremony. Her small baby bump on view to both families of who Xander really loved along with who was actually carrying on the blood line.

While her actions were a silent yet defiant part of the evening, she was also deeply enraged by the treatment of herself at the wedding. Those that would dare to look in her direction sneered at her presence. Most were baffled at her extended invitation, while the families did their best to save face in the situation, not wanting to cause a scene. Either way, Nadia was treated like a dirty secret instead of the mother of Xander's children.

Staring at the photo of Xander and Evette harder, Nadia had a sneaky suspicion she had seen her somewhere before that night. Where, though, she couldn't place at the moment. When they were younger, they hadn't run in the same social circles, but because of Xander, they did attend the same events and parties. Nadia couldn't pick the old Evette out of a crowd of debs if she tried, but the older Evette looked to command herself differently. This was the version of Evette that stuck out to her. She had seen this woman somewhere in the last few years.

Tossing the newspaper back onto the table, Nadia pondered if her cousin could dig up some dirt that would persuade the Hulston family to call for the annulment of the marriage. She would remind herself to give Victor a call later that afternoon to see what he could handle for her. For now though, Nadia remembered there was once a missing persons case opened on Evette Cason. She hoped it was still active. If it was this would tie the pretty little bitch up for a little bit while Xander and her took the honeymoon trip to Aruba instead of her. Nadia would make it a point to call down to the station and talk to a few of the boys on the payroll.

The bright rays of sunshine showed through the cracks in the blackout curtains that Piper had installed in her bedroom. She hadn't realized in all the years she had been gone how much she detested the early morning sun. Her thoughts on the matter were more towards how Nicky liked the whole house to be dark. Piper snickered, throwing her arm over her face, at the Italian Vampire, which is what she would call him when he would emerge hissing at the light.

The burning in her chest at not knowing where he was or what he was doing caused tears to slip from her eyes. Piper grieved for what could have been more than the fact she had sacrificed her own freedom. She began to wonder if this was Karma raising her ugly head for all the times she should have said something to Nicky about her feelings, or not openly going to the cops over what Xander had done all those years before. Piper could admit she hadn't been a saint but this was far worse punishment than Hell could or would allow.

She was certain she was in her own personal hell. What could be more damning than a loveless marriage and a husband that preferred the company of his mistress? Not that Piper intended on giving Xander a honest chance but she was willing to play the game that would end with him at the end of a hangman's noose. That would be a suitable punishment for the lives he destroyed in pursuit of being the biggest playboy on the block.

Piper's phone buzzed with a text. Groaning, she rolled to the night stand to see who was trying to contact her, secretly hoping it was Nicky. Her face fell when she saw the text was from her mother-in-law reminding her of brunch at the country club. "Appearances must be maintained." Piper could hear her mother's voice ringing in her ears.

Dragging herself from bed, Piper was determined to find a few moments to contact Nicky and see what was going on back home. After all the last accounts she had, Nicky was on his way and apparently pissed for whatever unknown reason. Something inside her said she should have pressed Mark and Kris for more information but there simply wasn't time. Yes, she could have made time to tie them down and extract the information with extreme measures, but that might have caused a huge mess she didn't want to deal with at that moment. Simply put, there never seemed to be enough time for anything.

Retreating to the bathroom, Piper took a few moments to take a good long look at herself in the mirror. She wasn't the obedient daughter she had been when she had returned from college, which seemed like a lifetime and a half ago. Piper learned in her time away that there was more to life than parties and social standings. She had gotten her hands dirty in more than one way, and there was no doubt in her mind that it had molded her into the woman she needed to be to handle the situation before her.

Piper was lost in her thoughts, readying herself for the day's events, when the knock came to the door early that Saturday morning. Looking through the open living room windows, Piper wasn't prepared for there to be a police cruiser sitting in her driveway. Something deep in her gut told her shit was about to go sideways, but she put on her best poker face when answering the door.

"Good Morning, Officer. What can I do for you?" Piper's best beaming smile on display.

"Good Morning Ma'am, Are you Evette Cason?"

"Hulston, now but yes I am Evette. How can I help you?"

"I'm Officer Jenkens from the Parish Police Department. Do you have time to answer a few questions?"

"All depends on what this is about." Piper kept her voice steady but something was definitely off about this.

"Your disappearance. As you know you have been a missing person for the last twelve years."

"No, actually I had no idea. I simply left town to study abroad." Piper kept her tone even, looking for any sign of why he was really there.

"I see. Can anyone vouch for that?"

"Officer, is it illegal to leave the country?"

"No ma'am, just trying to close out this cold case." His demeanor shifted but Piper caught the snippy tone. As if, he was more on a hunting mission than a well check.

"My now husband saw me off that morning. Unfortunately, he isn't here and I am now late to meet him and his family for brunch."

"Yes, ma'am. I will reach out to him to check the..." the officer stopped cold looking down at the papers he had brought with him. "But he said he didn't see his fiancé at all that day."

"Excuse me?"

"I'm sorry ma'am, Xander Hulston said during the investigation he didn't see you at all that day." The officer's eye brow was raised looking at Piper as if he knew there was more to the story. Possibly, he was also barking up the wrong tree.

"Well Officer..." Piper put on her best southern smile "Jenken's was it? I don't know what to tell you. I was out of the country, I'm back, married to Xander Hulston, and now if you don't mind I must ask you to leave. I have to be at the club in less than 30 mins and you are causing me to be late. Since, the last thing I want to deal with today is an angry mother-in-law."

"Yes, ma'am. If I have any other questions I'll be sure to reach out to you." The officer turned and left but not before giving Piper a hard look.

It didn't go unnoticed to Piper that he grabbed his phone off his side and placed a call even before getting in his cruiser. He had looked back at the house several times before raising his voice, but not loud enough for Piper to make out what he was saying or who he was talking to. Once he was in his car, screaming could be heard then he pulled off like a bat out of hell. Piper had half a mind to call down and talk to the Chief of Police, but deep down she knew she would get the runaround.

Staring at the place in the driveway the cruiser once sat, Piper tried to decide whether or not she would let this slip while she was at brunch. Maybe her new mother-in-law would like to know someone was harassing her, or maybe even her parents. Personally, she just wanted to see the look on Xander's face to see if he was the reason the cops had shown up to question where she had been these last twelve years.

One thing was for certain, she would have to tread lightly for the time being, keeping her mask up at any and all cost. The last thing she needed was police poking around in her past.

CHAPTER 14
TURNING UP THE HEAT

Nerves were about to bubble over as Piper sat in the car waiting for the valet to walk over and take the monstrosity she was driving away. She hated SUVs. They reminded her of overly inflated, self entitled sports moms she had encountered in her travels. It was a status symbol plain and simple. The one she drove was no exception. It was a sleek looking blacked out Denali with all the bells and whistles that anyone would ever want. Well, anyone but Piper.

Piper missed the faded leather seats of her Plymouth Duster. The simple AM/FM radio that always seemed to pick up two stations at once. Her ability to hit the gas, lighting the tires up. While she had not grown up with the knowledge of American Muscle, Piper could admire the beauty in the intricate simplicity of the old cars. Her chest began to tighten at the thought of Nicky buying her that car and teaching her how to make it shine once again. The car like herself had been reborn from the ashes of a horrible tragedy but now they both stood as a testament of determination.

When the knock came at Piper's window, she had nearly jumped out of her seat. A well dressed young man smiled at her putting both his hands in plain sight to calm her. Signaling for her to roll the window down, Piper steadied her heart knowing that being a part of this life was going to be a little more tricky than she had intended for it to be. She had come accustomed to looking over her shoulder, and now it was making her jumpy, which is something Nicky would tease her for if he was there.

"Yes." Piper tried to keep her tone even.

"Your car ma'am." The young man looked slightly confused but kept his warm smile.

"I'm sorry. Podcast caught my attention." Piper remarked trying to play off the awkward situation.

"My mom gets so involved with those things that just walking through the house will cause her to jump out of her skin. I understand. Here is your ticket." The boy tried to cover his giggle by clearing his throat offering her the valet slip.

"Never been much into unsolved crimes. But I can see the appeal." Piper exited in the car and walked toward the entrance of the limestone country club.

Everything was just as she remembered it from the founding father's and board member's pictures hanging on the walls to the women walking around in tennis skirts, even though they hadn't stepped foot on the court. Piper's stomach pitched when she realized she was once one of these young ladies. With all the time that had passed, she hoped she would never have to be that again. She had no doubt she could still play the part but for now she would do what she came to do.

"Angel Face," Xander called out waving her over to the table, as Piper cringed at the pet name.

Piper plastered on her best smile as she strolled to the center of the room. Xander rose from his seat to pull out her chair and place a light peck on her cheek. She wanted to throw up right then and there. Keeping her composure, she played it off as a woman still navigating the parameters of newlywed life with a man she hadn't seen in twelve years. She was thankful that neither family had noticed the uncomfortable awkwardness that seemed to engulf the two.

"Angel Face, what kept you?" Xander's sickly sweet tone coupled with him placing his hand on hers at the table tested her resolve.

While she had debated over and over again on the ride mentioning the morning's events to the families, Xander's peculiar tone of blaming her for being late was pushing her over the edge. "I'm sorry for my tardiness, but I had an unexpected visitor this morning. Coupled with not knowing where my husband was or whether we were coming together caused a bit of confusion this morning."

"That time of the month." Xander's disgusted expression earned him a snicker from not only the men at the table but also most of the passers by.

"No, husband. An Officer Jenkins from the Parish police department. He was asking questions about my disappearance." Piper's eyes never faltered as she stared daggers at him, ignoring the gasps from the room pretending not to be listening into the conversation. "He gave me some interesting information while he was apparently doing a well check."

"And what was that dear." Jamie Hulston spoke up, breaking the intense staring competition between the two.

"Apparently, Xander had told him he didn't see me at all on the day I disappeared. I told him that he must have had the wrong information as Xander was the one that had taken me to the airport. I believe the cold case, as he called it, will be closed." Piper side eyed Xander one more time before turning to the others at the table with a brilliant smile.

Awkward glances were shared among not only the people at the table but others in the room. She had no intention of letting anyone save face here. Most of all, the man that caused her to nearly die. Piper had a plan to deal with him but it would be slow and calculating. The same way he had planned on getting rid of her. Oh yeah, Piper found out that bit of knowledge while she was getting ready to return back to New Mexico.

"But you weren't a missing person," John Hulston had said trying to save themselves from the mountain of gossip that was being spun as they sat there.

"And that is exactly what I told Officer Jenkins." Piper batted her eyes toward her father-in-law. "I was simply studying abroad for the company. When he asked who could corroborate my story, I simply told them to talk to Xander."

"I'll call down to the station on Monday and talk to the Chief. He'll be able to put this all to bed," Larry Cason spoke up loud enough for most of the rubberneckers to quiet down.

Trying to turn the topic of conversation, Betsy spoke up with an intense enthusiasm. "So, how are the two love birds getting along? I know it's only been a week since the wedding but have you thought about when you will be taking your honeymoon yet?"

"We are getting along fine, Mrs. Cason." Xander quickly responded before his lovely bride could blow him out of the water.

"I've told you a thousand times we are family now. Call me, Betsy." Mrs. Cason blushed at his manners.

"Betsy it is then." Xander relaxed a little, putting a light squeeze on Piper's hand, instinctively telling her not to embarrass him.

"Personally, I've been so busy setting up the house and all the newlywed things, I don't think I really see Xander all that often. It'll be nice for the honeymoon. You know just the two of us. No real escape from having to get to know each other better after being away from each other for so long." The information was clear to anyone that could read between the lines, and Piper had no problem sharing.

"Yes, with all the big projects at work, I have been coming home late into the night, and leaving well before Evette gets up in the morning." Xander tried hard to cover his ass. "But our honeymoon will be different. With no work for two weeks, we might be able to really get to know each other and maybe even start our family."

With the words that erupted out of Xander's mouth, both mothers gushed at the thought of the couple starting their family. Piper's expression hardened quickly. She had no intention of ever allowing him anywhere near her sexually, especially after what he did to her prior when she told him no. It would be a cold day in Hell before she would carry one of his children.

"I guess we will see what happens." Piper was left between a rock and a hard place on responses she could give in that moment.

The families had sat there for another twenty minutes before John had looked down at his watch and began to clear his throat. "Ladies, I'm sorry to interrupt but it is nearly tee time. Son, will you be joining Larry and I? Evette, you don't mind if we steal away your husband for a round of golf do you?"

"No, he's all yours," she said, smiling back at the three men as they rose from their seats. "If you're going to be late for dinner I'd appreciate a call or text," Piper shot at Xander.

"I have to run back to the office this afternoon, but I should make it home in enough time for dinner," Xander responded before walking away, his father slapping his back.

A thunderous silence fell over the woman before Jamie had finally spoken up. "Evette, darling, I know this is a lot to get used to, but becoming a corporate wife isn't all bad."

"Never knowing if your husband is coming home or headed to his mistress'. Yeah, I can say it's been more than a little hard to get used to." Piper's voice was barely a whisper but she might as well have screamed it with the way the two women placed their gloved hands over their mouths.

"Excuse me?" Both Betsy and Jamie responded.

"We've been married for a week, and he has not spent the first night under the same roof with me. I know where he is. With the same woman I caught him in the coat closet with at our wedding. So, please, don't treat me like I am the problem here." Piper glared at the women but her pleasant expression never faltered.

"I'll be right back. I need to have a chat with my husband about our son while they are out on the course." Mrs. Hulston looked at Piper with a pitying look before rushing out of the room.

"Honey, this will be an adjustment for everyone. You have been gone for so long. Of course it's going to take some time to adjust to married life." Betsy's words seemed to infuriate Piper more than comfort her, as each word dripped with condescension

"Mother, with all due respect, if you knew father was having an open affair with no signs of ending said affair, what would you do?" Piper's voice was cold and calculating as she spoke.

"I would give him time to realize what was really important to him before throwing my hands in the air and ending it." Betsy could see what her daughter was really hinting at.

"Sometimes you have to gauge the situation on whether it is worth fighting for or not. Xander doesn't want me. He never did and now here we are sipping overpriced cocktails pretending everything is okay, when it is not."

"Sweetheart, you have to try to be a good wife to him, and maybe he will do what is right and be a good husband to you. But as of right now, you're experiencing growing pains in the relationship." Betsy sipped her tea and cleared her throat. "Now, let's not let this spoil the mood for the day. All will be well soon, you will see."

Piper remembering the mission at hand, "Whatever you think is best, mother."

"Very good. Now, I have some things from your old room back at the house that I think will make your place feel more like a home. If you would like I can drop them off later today. Oh and the wedding photos should be arriving in the next week or two. I know the one of Xander and you will be lovely over the fireplace."

148

"I would love the old pictures from my room. Thank you." Piper sat there quietly for the rest of the lunch counting down the minutes until she could leave.

When Jamie had returned back to the table, she had noticed her daughter-in-law's demeanor had shifted. She was unsure of what had happened while she was gone, but knew whatever it was had set a somber atmosphere over the rest of brunch. She hardly looked at anyone, and wouldn't join in the conversations but nodded along. It broke her heart to see the spirited young woman dealing with such problems not long after she was wed.

As Piper sat quietly watching the room, she tried to plan the best way she would be able to leave without having to have a further confrontation with her mother. It was clear that her mother either didn't understand or didn't want to. Was public image so important that she would sacrifice her daughter? She had done it once behind her back but now her eyes were open and Piper didn't like what she was seeing.

When a break in the conversation finally came after an hour, Piper took it upon herself to exit stage left. "This has been a great afternoon, but I have other things that I have to get done today." Piper rose from her seat and grabbed her purse.

"What else do you have to do?" Betsy looked more annoyed by her daughter's attempt at retreat.

"Well there is the grocery shopping. I have to stop by the cleaners, and I have to check in on some work that I have neglected since returning back here." Piper's tone was colder than she would have liked but she wasn't getting roped into another two hours of mindless small talk.

"Your maid doesn't run errands for you?" Jamie looked a little confused.

"I don't have a maid. We have been in the house a week and I haven't found time to hire staff. Not even sure if I want any at this time.

149

It's not hard to keep up with a house when you're the only one in it." Piper's final jab at two women was oddly satisfying.

"Well, my dear, I'll send over two of my maids until you can hire your own." Betsy scoffed at the thought of her daughter doing actual chores around the house.

"Mother, there is no need for that. I'm sure I'll find someone soon but for now it's not necessary. Good Day." Piper walked from the room with determination. She couldn't stand being a part of this fake world a moment longer.

Walking to the front door of the country club, Piper had overheard a few young ladies gossiping. While trivial things like this wouldn't have caught her attention so easily, hearing her name had her damn near stopping in her tracks. She knew she would be the focus of a bit of gossip but hearing Nadia's name mixed with hers in the same conversation had her blood boiling.

Most of the women thought she was a fool for marrying Xander, while others pitied her for being put in a situation that was a loss from the beginning. Intuition told her that playing this part was going to be harder than expected. Especially since Xander had no shame in openly being with Nadia. She would have to work on getting her father and father-in-law to see reason, even if the ladies of the house didn't.

Returning home to the empty house filled Piper with a sense of longing she hadn't had to deal with in the last decade. It didn't matter if it was the Valence home or Nicky's, there was some sort of sound or movements. Guys arguing over a card game to Valence Jr..'s latest conquest being spoken about. Valence Sr. screaming for everyone to keep it down while he was in his office. She missed it all. Realizing it was too late to go back now, Piper moved with her bags to put the shopping away.

She was lost in her thoughts putting things away when movement out of the corner of her eye caught her attention. Piper grabbed a knife from the drawer, not letting on that she had noticed she wasn't alone. When the shadow on the floor gave up the person's whereabouts, she crept over ready to defend herself. Holding her breath, she rounded the wall thrusting the blade and then screamed.

"What the hell are you doing in my house?" Piper looked into the eyes of a petrified maid ready to drop the boxes she was carrying.

"I was sent by Mrs. Cason." The poor woman's voice was barely over a whisper.

Piper dropped the knife onto the kitchen table before speaking. "I am so sorry. I thought I was being robbed."

"No ma'am. I should have knocked but your mother gave explicit instructions to just come in and begin tidying up. I'm so sorry that I startled you." The woman placed the boxes down on the table, hoping this would not be the end of her employment with the Cason family.

"What's your name?" Piper tried to breathe as she sunk into the chair next to the knife.

"Mary ma'am. Mary Travis."

"Mary, let's just keep this between us. I don't want to have to explain my reactions to my family."

"Oh absolutely. Should I put these things away?" Mary looked extremely uncomfortable but was happy she wasn't losing her job or her life today.

"Well, that would depend on what you have there." Piper gave her a wry smile.

"This box..." Mary motioned to the top box. "has old pictures and things from your room at the Cason house. The bottom box has about a week's worth of frozen meals from the Chef. Your mother didn't know what you would like so she sent a little bit of everything."

"That sounds like her." Piper ran her fingers through her hair. "You take this kitchen box and I'll take the pictures. This house needs a little familiarity anyway."

"Yes, ma'am." Mary placed the top box on the table as she went to the kitchen to start unloading the other. She turned back to ask. "What would you like for dinner?"

"I already picked something up to cook a little later. Don't worry about leaving anything out."

"No, ma'am you misunderstand. Your mother has entrusted me to care for you and your home until you can retain your own help." Mary looked at her confused.

"That's not necessary. I'll be able to manage."

"But Mrs. Cason was very clear with her instructions."

"Of course she was." Piper's temper was beginning to simmer when she realized it wasn't Mary's fault her mother couldn't understand. "Mary, do you want to make dinner or do you want to go home early?"

"I'd lose my job if your mother found out."

"Fine." Piper raised her hands in defeat. "I was going to make fajitas for dinner."

"Very good. Would you like fresh guacamole with that or pico?"

"Either or is fine." Mary smiled and walked into the kitchen with the oversized box.

Piper merely rolled her eyes. Had all the maids been that way? She couldn't remember any of them being so forceful. Piper could admire a woman that didn't take no for an answer along with following orders. She pondered how much she could be making under her mother. Piper would gladly double it to keep Mary's help.

Smiling towards the kitchen, she took the box into the living room and began to start unpacking all the trinkets. The old photos made her conscious of her age, of how much time had passed, and of what an interesting life she'd had. Too bad, it was all a sham. Piper had picked up a carefully wrapped frame holding a photo of her on her 16th birthday. Placing it on the mantel, she picked up another. This one was of her and Ethan on the camping trip just weeks before he died.

Someone once told Piper "you can bring a person back to life just by remembering them." She wished it was true. All of her life, Piper wished by looking at the old pictures of Ethan he would appear out of thin air and rescue her from the horrible nightmare that ensued after his death. It wasn't all bad, she could admit to herself, but knowing that Xander was just playing his part, as she was now, made her die a little inside.

"I miss moments like this more than anything." Piper whispered as she ran her hand over Ethan's face.

Piper sat quietly for a long while unwrapping every trinket and picture. She missed the young girl so full of hope and promise. Her heart broke for the innocence that was lost not long after, and while she mourned for that little girl, Piper couldn't help but admire the woman she had become. All thanks to Nicky.

Hearing Mary clear her throat behind her, she turned from the task of unwrapping the box. "Dinner is ready, Mrs. Hulston."

"Mary, could you do me a favor?" Piper couldn't stand the reference to Xander's last name.

"Yes, ma'am."

"Please either call me Evette, or..." she trailed off, not sure if she could trust her with the name she had chosen for herself.

"I get it. I will simply call you Evette." Mary wanted to say more about Mr. Xander Hulston but at the same time she needed to keep her job.

"Thank you." Piper greeted her with a warm smile and followed her into the dinning room where Mary had placed her dinner.

She had forgotten what it was like to have someone to take care of her instead of her taking care of everyone else. It was nice. Nothing she would get used to, but it was great not having to cook a big meal to have no one to eat it. Or a spotless house, she spent hours cleaning to not have anyone really appreciate it. Nicky and Dom would tease her calling her the ball and chain when she would get on to them for leaving their shit all over the house. Piper wondered what they were doing right now. After all, it was Saturday night.

By the time dinner was done and Mary had departed for the evening, Piper sat on the cream colored sofa staring into the fire she had made. The logs popped and crackled, while she watched the flames dance in the hearth. She loved the peace she had in the solitude of the house, and dreaded when she would eventually hear Xander's key hit the lock. He would have to come here sometime if he wanted to keep up appearances.

As she went to rise from the couch, her unspoken dread became a reality. Piper hadn't even heard his car pull up in the driveway and from the state he was in when he crossed the threshold, she knew why. Xander was about ten sheets to the wind with a bottle still in his hand. Piper was always prepared for a lot of things but a drunk Xander wasn't on the Bingo card for that night. She wondered if she could possibly skirt around him and head for her room.

"There's my blushing bride." Xander's words came out slurred.

"There is my no good, cheating, lying, husband. What happen? Your whore didn't want you tonight?" Piper was squared up hoping that a little shove would knock him on his ass.

"Don't you talk about Nadia that way. You're just jealous." He gritted his teeth as the room began to spin.

"I am most certainly not jealous, but I am disappointed. Now I'm tired and going to bed. You can either sleep in one of the other rooms, if you can manage to make it up the stairs or fall face first into the gutter, I don't really care which. But do understand I am not dealing with your ass tonight." Piper's voice went low and menacing to prove she wasn't playing with him.

"I'll do whatever I want with my house and my wife." Xander reached out and grabbed her by the arm and attempted to swing her around like a ragdoll. Piper shook him off, resulting with him landing on his ass on the hard granite tiles.

Piper didn't stop until she was safely inside her room with the door locked. She knew she could take him in this state, but she also knew if the cops got called they had both been drinking. While she never left the house, it would be irrelevant. They would both be led away in handcuffs. If Piper could prove force, or he kept coming after she left the situation, only he would be spending the night in a cell.

She began to calm her nerves until she could hear him muttering something to himself. Then Xander started kicking at the door. First one kick, then two, then a thud and cussing. Piper didn't take any chances. She grabbed two things. Her gun and her phone.

As she was disengaging the safety, Piper called John in hopes he would come get his son and put an end to the madness. As her father-in-law picked up his phone, Xander's next swift kick splintered the door. Piper stood there phone on her shoulder and a 9mm pointed at Xander's heart.

"Evette, what's going on? Are you hurt? Who's trying to kick down the door?" John Hulston's voice was panicked.

"Your son just came home drunk. No, I'm not hurt. Xander took it upon himself to kick my bedroom door down. Now, if you want to see your son alive again, I suggest you get over here and collect him. If he comes at me I will open fire." Piper's tone was even but not because she was calm.

"Open fire? Evette, what are you saying?"

"I'm saying I'm giving you one opportunity to save his worthless life. I have a 9mm pointed at his chest and have no problem unloading the clip if he comes anywhere near me. Now come get him or so help me." Piper dared Xander to even blink wrong. She had no problem with ending him right then and there.

"I'm on my way. Don't do anything rash." Xander's father hung up the phone.

"Now, I'm going to give you two options. Listen carefully I will not repeat these again. 1. You go downstairs out the front door and wait for your father on the curb like the trash you are. 2. You take even a step toward me and I make you Swiss cheese. Blink once if you understand me." Piper watched as he blinked.

Xander, not wanting to take the chance that she would make good on her promise, backed out of the room slowly and down the stairs. It wasn't but a few seconds when she heard the front door close and the deadbolt slide to lock the door. Piper breathed a little easier putting her gun on the bed and using her phone to take pictures of the damage, sending it to his mother and father. Caption reading: Strike one.

CHAPTER 15
TRUSTING THE
EXECUTIONER

The Hulston family trusted me with Xander's life; they really shouldn't. Trust is something earned not given freely, this was something Piper had learned over the years. Keeping oneself guarded from the cruel world seemed to be a better lesson to live by since you couldn't be hurt if you already saw it coming.

After Xander's explosive episode, which caused her to take drastic measures, the families called a meeting. They had made Xander apologize and promise never to do it again, Piper didn't trust him as far as she could pick him up and throw him. With Xander, now peacefully sleeping at her side three thousand feet above the ground, Piper envisioned what his reaction would be if he was thrown from the plane. Would he be shocked? Scream? Would he have that moment of clarity as she did before, what he would hope would be the end? The internal war raged as Piper wondered what exactly to do with the coward that slept next to her.

A deal was a deal and as such, she would play her part. Though in the back of her mind she was envisioning herself anywhere but on a plane headed for Aruba. She had begged for them to take separate trips, but Xander's logic was what would happen when people want to see the honeymoon photos. Piper simply replied with "Tell them we were too busy to take any."

Unfortunately, this wasn't a battle she was willing to fight at the moment. If she would have had it her way she would have flown to Italy and figured out a way to send word to Nicky to meet her there. It bothered her greatly that he had not reached out, and Piper began to wonder if she had meant anything at all to him. Deep down she knew the answer to that question, but as it had now been nearly a month and a half, she was beginning to doubt herself and the understanding she thought they shared.

Pushing the overwhelming feeling from her mind, Piper checked to make sure Xander was still knocked out. His loud snoring, which made her want to smother him, was a good indicator. Pulling out her leather carry-on, Piper went over the file on the individual she would be dealing with once they landed. She was thankful that Mark and Kris had already arrived at the resort and was waiting to make contact with her.

Closing the file and stowing it away, Piper couldn't help but feel overwhelmed by the whole situation. This would be the first contract she would complete without Nicky and it didn't feel right. While she had done dozens of jobs on her own, Nicky was always ten steps behind her. He watched her back, now she would have to rely on Kris and Mark. Debating on whether or not they would get her killed, Piper stared out the window taking in the breathtaking view of the ocean.

After what seemed like days on the plane without sleep, they landed in Aruba. Customs was a fun experience, as the reason for their arrival was a honeymoon neither of them wanted to be on. The other, not so fun part, was having to walk off out of the airport looking like two people in love. This was more of a task for her than him, as he made sure to have his hands on her at all times. She internally cringed at his physical touch.

She swore under her breath as they walked toward the driver holding up the card with Mr. and Mrs. Hulston on it. Piper smirked when she recognized the driver. Of course, Valence Sr. would send the local driver for her arrival. After all, this honeymoon was a gift from him, though everyone thought it was something planned by the families.

"Let me take the bags for you." The driver smiled.

"Thank you." Piper sighed as she climbed into the back of the Rolls Royce.

Of course they wouldn't be staying at the resort they had booked months ago, when Valence Sr. reached out with the information. He would have made sure to see to their privacy along with leaving her close enough to handle the mark. Groaning internally, Piper plastered on her best smile for any onlooker. After all, this was her honeymoon even if she would rather stick her tongue in a light socket.

"The resort really knows how to treat their guests." Xander boasted, trying to play big dog, climbing into the back of the car.

"I take it you've never been to Aruba before?" Piper questioned, knowing the answer before he had opened his mouth.

"No, have you?" Xander looked puzzled.

"Not in some time, but it was an enjoyable place the last time I was here." Piper said more conversationally than a jab at the fact he had no idea the places she had been.

"You know you don't have to pretend." Xander glared, ego slightly deflated.

"Who said I am pretending?" Piper said through the gritted teeth, as the car pulled away from the curb.

"How have you been here before?"

"Xander, I had a whole life and lifetime worth of experiences in the 12 years after you left me in that hotel room." Piper's voice went low and menacing, "and I'll return to that life or even start a new one once this sham of a marriage falls apart. The best thing for you to do is stay in your own lane."

"Well I guess..." Xander's voice trailed off when he saw the driver look back in the rearview mirror.

The tension in the car grew, as they headed past the resort. Xander looked confused, glancing over at Piper. The priceless look on his face made her stifle a giggle. As they pulled outside the two story beach front property, Xander's eyes went wide.

"You know, I really hoped I'd never see this place again. At least not like this." Piper huffed, waiting for the car to come to a stop. Fitting for Valence Sr. to send her to the place, where each and every Valence family member had their honeymoons.

The last time she was here, she had thought Nicky was going to profess his love for her. It was one of the few times they were on an honest to god vacation. Nicky had been fumbling over himself all day. Piper thought she had seen him with a box, and she did. As she absently touched the locket around her neck, she felt the tears prick the back of her eyes. Not that Xander had noticed.

The compound was built in the late 1930s as a wedding gift for the OG Don's now late wife. The beautiful white stone house with the antique clay shingles gave a homey feel to the landscape. It was as if, even after all these years, it evoked warmth, happiness, and above all love. Piper didn't feel love at the moment. She felt spite, anger, and vengeance.

"Should I carry the bags in for you, Mrs. Hulston?" the driver spoke up, breaking Piper from her thoughts.

"No, Sean. We will manage." Piper sighed walking to the back of the vehicle taking her suitcase. Looking around to see Xander staring out over the water, "Tell Kris and Mark, I have arrived, would you?"

"Yes, ma'am. Are you going to be needing the car this evening?"

Piper looked at her phone to get her bearings on the time. "Yes, around seven. I believe the reservations were made?"

"Yes ma'am. Mr. Valence was very explicit with his directions."

"I'm sure he was. Thank you, Sean." Piper tipped her head at the man and walked toward the front door.

Xander, oblivious to her actions, continued to admire the view until he heard the car pull away. With a scowl on his face, he walked over to where his bags had been abandoned in the drive. Snatching them up, he followed the path to the front door to find his bride talking to a woman he assumed to be the housekeeper. He couldn't understand her obsession with being friendly to the help.

"Yes, Ms. Davis, it is good to see you again. Were both rooms prepared?" Piper leaned in and embraced the older woman.

"Yes, ma'am. Also, your itineraries are on the night stands. Did Sean talk to you about the car service when he dropped you off?"

"Yes, Ms. Davis. He also confirmed he will be back around to collect us at about 6:30 for the dinner reservation."

"Very good. I reminded him before he left to collect you from the airport. He's getting forgetful in his older age." Ms. Davis patted Piper's arm.

"Is Billy not taking over for him soon?"

"Oh he is, but you know Sean. He doesn't like anyone driving the good cars but him."

"I'm sure Mr. Valence appreciates all the care he takes with those cars." Piper had continued chatting with the woman while Xander stood their red faced from carrying all his bags.

"Hello..." Xander's tone was aggressive. "A little help here."

"You look like you have it just fine. I told you not to pack what you couldn't carry." Piper rolled her eyes, while Ms. Davis stifled a giggle. "Your room is at the top of the stairs down the first hallway, third door on the left."

"My room?" Xander's puzzled expression was almost comical to Piper.

"Yes, your room," she repeated. "I agreed to go on this honeymoon. I didn't agree to share a room with you."

"Where is your room?" Xander scoffed

"Wouldn't you like to know. Ms. Davis, this is Xander Hulston. Please show him to HIS room, so he doesn't get lost. You know the house has a tendency to make people disappear." Piper smiled sweetly at the woman, and Ms. Davis understood the meaning behind her words. She had worked for the Valence family long enough.

"This way, sir. Ma'am your usual room is ready. You can find your way right?"

"It's been a few years, but I'm sure I can manage."

Piper had waited until they had disappeared up the stairs before she had grabbed her bags and made her way out to the bungalow on the other side of the pool. She didn't like staying in the main house for a variety of reasons, the main one being, Nicky wasn't there. The second one being the large security team that popped out of every corner of the house. She liked her privacy and the bungalow gave her that.

Xander's room, also known as the honeymoon suite in the house, had a balcony that overlooked the sprawling backyard. It wouldn't be long before he found her but it would give her time to plan how the next week and a half would go. If he played nice and dropped the attitude, she might rein back the hostility, currently it wasn't looking to be going in that direction.

Using the key that had been specially made for her, Piper entered her room. She had noticed Ms. Davis had outdone herself with all the little touches. Fresh flowers on every surface, a fully stocked kitchen, and even her favorite snacks in the mini fridge that was in the office. A smile had crossed her face, hoping this meant more, as there were some things only Nicky liked among the items prepared for her.

Collapsing on the bed, Piper tried to relax before putting her things away. She didn't want Ms. Davis' job to be any harder than it had to be with the two of them there. She was already going to have her hands full with Mr. Needy upstairs. As she went to stand the in suite phone rang. "So it begins."

"Hello."

"Took you long enough to get here." Kris' unmistakeable snark came rolling out.

"Would you believe we ran into traffic?" Piper smiled.

"Likely story with you. How are you settling in?"

"Ms. Davis did a wonderful job getting things ready."

"The Husband?" Kris snickered.

"For the love of god, do not refer to him as that again or you will know what the other end of your manhood looks like. Up close and personal, get my drift." Piper's temper flared as she gripped the phone.

"Yes ma'am. Sheesh. You do not travel well."

"Kris, I don't have time for your shit. Now did you call for a reason or just to poke the bear?"

"A reason. Poking the bear is just a bonus from this distance."

"For fuck sake." Piper growled. "I'm gonna hang up."

"Chill little momma. Damn so grouchy. The meeting has been set."

"When?"

"Tomorrow. 11am brunch over here at the resort."

"Okay that should be doable. You guys going to be at the restaurant at 7?"

"Yep. What's the plan?"

"Who's going to the meeting with me?"

"Mark. He's gotten buddy-buddy with two of the guys, men."

"Cool... Cool... Cool..." Piper talked as she went for a water. "Okay so here's the thing. Y'all will approach the table, make conversation, and play into his ego. Then talk about the place on the other side of the island that rents Jet Skis."

"Does he even know anything about Jet Skis?" Kris retorted.

"Not a clue. You guys will stay out for most of the afternoon and meet us back at the compound for an early dinner. By the time you two get back, he should be worn out and heavily sunburned."

"That sounds about right."

"He'll pass out early and I'll finish the job." Piper sighed. "With you two keeping him occupied I might get a little peace on this trip. Hoping after everything he'll want to go home early."

"So we have to keep him alive?" Kris chuckled.

"I didn't say that now. Accidents happen..." Piper looked down at her watch seeing it was nearly 4 pm. "Gotta go. See y'all in a few hours. Oh and by the way."

"Yea, boss."

"Don't forget plan B." Piper hung up the phone and dropped it to the bed. Running her hands through her hair, she had become agitated by the whole situation. Deciding a quick swim would calm her nerves, she grabbed her bikini and changed. She always felt better after she came out of the water.

As Piper began to dress for dinner, her mind raced with thoughts of what could have been. She had tried hard over the last few weeks to deal with her disappointment in Nicky not busting in guns blazing to save the day. Piper had pushed it all down, but now being here caused everything to come back to the surface like a raging title wave.

She had written him a letter, several in fact, over the past month, and she was hoping that Kris and Mark would be kind enough to deliver them. She knew it was a long shot, if he wanted to talk to her, he knew how to get a hold of her but down right refused. She needed closure to close this chapter of her life. If Nicky didn't feel the same way about her, then she would have to live with it.

A knock came at the door as she smoothed her cotton maxi dress, and slipped on her shoes. "Yes?"

"The car is here, Miss." Ms. Davis called from the door.

"I'll be there in a moment. Please tell Xander, we will be leaving in five minutes."

"He is already in the foyer, waiting for you." Ms. Davis had a particularly aggravating tone in her voice.

"Okay. Thank you." Piper would have to remind herself to leave Ms. Davis and Sean a big tip for having to deal with Xander on this trip. Walking out of the bungalow for dinner, Piper grabbed her purse with the letters inside.

The evening was humid and the sky was a brilliant starburst orange. Piper marveled at the setting sun as she walked through French doors to the main house. When she locked eyes with Xander, her pleasant mood had disappeared. He was standing by the front door tapping his foot as if he was being inconvenienced. She forced a smile that didn't reach her eyes.

"Took you long enough. We are going to be late." Xander barked.

"Xander, do I need to remind you of what happened the last time you talked to me in such a manner? You can go home in a body bag and I can be a not so grieving widow." Piper's eyes flashed a warning. "Plus, this is our honeymoon. We are supposed to be enjoying ourselves, not bickering like children."

Xander looked at her with shock plastered on his face. The night he busted into her room coming to the forefront of his mind. He was partially sure she didn't have a weapon on her, but wasn't willing to take that chance either. From what he could tell, the people that worked for Mr. Valence seemed to like his wife very much, and would probably help her get rid of him, if she asked.

"I'm sorry, Angel Face, where are my manner?"

"You know I have been wondering the same thing since I came back, maybe you'll find them on this trip." Piper cut her eyes, as she applied her lip gloss in the mirror by the door. "Shall we?"

They exited the house the same way they had the airport. Xander with his arm around her, and Piper trying hard not to throw up on his shoes. As they had gotten to the car, Sean merely nodded seeing she was visibly uncomfortable by the embrace. He held open the door taking Piper's hand to usher her inside. Xander had practically skipped to the other side and climbed in next to her.

"So. Where are the reservations at?" Xander bubbled with excitement. The same that once caused her stomach to flip seeing his anticipation, now it flipped for other reasons.

"Oh it's this little place out in Santa Rosa. Mom and pop run kind of place. Real down to earth, but super popular with the tourist crowd. Hence the reason, you need a reservation if you want a good table." Piper said, staring out the window watching the scenery fly by.

The place was packed by the time they had gotten there. Piper had no idea that they had done live music. It made her smile as her mind drifted for a brief moment back to Mexico, and she absently reached back to touch her tattoo. They stood in line for a few minutes before the hostess asked them if they had a reservation.

"Yes, ma'am. It's under Valence," Piper responded as the hostess' eyes went wide.

"Is Mr. D'Angelo here with you this evening?" She swooned.

"No ma'am, not this time. He placed the reservation as part of my wedding gift."

"Oh, so you shall have our best table. Would you like to be closer to the bar or the band?"

"Bar please. I would like to have my hearing tomorrow." Piper chuckled.

"Not a problem." She grabbed up a few menus. "Follow me please."

Piper scanned the room while they were escorted to their table. Her nerves were on edge, until she spotted two familiar faces in the crowd. Mark and Kris were sitting two tables away. They looked to be a few drinks in and Piper had hoped they weren't too tipsy. She knew they could handle their liquor, but they had a tendency to get hammered, fucking up the entire mission. Piper prayed they could hold it together at least for the night.

"Can I start you off with some drinks or maybe some Champagne?"

"We will take some champagne, after all this is a celebration," Xander boasted loud enough to cause both Kris and Mark to almost choke on their drinks.

"I'll take a 1990 Vintage Highland Park Limited if you have it, Jack and Coke if you don't." Piper cut her eyes toward Xander, ignoring what he said.

"Yes, ma'am coming right up." She looked between the two very uncomfortably.

"Why do you have to be a party pooper?" Xander pouted.

"Because if you knew anything about me, you would know I don't like champagne unless it's from a particular vineyard in Italy. I drink only top shelf whiskey, and if not it's Jack." Piper tried to keep her temper in check.

"Did I hear someone over here say champagne? What are we celebrating?" Kris stumbles over to the table breaking the very awkward eye contact between Xander and Piper.

"We just got married." Xander boasted.

"Oh we'll congratulations to the happy couple." Kris reached out to shake Xander's hand.

Piper thought it was comical to say the least, but was glad to know either he wasn't paying attention at the wedding or the men had changed just enough not to be recognized. Either way, Piper didn't care. This was going to work out in her favor.

"Thank you." Xander liked the attention.

"Hey, why don't me and my buddy over there join you. I can tell you all the great things to do while you're here. That would be alright wouldn't it?" Kris waved Mark over.

"Of course it would. You don't mind, do you, Angel Face?" Xander smiled over at her. "After all, having a good conversation over a meal is what memories are made of."

"Of course. Why don't you join us." Piper was happy he was playing right into her hand. "I'm Evette. The douche-canoe there is Xander. And you are?"

"Kris and this is my buddy Mark." Kris introduced themselves trying to keep a straight face.

"You'll have to forgive my lovely bride, Kris. She isn't happy with me right now." Xander was always quick with an excuse.

"I don't exactly hate you, but..." Her voice trailed off, taking the drink the waitress had brought to the table and drinking greedily from it. "If you were on fire and I had water, I'd drink it."

Both men busted out laughing, while Xander sat there slack jawed. "You got you a pistol there. Never seen a woman so quick witted." Mark retorted.

"Yeah, she's a real comedian." Xander's voice hardened, but Piper only shot him a look.

It wasn't long before the subject had changed and food was ordered. A comfortable rhythm had settled in with the group. Piper sat back, always the watching observer. She was grateful when Xander finally got up to use the restroom.

Piper waited until her husband was out of earshot, then signed in relief. "Before you ask, no that man never shuts up."

"Damn, you were getting brutal there for a minute. Trouble in paradise already?"

"Mark, I've already pointed a gun at him, and swore to be a grieving widow, what do you think?"

"I can definitely see why. He is a pompous ass." Kris raised his glass to Piper.

"Yeah, well..." She shrugged. "What can I do about that? Either way, I need a favor from the two of you."

"We can't make him disappear just yet. We have been seen together." Kris retorted.

"Huh, now there is a thought, but no. I need you to get these to Nicky." Piper pulled out the stack of letters that Mark quickly put in his coat pocket. "Please try to persuade him to come, for my sake."

"We can do what we can, but there are no guarantees right now." Kris shot a look over to Mark for back up.

"Piper, I think we need to talk about that later. Your husband is coming back over." Mark quickly diverted the conversation.

"So, Xander. I heard you want to go on some jet skis." Kris piped up when Xander sat back down at the table.

"Yeah, I really do, but Evette doesn't like the water that much."

"Well, I'm going out on some tomorrow, if you would like to join. I mean there is nothing like the feeling of wind in your hair, water in your face, and the whole ocean to play in." Kris talked up the experience.

"I would love to. You don't mind, do you, Angel face?"

"Not at all. I was going to have a spa day over at the resort anyway. You two go and have a good time." The vision of Xander being eaten by a shark or whale, almost had her busting out in laughter.

The rest of the night had gone smoothly and it wasn't long before they were saying their goodbyes. Xander was somewhere between tipsy and sauced when they were on their way back to the compound. With every swaying motion and pothole, Xander became a little green around the gills. Piper prayed he didn't puke in the car, as it was an expensive service to have it cleaned from the smell.

He held it together, and she had even done the nice thing and helped him out of the car. Though it took both her and Sean to carry him to the front door. Ms. Davis was only slightly amused by his condition until she realized two of the security staff would have to carry him to his room. Not knowing if Xander could hold his liquor or not, Piper cringed thinking about the mess that could potentially happen through the night.

After she handed him off to the security staff, Piper made her way to her room. She couldn't wait to climb into her bed and pass out for a few hours. As she replayed the events of the day in her head, Piper had a nagging feeling she was missing something. There was something about the look that was exchanged between Kris and Mark that didn't sit well with her, but Xander had returned to the table before she could press further. It was the same look they had exchanged the night of the wedding, for that Piper was sure of.

She played with the locket she had rarely taken off. Why did Nicky feel close by but she knew he was thousands of miles away. Opening the locket to the secret compartment she had found after arriving back in New Mexico, Piper stared at the funny photo of the two of them at Coney Island. She couldn't be wrong about this or about Nicky. He had cared enough for this simple gesture, but why didn't he care now?

Piper had a knack for driving herself crazy with the "what ifs", especially when it came to Nicky. The letters and slightly pleading to the guys to reach out to him was the last card she had to play. She had tried to reach out to both Nicky and Dom, with no response back. She prayed that nothing had happened to them, and Kris and Mark weren't trying to cover it up. Valence Sr. had even been a little shady, but the question was when wasn't he.

All the nervous energy had her pacing the room like a caged animal. Piper didn't like not feeling in control. It brought her back to a place and time she wouldn't dare let herself revisit. She wasn't that scared little woman anymore. The last twelve years hardened her like stone. The only kink in her armor, the only fault in her resolve was a brown eyed Italian boy that made her feel alive.

CHAPTER 16
NO DISRESPECT

As the golden sunlight danced across her face, Piper woke up groaning and growling. She had a total of three hours of sleep the whole night, and now the sun was reminding her it was morning. Between the "what ifs", the nightmares, and the sounds that kept startling her awake, Piper was in no mood to take on the day.

Piper threw her arm over her face screaming every curse word she could recall in every language she could recall it in. Why had she left the curtains open? Had she learned nothing in the years of being around Nicky? The sun was the hot devil that reminded them of what had been done in the dark. For her, it was about seven shots of Jose Cuervo to finally have her drunk enough to sleep. The buzzing of her phone had her yelling FUCK at the top of her lungs.

"WHAT!" Piper snapped into the phone once she found it.

"Well, Good Morning to you too," Mark responded, chipper as ever.

"Fuck all the way off."

"Awe, that's my girl." Mark snickered. "What has your panties in a twist this morning? Hubby not doing his job?"

"Mark, do you want me to cut you up and feed you to the fish?" Piper growled climbing out of bed, hair sticking up nine ways to Sunday.

"As temping of an offer as that is, we have a job to do today."

"I know..." Piper looked into the mirror almost shocked at her reflection. "Has Kris picked up the package yet?"

"Yep, they left about an hour ago. Ms. Davis called me to do your wake up call. Something about you getting into the liquor cabinet last night had her on edge. Do I want to know what you grabbed?" Mark chuckled through the receiver.

"Not really." Piper wanted to throw up just thinking about it. "I had a bad night. The nightmares are back."

"Are you going to be good to handle this today?"

"Don't have a choice, do I?"

"Okay then, wheels up in thirty."

"Is Sean coming to pick me up or are you?"

"Sean."

"Okay, see you in thirty. Order me a Bloody Mary if you don't mind."

"Will do," he chuckled before disconnecting the call.

Piper threw her phone onto the bed. She desperately needed caffeine to combat the intense hangover that started to plague her, but that required her to walk out into the bright sunlight. She wasn't sure if she was ready for that kind of blindness. Ready or not though there was a contract to handle, and Piper was the only one that could get anyone to sign on the dotted line. She definitely felt like this was going to be a "your name or blood." kind of situation.

By the time she walked into the main house, Ms. Davis was already coming to tell her Sean was there with the car. She had recounted some of the fun little details of Xander the night before, and an interesting conversation she had overheard early that morning when she brought him his breakfast. Piper was thankful that Ms. Davis was on her side, because she knew that woman could be vindictive. She knew she would have to deal with Xander later, but as for right now, he was Kris' problem.

After Piper had arrived at the resort, Mark had escorted her down to the private outdoor patio where they were to be having brunch. She was cordial with the two men at the table, but it was their boss, who she had been there to see. Her patients and headache were wearing thin when he finally arrived fifteen minutes late.

Piper prided herself on punctuality and expected others to do the same. As she rose from her chair, she shot a look at Mark. He shook his head knowing this was not going to end well. Piper was already in a bad mood, and one of the four of them was fixing to bear the brunt of it.

"Where do you think you're going, Ms. Johnson?"

"To report back to Don Valence, on your blatant disrespect. We're done here."

"How have we disrespected you?" The two men moved towards her, which was their first mistake.

"The meeting was at 11." Piper turned slowly back towards the men. "It is 11:15. Which means you are late. First strike. I am sure you were made aware of my stickler for punctuality. Second strike: You didn't apologize or make anyone aware of the discrepancy. And Third..." Piper trailed off getting inches from the one guard's face. "Is wasting my damn time. Then questioning me about why I am leaving. I have cut mens balls off for less. Now, good day gentleman."

"Ms. Johnson, I think we got off on the wrong foot here." The older man stood up from the table to address her.

"That's all you got, sir, two wrong feet and some fucking ugly ass sandals. Now, I said good day."

"I deserve that. I apologize deeply for any and all perceived slights. What can I do to make this right?"

"Mr. Daniels, you take forty percent off the distribution costs. You front the first ten loads for Don Valence and you owe me lunch." Piper crossed her arms, staring the man in his eyes.

"Ten percent and five loads."

"Forty percent and five loads or we find someone else. I'm sure there will be a line of men waiting that won't waste my time."

"Mark, are you going to say anything here?" Mr. Daniel looked at the man next to her.

"Not my show. I have been instructed to follow her lead. Plus, I might want to have children someday and I don't think I will be able to without my balls." Mark put his hands in plain sight.

"What's it to be Mr. Daniels? I have phone calls to make."

"Deal."

"Good man." Piper pulled the contract from her bag and handed him a pen. "Don Valence is a stickler for the paperwork."

Within the hour, the papers were signed, sealed, and delivered to the courier that was flying it back to Don Valence. Mr. Daniels had apologized with a lovely lunch poolside, while he and his men packed up to head back to the states. All in all, Piper thought it had been a productive day.

While Mark and Piper sat in the sun soaking up the rays, Piper took it as a sign to approach the subject one last time. She hoped for a more resolved answer, but knew there just might not be one to have. She braced herself before speaking, but of course Mark was going to beat her to the punch.

"I was able to get a hold of Dom last night." Mark started taking a swig of his drink.

"How's the boys doing? Is he able to get the message to Nicky for me?"

Mark took off his sunglasses before sliding them onto the table. "Piper, I'm begging you. You don't want to know what was said." He was definitely going to need to go to confession when he got home.

"Mark, just give it to me straight." Piper held back the tears as they pricked the back of her eyes. "Rip the Band-Aid off, so we can get this over with."

"Nicky's moved on. You were just another job for him. A damsel in distress that made him feel better about his life. Rumor back at the house is, he's been chasing skirts ever since you left. He was supposed to show up in New Mexico. He didn't. He disappeared for two weeks, came back hungover and had a blonde on his arm."

"Don Valence?" Piper's voice was low and harsh.

"He saw the cracks in Nicky's facade. He wasn't happy about losing you or you being so far away, but he's keeping things moving. Looks like a line of contracts for you in the next few months. Hell, he's going to be flabbergasted by the work you did on this one."

Piper didn't respond, holding her hand up to silence Mark. She became sidetracked when she had seen none other than Nadia Morang entering the outdoor bar. "What the hell is that bitch doing here?"

"Who?" Mark looked over his shoulder to see a pregnant woman saddling herself up to the bar. "Is that?"

"Nadia Morang? Sure the hell is. What in the fucking hell is she doing here?"

"I have no clue."

"We have to leave." Piper gracefully stood.

"Why?" Mark looked confused.

"It's not safe for us to be seen together. She knows the associates of the Valence family. She will be able to blow my damn cover if she recognizes you. Not to mention what she will say to Xander, because I was having lunch with another man. Now move your ass." Piper bit back.

"You're going to have to explain this to me later." Mark stood keeping his side to Nadia as Piper walked on the other side of him.

"The baby she is carrying is Xander's. That is his fucking mistress."

"Oh fucking hell."

"Yeppers," Piper said as they scurried to the parking lot.

Rage bloomed in Piper's chest. She didn't believe in coincidences. Not when it came to Xander and Nadia. The only thing she didn't know was whether he knew she was coming or not. As the thought passed through her head, Mark's phone buzzed with a text. Looking down and reading it, Mark went pale.

"What is it?" Piper barked.

"Kris just texted."

"And?"

"Xander is drunk off his ass and told him to keep a secret."

"That bastard flew her in."

"His exact words were..." Mark held his breath and let the words fly. "If he wasn't going to get any from his prude ass wife, he would have it delivered."

"Call Don Valence. I am out of here tonight no later than tomorrow morning. Make it happen."

"What about him?"

"Stay close until I'm gone. Once I'm out, his things will need to be moved out of the compound."

"I'll handle it, Boss." Mark began to start making phone calls, as Piper got into the waiting car with Sean.

It was by the luck of the draw that both Kris and Xander showed up at the exact same time as Piper. Kris could tell this was probably not the time to crack a joke with her, and hauled the drunken Xander into the house. Ms. Davis looked more stern as this was the second time in less than twelve hours this man was being carried in drunk.

"Is he ever sober? You know there are programs for that?" Ms. Davis tapped her foot at the three of them pointing the way to Xander's room.

"Ms. Davis, I'm letting you know the visit will be cut short this time. I am deeply sorry for all the work you have put in."

"Is everything alright? Did something happen with him?" She pointed her thumb up the stairs.

"You could say that. He will be going to the resort when he sobers up a bit and I will be headed back stateside. I promise to visit again soon." Piper hugged Ms. Davis as Kris came out on the landing. "I need a word with you." Piper pointed her finger up to Kris.

After some thorough questioning about everything from Nicky to Xander, Kris gave her the same song and dance as Mark had. When he spilled the beans on what happened out on the skis, Piper stopped him about half way through the play by play. Piper was hurt, angry, and was done with it all. She would not stay there a minute longer than she had to, and she made it crystal clear to both men.

Once Kris left the bungalow, Piper sat on her bed and sobbed. Her life to this point seemed to be one unfortunate event after another and she had reached her limit on the lifetime supply of bullshit. All she wanted was to love and have someone to love her in return, she didn't think that was too much to ask for. But here she was crying her eyes out, wishing it was all over. Some sort of bad dream, she couldn't wake from. Hoping that a hot shower would at least make her feel human again, Piper walked toward the shower ready to crank the hot water to the max.

Piper was sure after nearly thirty minutes she had run every bit of the hot water out on her side of the island. She was even feeling a little bit better after she had shed every tear she thought she had left. As Piper stepped out of the shower, enveloped in the scent of coconut that seemed to lighten her mood, she wrapped a towel around her. Wiping off the mirror, she felt the icy grip of fear caressing her spine. Xander was standing in her room, hands on the door frame of the bathroom glaring at her.

"What the hell are you doing here? How the hell did you get in here?" Piper shrieked, pulling her towel close.

"For some reason, I'm attracted to you, and you belong to me now. So, you will do your wifely duties." Xander's eyes were cold.

"If you touch me, you won't make it off this island. I can guarantee that." Piper inched toward the shaving kit that contained a straight blade razor she had used on her legs.

"Can't you just forgive me already and be a good wife?"

"You think I'm just going to forgive you?" she asked, voice tight with anger. "After everything you've done?"

"I believe you're required to by your vows to me. You know for better or worse and all?"

"You mean the vows you broke before the ink was even dried on the paper? Go to hell Xander. And get the fuck out of here, before I do something you will regret."

"What's in that bag and what are you hiding there?" Xander lunged for the shaving kit, but Piper already had her hands on the straight blade and placed it under his Adam's apple.

"Now are you going to leave quietly or am I going to have to explain to Ms. Davis, why there is blood all over the bathroom?"

CHAPTER 17
UNFULFILLED PROMISES

It had been over a month since Nicky had laid eyes on Piper. Her sweet seductive face, her eyes so full of promise, and the way she looked so peaceful as she slept were forever etched into his mind. As he poured over each and every paper for the dozenth time, he began yet another of his drunken stupor. Nicky was pissed, rightfully so, but each day of no news as to her whereabouts was like a sucker punch to his gut. He had promised to protect her at any and all cost, and now he had no idea where the hell she was.

He knew something had to have gone sideways, when he arrived home and she hadn't been there. Don Valence had added two extra pickups for him and Dom, so there was no way they were going to beat her back to the house. Though it was always a fun challenge to see which one of the three would get the bragging rights in the long run. Nothing felt out of place, and this wasn't the first time Don Valence had added to the workload while they were still on the road.

Nicky was given a bullshit story by everyone, including Don Valence, that Piper was put on an assignment by the old man and had Mark and Kris with her. Don Valence had been trying for nearly two years to divide Nicky's crew in half with Piper being the head of her own crew. His logic being that Piper could handle the brain work while Nicky would be her backup and muscle if needed. It would allow more contracts to be processed faster, increasing everyone's bottom line.

While both parties involved had no intention of allowing that, it looked like the old man had jumped the gun and did what he wanted to, or at least that was the way it looked to Nicky and Dom. Nicky was put on edge when he had found out. As the two in question had a track record of putting Piper into situations only her charm could get them out of. Thankfully, he had found out about those contracts before the three were too far into them.

The red flags started to appear almost immediately, even if Nicky didn't want to acknowledge them right off the bat. It started with him being told they had taken too long to get back to the house and Piper couldn't wait any longer for them. Sometimes contracts became time sensitive, and she had a habit of jetting off with whomever happened to be available, even if it was Mark and Kris.

While Nicky had a level of respect for both Mark and Kris, as they were part of his crew, Nicky didn't trust them to blow their noses let alone keep Piper from going off the rails. He knew all to well about her bad habit of going off on suicide missions, and on more than one occasion Nicky had to step in, cleaning up the mess. If this was that kind of situation, Piper would have surely waited for him. She would have made up some excuse, as she had in the past, to stall long enough for him or Dom to be at her side.

The second red flag came with him being told he couldn't leave the compound mere days after he had arrived home. Don Valence had told him there was to be a family dinner with three or four other families and he didn't want Nicky and Dom wandering off. Apparently, the heads of these families were bringing their daughters to parade them through like a livestock auction. In accordance with Don Valence, it was time for Nicky to settle down, and think about his future along with the future of the Valence family name.

The brightest of all the red flags though was how happy Valence Jr.. had become by the turn of events. He was ecstatic the beautiful women were being paraded through the house like a roaming buffet line, and even more overjoyed by Nicky being knocked down a peg or two by the old man. Nicky's pain made him weak, and that was one thing his father loved to play on. So much so, he spilled the beans about where Piper really was and why she was there to rub salt in the open wound that was starting to form. Nicky was enraged.

Storming out of Valence Jr.'s office, he headed straight for the garage and 1966 GTO. The bright blue paint gleamed under the overhead lights. He would need something fast and loud, and the GTO fit the bill. It didn't go unnoticed to Nicky that the Duster, Piper's pride and joy, was still parked in the spot next to his, but the Impala was gone. At least, he knew which car he was looking for, which put him one step closer to her.

Nothing was going to stop him from getting to her and/or tearing the heads off of Mark and Kris for letting her go through with this. He had no idea what would possess her to go back now to marry Xander Hulston. They had a good thing going and whether anyone liked it or not Piper was his in every way that mattered. His right hand in business, and matters of the heart.

Nicky had carefully backed the car out of the garage, lighting up the tires as he headed toward the main road. The GTO kicked up every bit of gravel its tires could grab, slinging rocks and debris over everything. The men that had run out of the house to see what the commotion was, were suddenly in the danger zone.

When Nicky passed Dom like he was sitting still out on the main road, Dom knew something had gone wrong back at the house. Jr.. had been picking at him for two days and Nicky had about enough of it. Dom knew whatever caused this outburst had been serious, as he didn't even stop and tell him what was going on.

Stopping at the gate, Dom called Manny to find out what in the hell had happened.

"Manny"

"Hey it's Dom. Someone want to explain to me why Nicky just tore out of here like a bat out of hell?" Dom sat back on his motorcycle debating on whether or not to pursue.

"Shit he's escaped the compound!" Manny yelled over to someone that started screaming to call Kris and Mark.

"Okay, someone tell me what the hell is going on?" Dom's temper started to flair, as he now knew something was amiss.

"He's going after Piper. FOLLOW HIM." Manny screamed into the phone.

Dom dropped the phone into his pocket, and turned the bike in the last direction he had seen that bright blue GTO. Opening up the throttle on the bike, Dom thought, *What has that girl gone and done now?*

The sun was setting in front of him on the old desert road, when Nicky reached the halfway point to New Mexico. The fire that had bloomed in his chest, when he had gotten the news, now rippled like molten lava through his veins. The GTO screamed down the highway echoing his fury and frustration. Never letting off the gas, he tore through every inch of road that stood between him and Piper.

When Nicky did stop long enough to get gas and something to drink, he had seen his phone had been blowing up for hours. Not giving a damn about anyone that wasn't Piper, Nicky went to throw the phone back in the car. It was Dom's ringtone that had caught him off guard. Deciding not to leave his best friend in a lurch, Nicky answered the phone.

"Where the hell are you?" Dom screamed over the rushing wind.

"Mile marker 118, Exit 121."

"You had that bitch wide open didn't you? I lost track of you when you hit the highway."

"I can't believe they let her do this!" Nicky's anger was still boiling over.

"You want to explain to me what the hell is going on?"

"You know that contract Don sent Piper on with Mark and Kris?"

"Let me guess they are in over their damn heads and put her in a spot again?"

"You could say that." Nicky tried to breathe but everything felt like raw ash stuck in his lungs. "The contract put Piper back in her old life."

"Please for the love of god, don't tell me they were that stupid."

"Piper didn't have a choice, because if she did, she wouldn't have done it."

"Do you have any other details?"

"She had to marry the son of a bitch that hurt her."

"Throttle is wide open. Wait for me there, we need a plan."

"Hold on a second, I got another call coming in." Nicky switched over, hoping it was Piper reaching out to scold him for jumping the gun. "Yeah."

"Son, where the hell are you?" Jr.'s eerily amused voice came through on the line.

"I'm headed to find her and bring her home. I promised to keep her safe."

Nicky's heart dropped and shattered like tempered glass at his father's next words. "You're too late. The wedding is in an hour at an undisclosed location. After the marriage license is signed and sealed, a copy will be delivered within a few days for proof of completion, there is nothing you can do to stop it."

"Why didn't you stop this? Why did you let this happen?"

"Better talk to the Don, he was the one calling the shots on this one. Now I could have stepped in, but where would be the fun in that." Jr. cleared his throat. "After all, she was just some broad. You'll find another to strike your match. She was nothing to get hung up on."

Nicky growled in frustration as he sank to the ground in front of his car, his phone disconnecting both calls. That's where Dom found him ten minutes later, bawling his eyes out, heart shattered, and begging for it all to be another bad dream.

Dom dismounted his bike walking over to his brother. Bending down looking straight into Nicky's tear soaked face, he shook his head. "Brother, don't make me have to be the voice of reason here."

Nicky, body still wracking from sobs, started laughing. "If your my only hope, we're fucked."

"Awe, that's the sweetest thing you ever said to me." Dom reached his hand out to pull Nicky off the ground. "Look man, we don't know what this contract entails for her, but you trained her well. She can protect herself this time."

"We don't know what he'll do once he has his hands back on her. It's not Piper being able to handle it. Xander might succeed this time." Nicky's rage had him screaming.

"You underestimate her. You always do. We should be more worried about her smiling in a mug shot than him laying a hand on her." Dom tried to give Nicky a little bit of perspective.

"So, then what do we do now?" Nicky wiped the tears away with the back on his hands.

"We need to go back to the house and make a plan. We can't just bust in guns blazing. Someone, mainly her, could get hurt. We need to look for every clue she would have left behind. Piper is a creature of habit, there is bound to be something either at the main house or yours." Dom tried to keep a level voice but the rage was getting to him.

"What are we going to do with Mark and Kris?" Nicky's eyes went black at having to mention their names.

"You let me handle them." Dom patted Nicky on the shoulder. "Now, let's get out of here."

Unfortunately, Nicky had also taught her well about how to cover her tracks. That's where the problem currently had the men stone walled. It had been two months with no sign, or contact from her. Piper stopped using her burner phone, the secondary accounts, or anything that would giveaway her whereabouts.

Nicky had even gone as far as to try and track Xander Hulston, her husband by law. Which wasn't hard, because he seemed to be a magnet for the society pages, but through it all he had never been pictured with Piper. In fact, the only picture of Piper and Xander had been the wedding announcement. Nicky's blood boiled at the thought of Piper having to marry the man she despised most.

It wasn't until now that he had come to terms with his feelings for her, and for good reason, in his mind. Nicky didn't want to hurt her. He didn't want her hurt because of him. They had a good thing going, and what was the point of messing that up? Besides Dom, Piper was the only one he could fully trust.

It hadn't been anything serious, at least that's what he had told himself time and time again. But there was that drunken night in Mexico with way too much tequila, and a promise that in the daylight was never uttered again. A permanent reminder he absently rubbed while looking over papers begging for any small clue as to her whereabouts.

While most of the crews refused to make eye contact, it didn't go unnoticed that Mark and Kris had avoided him like the plague. Every time either him or Dom had tried to corner them for information, and why they felt the need to sell out one of their own. Don Valence would have them vanish like smoke. He hated that this was all done behind his back, and before he could rush in and stop it, the contract was completed or at least part of it.

He was at a crossroads and whichever path he chose would ruin someone's life, though at this point he couldn't care less. Nicky would turn his back on the family for the chance to have Piper back in his arms. But if for any reason, Piper wanted the life she had been thrust back into, he had no problem walking away. It would kill him, there would be no doubt about that, but he would respect her choice. After all, he had no right to ask this of her and Nicky hoped it wasn't too little too late.

When Dom came busting into the house, all giggles and happy energy, Nicky wanted to separate his head from his body. As he poured himself another drink, Dom had come bouncing into the den like a kid hopped up on candy. Nicky tried to ignore him, but Dom had a way of getting his attention.

"What has you so happy?" he grumbled, never bringing his eyes off his glass.

"I know where she is?"

"Where?" Nicky jumped from his seat, almost spilling his drink over the papers.

"Aruba"

"Confirmed?"

"Yep. Mark and Kris landed there yesterday afternoon. Mr. and Mrs. Hulston..." Dom had put his finger down his throat to make him gag at staying the names. "I mean Piper. Will be landing in about an hour."

"Did you talk to Ms. Davis?"

"I did." Dom's expression was one of pure joy. "She sends her love, and confirms Piper will be staying at the compound for the next two weeks."

"Well then what are we still doing standing here?" Nicky went to rush from the room to pack. "Hold your horses there. There is more that I need to tell you."

"What could you possibly have to tell me that's more important than that?" Nicky stood there with red rimmed eyes that finally had a shred of hope.

"It's her honeymoon." Dom flinched ready to have something thrown at him.

"I'm still waiting for the point here." His anger bubbling close to the surface.

"Xander will be there. I think it's gonna be a little awkward."

"Oh that. Well, I'm sure if I know my girl, she will do whatever she can not to be anywhere near him. Call McNulty, tell him to get the plane ready for a search and rescue."

"Boss," Dom rolled his eyes.

"Dom, you can't just come in here and give me the best news that I have heard in the last two months, and not be ready to jet after. What could possibly keep you rooted to the floor, now?" Dom was ready to take his head off.

"The jet is in Aruba with Mark and Kris. That's how they got there."

"Oh for fuck sake."

"Yeah, you never let me finish." Dom refused to make eye contact. "I do have a plan B though."

"Spit it out."

"We are booked on the next flight to Aruba."

"Leaving?"

"Saturday Morning." Dom flinched again.

"But it's Thursday?"

"It was the soonest flight that wasn't economy."

"FINE." Nicky stormed out of the room slamming the door in his wake.

187

"Piper, for the love of god, come back." Dom sank onto the couch running his hands through his hair.

The next two days had a rollercoaster of emotion attached to them. Nicky would go from highs to lows giving Dom whiplash every few minutes. It was enough for him to contemplate hog tying Nicky and shipping him to Aruba snail mail, but he grinned and bore the brunt of Nicky's actions knowing all would be well once he laid eyes back on Piper.

One fourteen hour flight, two layovers due to mechanical issues, and the airline losing the luggage later, Nick and Dom see Sean standing outside the doors. Sean, a bit confused to be seeing Nicky and Dom, welcomed them with open arms.

"It's been too long, old friend. Isn't Billy supposed to be driving now, so you can enjoy your retirement?" Nicky inquired, putting his bags in the trunk.

"I don't let him drive the expensive ones. There will be no dings in Mr. Valence's prized collection."

"I understand. That man will have all our heads if something happens to one of these beauties," Dom chimed in.

The quick ride to the compound Nicky was practically bouncing out of the car. He was within miles of his goal and swore if she would have him, he'd never let her go. He had even gone to the jewelry store to prove how serious he was and bought her the biggest diamond ring they had. Nicky currently played with the box in his pocket, praying he wasn't too late.

He had barely waited for the car to come to a stop before running up the drive, down the walk and bounding through the front door. Ms. Davis was even caught off guard seeing Nicky standing before her. He didn't even say a word before running to the bungalow and throwing open the door.

The room smelt of her body spray and shampoo, but her bags and effects were nowhere to be found. Nicky tore through the room looking for any sign of her, but there was nothing. When he picked up the pillow and screamed into it, he saw a letter placed under the pillow addressed to him. Nicky turned it over and over in his hand, before opening and reading the contents.

It was dated for that morning, and from what he could make out from the tear-stained pages, Xander had flown his mistress in and she was done with it all. She hoped he was happy, while she lived in misery. He crumpled the paper in his hand, dying inside. Maybe he could still catch her, or maybe she was nearby.

When Dom came into the room, saying "Someone has been sleeping in my bed." Nicky had the paper smashed to his chest.

"She's not here." Nicky's voice was small.

"Did she leave a clue to where she was headed to next or even an address?"

"No. Maybe Ms. Davis knows something." Nicky rose from the bed and walked back into the main house.

After a few minutes of Ms. Davis recounting every detail of Piper's short visit, she had told Nicky that Piper left about two hours prior with Kris and Mark headed back stateside. The "husband", as Ms. Davis, referring to Xander, was moved over to the resort after the fight they had the night before, and she was sure he had not returned with her. Apparently, Xander had flown in on a young woman which had upset Piper, which confirmed what Piper had written.

Nicky was fuming wanting Mr. Hulston's head on a platter, but knew he could do nothing without her saying so. He had been a day late and a dollar short. This time, but the next he would be quicker. Nicky would buy his own plane if he had to and learn to fly it. Whatever it took to have her back beside him. He'd do it!

CHAPTER 18
BURN IT DOWN

There must be a point where you're allowed to be defined by
something other than what he did to you.

~ Kate Elizabeth Russell, *My Dark Vanessa.*

Only ten more miles, Piper reminded herself, as she pulled away
from the curb in the blacked out Toyota RAV4. It took everything in her
power not to just keep driving. Life had been unbearable in New
Mexico, which had her jumping at every contract like a lifeline. This one
was no different, and even now as she headed back to the airport, job
completed. She felt all the life being drained from her like a thief in the
night. Piper replayed the moments in her mind before she had left for
the airport.

It had been a long time since she had been to see Don Graves, and
for once he didn't pry into her condition. She was obviously thinner,
and had the appearance of a woman that hadn't slept in days. He could
see the hardened look in her eyes, making him want to reach out and
fix it. When Piper refused to talk about it, there was nothing he could
really do. Questioning her would cause more friction. He knew it had
something to do with a certain someone's absence, and the way she
would either change the subject or leave the room when he was
mentioned.

"Any big plans this week?" Don Graves asked as Piper packed up to
leave Montana.

"Nothing more than usual. I'm sure I'll have a party to attend or plan, when I get back home." Piper sneered at the thought.

"Parties can be entertaining if you allow them to be." Dana Graves replied, coming into the room to hand Piper the freshly folded laundry.

"Not when it's to celebrate the downfall of oneself or independence to do a man's bidding." Piper smiled, taking the pile and placing it into her bag.

Dana crinkled her eyes as she tried not to snicker. "Are you having to attend a wedding when you go back?"

"No, unfortunately. At least with a wedding I can sneak out half way through the reception and pretend I stayed for the whole thing." Piper ran her hands through her hair scanning the room to see if she had left anything behind.

Dana signaled her husband to leave while she had a word with Piper. A woman could always read between the lines and her husband was not someone to "girl talk" in front of. He might take things the wrong way, and well, that's how wars were started. Especially, with the attachment he had to Piper, Don Graves would set the whole desert on fire.

As soon as the door was closed and she had heard her husband's footsteps lead away, Dana looked at Piper scanning her face. "You want to tell me what's really going on here, or are you going to make an old woman use what brain she has left to guess."

"I don't know what you're talking about Ms. Dana." Piper tried to hide the madness and chaos of her feelings, but the cracks were starting to show.

"You had a ring on your finger, the tan lines give it away. We know it wasn't Nicky's, all the families would have heard about it and would have been in attendance." Dana stood there, hands on her hips waiting for an answer.

"I really don't want to talk about it." Piper tried to keep the emotion out of her voice, while also looking everywhere but at Ms. Dana.

"Fine. At least tell me how long."

"A year tomorrow."

"So what you're returning home to is?"

"An anniversary party. Where I have to smile and pretend I'm a happy little wife, and I don't have a thousand ways for him to die, one much more painful than the last." Piper's eyes were red rimmed but her voice remained level and cold.

"And Nicky? He couldn't be happy about the turn of events." Dana pushed a little harder.

"Couldn't tell by his actions. He abandoned me to my fate. It's fine. We all have to make decisions when standing at the crossroads of life. Some of us get forced down a path, other's get to skip their merry ass's off into the tequila sunset. I wish him all the happiness," Piper said, zipping up her bag, and placing it on the floor. "Now, if you will excuse me, I have a plane to catch and an ungrateful husband to deal with. Thank you for your hospitality."

Ms. Dana stood there in shock, not expecting that revelation to come out of Piper's mouth. "I'm so sorry, my sweet."

"Please keep this between us. I'd like to keep what bit of my reputation and his intact. All anyone seems to know is Don Valence split us into two different crews, and I don't feel like explaining myself every time I turn around. So, please?" Piper's crystal blue eyes seemed to steel.

"You have my word. If he asks?"

"Graves or Nicky?"

"Yes." Dana giggled.

"I'm just having a bad day, for Don Graves." Piper thought long and hard before responding. "Nicky, tell him I'm balancing chainsaws and haven't dropped one yet." She forced a smile.

Her ascension into New Mexico's Albuquerque International came with an overwhelming sense of dread. No one knew she was coming into town earlier than expected. Well no one but Mary, as she had been staying at the house while she was away. Something didn't feel right in her gut. Piper understood this feeling all too well. She was waiting for the other shoe to drop on what had been an unproblematic trip.

After making her way through the airport and out to short term parking, Piper sent one last text to Valence Sr., letting him know she had landed. Taking in a long steadying breath she turned off the work phone and turned on her personal one. Messages began flooding in faster than the phone could come to life. She thumbed through them as she found her car among the sea of over priced SUVs.

The texts that caught her off guard were from Xander. Apparently, he had taken it upon himself to move the anniversary party from the Hulston manor to her house. Piper saw red as the next few texts were from the event planner and the caterer confirming the cancellation requests along with reminding her about the deposits that would be lost. At least a dozen more individuals had reached out giving the same information.

"What's his endgame here? Does he think making me look bad will make him look good?" Piper huffed as she loaded her bags into the back of her car. With Xander, there was always a bigger picture. Keeping most of his plans hush hush, since she had returned back to all the family drama. Looking down at her watch, she noticed it was a little after 3pm. "He's not winning this round." and began calling the event planner to get the word out.

She was a little more than half way home when Piper placed the last call. Thankfully she had placed a password on everything before she had left. Whoever had called pretending to be her didn't have it and the vendors had sent out the text as protocol in case it was her. Xander was working with another female to make her look foolish, and her money was on Nadia.

Piper white knuckle gripped the steering wheel pretending it was either of their necks. She couldn't understand why she had been allowed to be put through the ringer in such a manner. The mothers kept telling her to give him time to adjust. Neither understanding why she had returned home early and without her husband from the honeymoon, or why Xander was not welcome in her home.

The fathers, on the other hand, were all about the dotted line. Her disappearance caused a rift between not only the two families but also the Cason/Hulston group merger. While it had gone through in her absence, it was on thin ice. Everything resided on her marriage to Xander, and their places within the company. Both were one shaky ground at best and an earthquake ready to swallow up the whole deal at worst.

Piper kept up appearances, when work allowed, but that was all she would do. With her being out of town on business most weeks, it wasn't hard for her to have an excuse for missed events. It didn't stop the rumor mill from speculating, especially when Xander had been seen with Nadia on his arm. To some, it looked innocent enough, but to those that caught wind of the affair, it became the main topic of discussion.

She had been so distracted between the calls and text, Piper had almost taken a wrong turn coming off the highway heading toward her house. "First the wrong left turn at Albuquerque, now the wrong exit heading toward the house." She mumbled as the GPS chirped, "correcting course."

Arriving home, Piper couldn't have been happier to see everything was quiet. Entering the house and disabling the alarm, Piper discarded her bags at the bottom of the steps following her nose and the sound of music coming from the kitchen. Piper had found Mary busy in the kitchen preparing dinner, humming along with the radio. Apparently, Mary didn't hear her come in. Which had become evident, when Mary turned around startled by her presence. The look of shock and the salad that had almost gone flying out of the bowl was enough to make Piper break out in a fit of giggles.

"Ms. Evette." She tried to steady her breathing.

"I'm sorry. I thought you heard me disengage the alarm." Piper was having trouble regaining her composure.

"No ma'am. I must have had the radio up too loud."

"It's fine. I didn't mean to scare you."

"You would figure after working for you for a year, I wouldn't be startled so easily."

"I don't think anyone is ever used to my movements." Piper continued to chuckle, dabbing her sleeves at her eyes.

"Well," Mary put down the bowl. "Are you ready to catch up on the gossip?"

"Can you give me ten minutes to shower and change?"

"Yes ma'am. Oh, dinner will be ready in about fifteen minutes. Would you like wine with dinner?"

"Okay, wine sounds lovely. It's been a long travel day. I'll be right back." Piper skipped out of the kitchen, and back to her discarded bags.

Within twenty minutes both women were gathered around the kitchen island, gossiping like school girls. Mary had filled her in on Xander trying to come over under the guise of "picking something up". He had a woman with him. The woman had looked cheap in her opinion but style had changed so much in the last few years, Mary wasn't sure if she had been dressed properly or not.

She had refused to let him enter and he started screaming it was his house. Mary threatened to call not only her but the police, which made him leave screeching tires. She had gotten some strange calls from an unknown name and number. When she would answer, the line would always go dead. Piper chalked it up to kids making prank phone calls.

She sat there intently listening to Mary tell the most animated story, about something that had happened at the Cason estate while she was gone.

"Oh and that's not even the best part." Mary's eyes went wide before telling the information.

"Really?" Piper leaned in like a co conspirator gripping her wine glass.

"He was seen coming out of the pool house in a "kiss the cook apron" naked as a jaybird."

"How has my mother not fired him yet?" Piper wholeheartedly laughed.

"Probably because she likes the view when he is trimming the hedges."

Piper's drink came straight out of her nose as the image flashed into her mind. "You know I can't unsee that right now right?" she choked.

"You're not the one that had the full visual. All I was there to do was pick up some things from the cook, I got dinner and a show." Mary cringed as she recalled the gardener and the upstairs maid getting caught red handed on the deck of the indoor pool.

"I don't remember things like that happening when I was growing up there. Or I was too young to notice." Piper tried to remember back.

"No people were a little more discreet when we were growing up. Take that so-called husband of yours." Mary pointed a fork full of food at her. "If a man had a mistress, you never knew about her. If you did, you didn't know who she was. It would ruin her reputation and any good society would turn their backs on the harlot, especially if she knew about the wife. Nowadays, women out here act like it's a flex. What has this world come to?"

"And it's not just the women. Men out there doing the same thing with little regard to who they hurt."

"I say we just get a big place in the middle of nowhere and start a farm. We can have all the animals we will ever need and no men to tell us how to run it."

Piper laughed. "Sounds good to me."

Piper missed moments like this more than anything. This is the only thing that's made the last year bearable. The normalcy she rarely had growing up and hadn't really experienced until Nicky. It was comforting to know that something good bloomed out of the difficulties of the past. The light at the end of the tunnel had been real once and she hoped she would find it again.

The conversation lasted long into the evening discussing party plans and when each of the people would be there for set up. Mary would be the "go to" person to take a little off Piper for the day. After all, the party hadn't just been moved to her home, but moved up by five hours. Instead of a 7pm cocktail hour followed by dinner and dancing, it was now a 2pm cocktail hour followed by a late lunch.

Piper had found out, through the grapevine and Mary of course, he had told everyone they were headed to Aspen for their anniversary and had to move the party up a few hours. Xander apparently wanted to show off all the improvements she had done to make their house a home and that's how the party got moved there. As more and more information came to light, like the three packages that had been delivered there in his name, Piper went to bed hatching her plan that would destroy Xander the same way he had tried.

The clock on the wall ticked louder than her heartbeat as Piper stared at the reflection in the full length bathroom mirror. She had chosen a simple light blue retro style dress with a full poofy skirt. If he was going to tell everyone she was a 1950s style housewife, Piper had no problem playing the part. Especially since it was going to make him look like the asshole in the end, and her the injured spouse.

Piper had never resigned herself to being someone's punching bag, whether that was physically, mentally, or emotionally. She had accepted her current path, but not without a significant amount of personal heartache and emotional pain. While Xander was out there living his best life with a woman that had three children all by him, Piper was diligently keeping up appearances hearing all the whispers of his affair aired out like dirty laundry in public. It didn't matter if it was at the office or the club, Piper heard all the unsavory things said on both sides of the issue.

"It was all going to be over soon." She whispered into the reflection she barely recognized.

A soft knock at the door broke her reverie. This was her signal that it was time to put on the best performance of her lifetime. With one last touch up on her lip gloss, Piper called out. "Yes?"

Mary had stuck her head into the room. "Ma'am, the guests are beginning to arrive. Would you like me to show them to the back yard?"

"Yes, Mary. Thank you." She let out a breath, steadying herself. "Oh, Mary?"

"Ma'am?"

"Remember what I told you about the purse this morning." A wicked gleam shown in Piper's eyes.

"I have it all under control. All you need to do is enjoy the party." Mary winked at her before departing to handle the guests.

The anniversary party was not a celebration. It was a reminder. A reminder of everything she had been promised and lost. Now, it was time to make him regret everything he had done. Piper hoped he was smart enough to learn his lesson, but doubted it.

Walking out onto the balcony that looked over her backyard, Piper noticed several people she didn't invite. The one she had her eyes trained on was standing dangerously close to her husband, arms interlocked and looking rather cozy. Piper could tell from the onlookers and those gathered closer to them, the two were going to openly play into her hand.

She descended the stairs with the grace of a southern bell, catching most of the guests off guard. Xander had barely looked up from his drink or conversation to acknowledge her presence. His look of annoyance evident on his face, as if to tell her without words she was late. He broke away from the group for a moment to be seen with her.

"Took you long enough." His voice was low enough that she was the only one that could hear him.

"Surprised you noticed. You look awfully cozy over there." The smile on her face did not reach her eyes.

"You're being paranoid, and just a reminder everyone's watching you. You're seeing threats that aren't even there. You need to learn to trust me more." His condescending tone was like nails on a chalkboard to Piper.

"It's not me being paranoid, when I, along with everyone here, sees it too." Piper batted her eyes.

"I don't know why you're upset. You should know by now that I do everything for you." Xander's menacing smiling shot a warning, Piper chose to ignore. "Remember what happened last time you got mouthy with me? You always get so emotional over nothing. I had no choice but to do it." He was taunting her as he walked away.

Piper gritted her teeth, but decided she wouldn't be the one to strike first. Where would be the fun in that? No, she'd let him think he had her scared into compliance. Getting comfortable, as he always did, and he'd make a mistake. Then she could hit them where it hurt the most.

While making her rounds through the party guests of family and business associates, Piper was very careful not to get pushed to their side of the yard. She mingled among the crowds, when she had come across her in-laws looking disappointed. Xander hadn't heeded any of his father's warnings and was now making a mockery out of them as well.

When her mother found her in the crowd talking to her in-laws, Betsy was red faced. She pulled her daughter away from the Hulstons under the guise of some detail that needed her attention. Betsy took it upon herself to start the questioning, as soon as they were out of ear shot.

"What the hell are you doing over here when your husband is over there?" Betsy quietly shrieked at her daughter.

With a fake plastered smile, Piper responded. "Because my husband decided to bring his bitch to the party. So, I don't catch a charge, I'm far away from them until I have to be."

"You need to stand your ground with him. Show him you can be a good wife. I know I didn't raise you this way."

"Why, Mother? He isn't a good husband. Why should I waste my time, energy, or even my breath on him?"

"He's making a mockery out of you."

"No," Piper corrected. "He's making a mockery out of the marriage. If you can even call what we have that. Now you want me to do something, I'll do it. But I'm very sure you're not going to like my brand of justice. Might be a little messy for you."

"Evette Hulston, I don't have time for your childish games. You march your butt over there and claim your husband. People are talking. It's your job to shut them up."

"My job is to be a good hostess, and that's what I was doing before you rudely pulled me away." Piper's voice was stern and firm with her mother, as she tried to avoid bloodshed.

"Do something NOW!" Betsy's eyes went red.

"As you wish, mother." Piper looked at her mother, as she did not understand the monster she was unleashing. "Dad?"

"Yes, honey," Larry had called from inside one of the nearby groups.

"Have the checkbook ready will you." Piper gracefully walked over to the group of people that now surrounded the pair.

She stopped short of pulling Nadia's arm away from Xander, as Nadia was telling a joke and she wanted to hear the punch line, before she became the punch line.

"What's the best way to cut a woman down to size?" Nadia laughed while the others looked uncomfortable around at each other. "You flirt and steal her husband."

As the red stain spread over the flawless cut lawn, everyone fell silent. Piper had grabbed Nadia's arm, spun her around, and delivered a right hook Mike Tyson would have been proud of. Hearing her openly disrespect her, something in Piper's mind broke free. Past, present and future converging into one, as she began to land blow after blow on to the whore her husband openly paraded around.

The party went splendidly until Nadia's blood splattered onto Piper's favorite outdoor pillows. It was even tolerable, until Betsy had stuck her nose where it didn't belong. But now here they were Nadia pouring blood and Piper standing over her ready for round two.

"The way you flirt is shameful. Know your place or I'll put you in the ground." Piper's words came out overly sweet and harsh at the same time.

Xander immediately jumped between Nadia and Piper in a protective stance. "Tell me you're not serious, and you didn't just attack her unprovoked" Xander was wide eyed, trying to control Nadia's bleeding. "You can't be this insane," he shrieked.

"I never meant to come between you and him. We are just friends? How could you think anything else? No one was disrespecting you." Nadia cried holding her face. "Evette has lost it Xander, completely lost it."

Piper ignored the bitch's sobs as she glared at Xander, as he had gone to her aid. "You're taken that bitch's back and won't even cover mine? You can't be fucking serious?"

"What do you want from me?" Xander stood toe to toe with Piper as everyone stood back and watched the train wreck unfold.

"LEAVE HER. Take her out of here. Throw her rank ass off a damn cliff for all I care. Send her on her way and never speak to her again. Would probably be the best option though." Piper laid out the ultimatum not caring who was around to see the carnage.

"How could I abandon a single mother or the children I help her care for? You won't give me a child, and her children look at me like a father figure."

"I don't want to have a baby, at least not one you fathered." Piper was ready to start swinging on Xander, when Larry grabbed his daughter's arm.

"I think he's gotten the point, dear. And if he knows what's good for him, he will leave until he can learn to respect his wife."

"I'm not going anywhere." Xander puffed his chest out until he saw his father walk over and stand on the other side of Piper.

They were in a bit of a standoff until they heard screaming coming from the house. "Where are my pills? Who's seen my pills? I need them!"

"You mean the birth control pills that were in your purse?" Piper's eyes flamed, never taking her eyes off of Xander.

"Yes, what did you do with them you crazy bitch?"

"You don't think that was just lemonade in your glass, do you? Maybe it'll take you a little longer to come up knocked up this time. Or maybe not, you had missed nearly a week. I was just helping you out." Piper feigned innocence, before looking over at her father. "Get everyone out of here, party's over, and I'm going to my room."

Piper turned her back on the shocked guests and walked into her house still hearing Nadia's faint screams, as John had grabbed her to lead her away. Xander, on the other hand, followed Piper into the house to make her pay for what she had done. He had no idea that both mothers and her father were hot on his heels to referee whatever altercation came to be.

When he grabbed Piper's arm to spin her around and force her to look at him, she rounded on him. On her way past the refreshment table that held the cake they were due to cut, Piper had grabbed the large knife, which she now had pressed to his throat. His back to the staircase, Piper felt a kind of sick pleasure seeing the fear dance in his eyes. The same fear she had seen in Aruba. The same fear he would never be able to invoke in her again.

"Honey," Piper could hear her father's voice but the sound seemed so far away. "Baby girl, I need you to let him go. We can solve this another way. His life is not worth you losing yours." Larry inched closer to his daughter, gently putting his hand over hers to take the knife.

"You're right, father. He's not worth it." Piper broke eye contact with Xander to look at him. "Get him out of my sight." Her voice was barely over a whisper.

Xander's mother grabbed his arm pulling him away from her reach. "I know things have been tense between you two, but this is unacceptable."

"What is unacceptable, Jamie, is the piss poor excuse of a man you raised. I want a divorce. If he is openly going to parade around that whore, disrespect me, the families, our marriage. Then I'm out." Piper was colder than she had ever been toward her mother-in-law.

"Just because of a few issues you're going to throw it all away?" Betsy screeched jumping in on Jamie's defense, like she wasn't the one a few minutes ago to push her to the outcome at hand.

"Look, everyone is a bit on edge today. Things were said and done, that don't look good on either party here. I think the best thing for all is to have a breather for a little while. Look into couple's counseling, and see if this can't be fixed." Larry tried to play the peacemaker. "Xander, I think it's best to leave with your parents and reflect on your actions. Piper, why don't you go upstairs and get cleaned up. I'll send Mary upstairs so you're not by yourself. We will all have a sit down in a day or two to discuss the options to move forward from this."

Piper nodded her head as she walked up the stairs to her bedroom. She was about half way up, when she stopped to turn to the family gathered below locking eyes with Xander. "Have a nice time in Aspen. I hope you make it there this time without any unnecessary stops along the way this time."

As she continued up the stairs, Piper could hear the questions on what she had said bubble over. Her words might have been cryptic, but Xander knew exactly what she meant. This was far from over, and she was playing the long game. Though she didn't know how much longer she could continue playing it without her true nature coming to the surface. Just the sight of the two made her want to strike out irrationally, and Piper prided herself on keeping her cool.

Looking down at the state she had allowed herself to be pushed into, she noticed her dress was ruined by Nadia's blood that now stained the intricate fabric. Not that Piper had ever planned on wearing the retro dress again, but she liked the color. Now it was either to be discarded or kept as a fond reminder, she smiled murmuring to herself, "Never kept a trophy before."

CHAPTER 19
ON YOUR FEET

Dom stormed into the den with a little more gusto than he would normally, but something had to give. It had been days since Nicky had showered or even eaten something that didn't come out of a paper bag. He refused to go to the main house for anything for fear of yet another altercation between the Don or his father. The last had Dom pulling Nicky off of Jr. before he had choked the life out of him.

Valence Jr.. knew what he was doing that night by taunting Nicky over Piper. He knew what his reaction would be, and he still stupidly stepped up to the wounded lion like nothing had ever happened. The last year had been a living hell for Nicky, especially with mounting tension between the family. With every assignment, Nicky hoped he would get some sort of news, but when push came to shove, Dom was the only one he could rely on.

The breaking point for Nicky was his great-grandfather's funeral. Dom and Nicky had to fly to Italy to represent the family, and they both could have sworn they had seen Piper at the gravesite. After Nicky had Dom chase the woman down, his heart fell to find out it was one of his cousins. He had begun to see her everywhere, and when the realization showed it wasn't her, Nicky sank further into the abyss.

Nowadays he had been drowning his sorrows in tequila and bourbon. He refused to give up on the search for her, but in reality it had been nearly eighteen months since anyone credible had laid eyes on her. He'd scoured over every document, each night while he drank himself into a stupor. Nicky had jumped and ran at even the smallest hint, but Piper had become like smoke, something nobody could catch with their bare hands.

He had enjoyed over a decade of being totally irresponsible when it came to his love life. Had he told her in Mexico, or any of the other times after, how he really felt, Piper wouldn't have been put in the position to make that choice. Instead, Nicky played it off as it was just a moment of weakness that would undoubtedly be repeated. Dom knew Piper would have gone to the ends of the earth for him. Now, he looked at a shell of a man desperate for any word.

The only two that knew where she was weren't talking, and conveniently left every few days if not at least once a week to "handle something" for Don Valence. If Nicky hadn't been the drunken mess he currently was, he would have the sense to have them followed. Therefore, Dom had to make the call on that, and he was none too happy with what he found. Hence the reason, he was standing in Nicky's office ready to knock some sense into the one man he respected most.

Dom, being the clever little bastard he was, snuck into Don's office and found the files. After some quick work with a copy machine, he brought Nicky everything. Looking at his best friend, Dom studied his unconscious form. He debated how drastic he would have to be to wake the corpse from his slumber. With what he had in his hand, he figured full ham would be appropriate, dealing with the aftermath later.

Picking up the empty Jack bottle that Nicky's hand still barely gripped, he slammed it into the metal trash can. As the glass shattered, he startled awake, jolting forward, and lost his balance as the chair shifted the other way. Nicky flipped sideways out of his chair landing face first onto the carpet. Loud growls and curses erupted, as he unceremoniously dragged himself off the floor. Nicky glared around the room ready to take the head off whoever dared to wake him. When he locked eyes with Dom's smug face, he realized why his heart was racing out of his chest.

"It's you! You woke up for me." Dom's attempt at a singsong voice had Nicky sending him a death glare. "Ah, there's my loving boss."

"What the fuck was that? Do you not know how to wake anyone up without nearly causing them to have a heart attack?" Nicky braced himself on the side of his desk.

"Did you hurt yourself? Did you die?" Dom looked at him with more than pity in his eyes.

"I could have. What the hell do you want?"

"I want for you to go upstairs, take a fucking shower, sober the hell up, and meet me in the garage in 20 minutes."

"What the fuck for?" Nicky's head was throbbing more from the impact than the hangover.

"Because I have some information that can't be said within these walls." Dom shook the packet of papers at him.

"I have plans" He looked over at the open door waiting for his nightly delivery of food and booze.

When no one knocked and the cameras didn't show movement, Nicky looked at Dom with a puzzled look. Dom ran his hands through his hair and glared at his best friend. "No one is coming to keep you satiated in your misery. I have told Don Valence that I'm taking you out to clear your head and talk some sense into you. Now don't make me drag your ass from that spot."

"Talk sense into me. Have you ever been in love? Do you know what it feels like to have your heart ripped from your chest?" Nicky's red rimmed eyes broke what heart Dom had.

"You know I do, but this isn't about me." His eyes heat in response, trying so hard to control the demons within.

After what seemed like a forever long staring contest, Nick finally shook his head and stood up to leave the office for the first time in nearly a month. He knew Dom was right and he could at least use the fresh air if nothing else. He hated to admit there was no getting over Piper, no other woman had ever understood him the way she did. Now it seemed like she was gone forever, and he was doomed to become a version of either his father or grandfather.

"Fine, but you're buying." Nicky growled as he walked toward the door tripping over his own two feet.

"I swear you could trip over your own shadow in your state." Dom chuckled.

"My shadow's a tricky little bastard. It likes to see me fall to its level."

"Well let's not stay there at least. It might start complaining about the smell. Make sure to scrub twice, You smell like the inside of a landfill."

"Are you sure that's not your upper lip?" Nicky shot back leaving the office.

Dom smirked at the half hearted remark. He understood long before Nicky had admitted it that Piper was the one. He had caught the two together enough times in the last decade. Dom was actually surprised there wasn't a little Nicky running round, but there would be time for all that when she was back within arms reach.

Heartache bloomed within his chest, as other thoughts came to the surface. He wondered where his raven haired beauty found herself now. When this was all put to bed, he would have to make a trip to Nashville and see if she was still working for the Tootsie family. For now though, he would push his affairs to the side, and tend to the issues at hand. First being the state of Nicky's office and the god awful smell of what he hoped was uneaten food.

Nearly an hour later, the two men had found themselves in the back room of the Dustbowl Bar and Grill. They need a place to fly under the radar, and of course Val was working that night. When she had caught wind of the situation, Val had been fit to be tied with a few colorful things to say about Don Valence.

She couldn't believe her ears when word had gone around about Piper and the situation that put her back in the grip of the bastard that had hurt her. Val was ready to drive up to New Mexico herself and give that boy a what for, but Dom had convinced her to let them attempt to handle it first. After all, Dom had no intention of having to explain why a 5'6" Italian woman was smiling in her mugshot.

Val had made sure there was plenty of food brought, citing that Nicky looked to be too skinny. At the same time, she limited the amount of alcohol that was being brought in and out. She had heard that Nicky turned into a bit of a lush in Piper's absence and wouldn't tolerate him getting sloppy drunk on her watch.

After food was consumed and Nicky was thinking with a clearer head, Dom laid out every bit of the information he had painstakingly dug up over the last year. He started with the prize winning piece of information first, the contracts. When they realized there was a bigger price on her head than either of them knew, their jaw dropped.

"TWO MILLION!" Nicky growled, pouring over the documents Dom had nabbed from the old man's office.

"Looks like it. Four contracts. A million just from the Cason's wanting their daughter returned safely." Dom showed Nicky another set of papers. "The other million busted up in a few different ways from the Morang family. The last 250 thousand, though, relies on her cornering..." Dom's voice trailed off as his eyes saw the name.

"Who?" Nicky snatched the papers away from Dom, reading them for himself. "Victor? You have got to be fucking kidding me."

"If anyone could catch him it would be her." Dom winced.

"Yea with back up. The last time she put him on his ass, she had us as back up." Nicky rubbed his temples.

"That's not all." Dom's face fell. "I know why we can't track her by the money."

"Cash? That kind of cash would be hard for even her to explain." Nicky hated the feeling she was in deeper than he could get her out of.

"Nope there is a separate account. Looks to have been created while we were still dealing with the shit in New York."

"By who?"

"Don Valence. He's kept her working while she's been gone. The amount in the account is substantial."

"Why would he do this? None of this makes sense."

"From what I found out, he was hoping, by Piper being gone, you would settle down. Looks like he is hoping to pass the mantle of the family to you and not your father."

"How does Mark and Kris play into this?" Nicky's patience was wearing as thin as his sobriety.

"Remember about five years ago when Don wanted to split the crew in two? Piper would be the head of her own crew. Started a huge fight between the two of you, when you didn't believe this wasn't what she wanted?"

"Oh god, don't remind me."

"Yeah, well this was Don's way of making it happen. Mark and Kris are her muscle now whether she likes it or not. They also report straight back to Don Valence instead of you."

"So, how do we fix this? How do I get her back?"

"I know a roundabout location for her."

"When are we leaving?"

"Tomorrow, after you have a heartfelt conversation with your grandfather." Dom raised his glass to his friend.

"Tonight, we celebrate her pending return." Nicky mirrored his best friend, as the embers of hope began to ignite in his chest.

210

CHAPTER 20
FOLLOWING THE
BREADCRUMBS

Nicky's world had been turned upside down once again after Dom had told him everything he had found. From his grandfather getting Piper out of the way to Mark and Kris being the muscle behind it all, Nicky's heartbreak blinded him with the engulfing rage that built within. They had played a smoke and mirrors game all too well with Nicky. Letting slip little details that would send him off on a wild goose chase knowing he would never find her. He was set up to always be a day late and a dollar short, but his darling Piper had left clues. If he had only not been so enraged and quick to dismiss what was plainly in front of his nose. Dom, on the other hand, had seen it all, keeping detailed records for when Nicky finally came to his senses.

Everyone thought, by her being out of the way, Nicky would at least attempt to settle down with any number of available young ladies. Don Valence believed Nicky would seek solace to ease his broken ego, as Valence Jr. did when he happened to be rejected. Roxie's name began to be one the most prominently brought up in conversation, when anyone was actually listening to the old man. Nicky had no intention of marrying a woman that wasn't his equal in every way. Piper had checked all the boxes and so many more for him.

His heart ached at the thought of all the nights they had spent together, while his hot head tendencies and pride kept him from showing his true feelings. He couldn't stand the thought of her being in another man's arms, and would rather rip the offending appendages from their host. Nicky had to come to terms with the fact he had never felt like this with anyone else. Piper knew when to amp him up and when to rein him in, that was more than even Dom could do most days.

While this wasn't his direct doing, Nicky felt more than responsible for Piper not only being in this situation, but also remaining in it. Had he kept her true identity between Dom and himself, his grandfather wouldn't have had the leverage to use against either of them. Hell, had he convinced her to take option A instead of letting her take B, she would be living her life far from this. Nicky couldn't go back and change the past but he could damn well make sure they didn't repeat it in the future. This led the two hatch a half baked plan, that they were semi sure would work out in their favor. They told a few white lies and set the bait for Mark and Kris to tip their hands.

Don Valence and the others were told that Nicky and Dom were headed to Italy to blow off steam. Nicky would work on clearing his head, sowing some wild oats, and finally once and for all forgetting about Piper. In all reality, Dom and Nicky were headed to New Mexico with the hopes of fulfilling a promise of finding and bringing Piper back at any and all cost.

Before they had left Texas, Dom had found out one more pertinent piece of information that put Nicky on edge. While this cemented their resolve to carry out the search and rescue mission, Dom knew it would make it harder to keep Nicky under control for any length of time. After all, no one likes finding out they have been played a fool for damn near a year.

Dom was sure that Piper had been kept in the dark with lies and spun tales from all sides. He knew Nicky had been, and when he didn't accept the answers he was given, he tracked her chasing his tail in the process. While Piper was more than rational and intelligent, she would have no choice to believe what she had been told if Nicky wasn't reaching out to make contact in some way.

Neither had known that Piper's phone had been switched on the day of the wedding by Kris and Mark. Each of them had four or five burner phones all loaded with the exact same information, therefore blocking all contact from that number to Nicky and vice versa wouldn't be that big of a challenge. The rest would merely be turning off the swapped phone and never speaking a word of it to anyone. But they had gotten drunk on this last return trip, Dom guessed the bottle was easier to deal with the priest in confession, and spilled their guts. Of course, they had been so plastered, neither remembered a thing the next morning except for the massive head splitting hangover.

Dom still wasn't sure how they had accomplished it, as Piper normally never let her phone out of her sight, but they somehow did. The bigger problem was they had no idea which phone she currently had with her, since the rest of her things had been removed from the main house before they had returned back from the New York run. It was almost as if Don Valence had hoped to erase Piper, and with time and parading beautiful young women in front of Nicky, things would go back to the way they were before she had ever entered the picture.

As the sound of laughter drifted up from the street below, Nicky stood smoking a cigarette on the balcony feeling very much alone in this new town. He hated small towns even though he had grown up in one all his life. Nicky supposed the traveling had a lot to do with that as he had gotten older and joined the family business. The small town in Texas was home base and a place to lick one's wounds if things had gone sideways on a job. It was quiet but still had all the charms of nightlife.

New Mexico was a different beast altogether for him. It didn't help that they happened to be on someone else's turf. The Morang family wasn't known for playing nice with other families, especially if Victor happened to be around. There had been some tips handed over to the family on his moments, and Nicky knew of the contract to rein Victor back in. If he could handle it while they were there, then it was two birds with one stone.

For Nicky though, this wasn't about another contract or even about the small suffocating town, Dom and him found themselves in. It was about finding the one person that could make him whole. If this was where she was, he would endure it for her. Nicky would move the heavens and earth to have her back by his side. He would have to play it cool, but patience was not one of his strong suits.

Flicking the ashes from the balcony, he brooded over being in the apartment alone. Dom had gone out for supplies, as they agreed he would be the one less likely to be recognized in the small suburban area. Keeping a low profile was key, if they were going to get close enough to Piper and not to cause a scene or cause her to run.

They had settled for a furnished two story apartment off the main street that rolled through the center of town. It wasn't their ideal choice, but the man was quick to rent it and didn't ask any questions when they handed him a years worth of rent in cash. The only reason Nicky liked the place was due to the balcony. He could sit and watch passersby in hopes of catching a glimpse of Piper.

Nicky flicked the ash from his cigarette and remembered her always being a creature of habit. From her morning coffee to what she bought at the grocery store, Piper had to have things a certain way. It was one of the many things he teased her over when they were out. It was little things like that he missed most of all. She stayed on top of everything, and when she was gone, he had become lost without her. Twelve years of always having someone there and then poof.

He was lost in his thoughts, feeling sorry for himself, when Dom burst through the door panting with his arms loaded down with supplies. He looked like a kid in a candy store with the grin that was plastered on his face. Nicky wasn't in the mood for his playful banter, but as he approached to take some bags from him, he caught a familiar scent. Piper's body spray practically swallowed him whole.

"You've seen her," were the only words Nicky could choke out.

"I did indeed, brother." Dom's eyes sparkled with wicked delight as he put the bags down in the kitchen. "I mean what are the odds of being here three days and just running into her."

"What did she say? Did she recognize you? Why are you just standing there? Tell me!" Nicky rattled on like a schoolgirl finding out the Basketball player had a crush on her.

"Yes, she recognized me right off the bat." Dom paused for dramatic effect and knowing it would piss Nicky off further. This was the first time he had seen fire in his eyes in over a year, and he was going to savor it.

"And?" Nicky's patience was wearing thin.

"She looked shocked to say the least. I played it off looking at her confused and called her Piper. She said I must be mistaken. Her name was Evette. I apologized and told her she looked just like an old girlfriend of mine named Piper Johnson. That's when she dropped the code word." Dom was strutting around putting things in place.

Nicky raised his eyebrow at Dom as his voice went low, "Which one?"

"I must have a twin." Dom snickered at Nicky's reaction. They had many code words that would set different things in motion. Twin was one that they used to acknowledge but signal they couldn't react.

"Anything else?"

"Well there was a lady that approached her asking about the charity ball this evening. I'm sure with a few calls I could get us an invite."

"Handle it. I'll pull out my black suit" Nicky turned on his heels for the bedroom.

Dom stood there for a moment staring at the spot Nicky once occupied. He shouldn't have been surprised by his partner's reactions to him laying eyes on her first. Her pungent perfume followed him back to the apartment like a lovers greeting for Nicky. But there was more to the encounter than a chance of fate, she had told Dom something he wouldn't dare share. Dom felt horrible lying to her about Nicky's whereabouts, but he knew it was for the best. Both had that wildfire spark in their eyes, and who was he to put it out. For now though, he would bide his time and see if having them in the same room would rekindle the embers.

"You do realize this is a masquerade ball right?" Dom called over his shoulder fixing his tie for the tenth time. "You know I'll be even more happy about Piper being back than you will be." Dom had sent another not so subtle jab at Nicky.

"Yes, I'm aware. Otherwise, we would look like entertainment instead of guests in these masks." Nicky practically growled, unable to get his own tie straight. "And what gives you the notion, you will be happier than me?"

"Because she did the ties. She would never let us leave for any event with a crooked tie. Plus, let's face it, you can't cook." Dom chuckled, finally getting the knot to slide up without damaging the finished product.

"I can cook." Nicky huffed nearly choking himself with his tie.

"No, you used to be able to make something edible. Now, I wouldn't feed it to the dogs." Dom chuckled knowing exactly what buttons to push on the Italian man.

"If we didn't have somewhere to be in an hour, I'd..." Nicky trailed off as his phone rang. He sneered at what was now the third call from his father. He didn't have time to hear about his last conquest or

217

heartbreak, whichever way it happened to fall at the moment. His mind was on a raven haired beauty.

Valence Jr.. had lectured him thoroughly before he had left for this trip, telling him all the things Nicky didn't want to hear. He never liked Piper. Nicky thought it was more because she wasn't Italian, but there was something more behind the snide remarks he had made about her before and after she was gone. Valence Jr.. didn't like or even tolerate Piper, because she had shut him down on more than one occasion. Piper had been loyal to the Don and Nicky, nothing more.

While she had always been cordial, Nicky knew Piper didn't respect his father. He was the self proclaimed ladies man, and she was one of few that didn't buy into his bullshit. Though he couldn't prove it, Nicky was sure it was his father that happened to be in on this with the old man. Valence Jr.. had been a little too happy over the last two years, watching his son fall into a shell of his former self. Nicky had let him believe it was his idea to get away for a while, but they all played right into his trap.

Dom stood in the doorway watching the smoldering look dance across his best friend's face. Unfortunately, he knew it was only one of three people that could invoke a reaction like that out of him. One of which, they were due to come face to face with in less than an hour. "Father or Don?"

Nicky cut his eyes dangerously towards Dom in the mirror. "Jr."

"Do you think he knows where we are?" Dom leaned in on the door frame gauging his demeanor.

"No, I don't think so. We haven't had the calvary show up to stop us."

"Well, this is the Morang area. It might not be our calvary we should be worried about." Dom looked a little more somber at the thought.

"We are fine," Nicky bit back.

Dom held his hands up half heartedly in defense. "I'm just saying."

"Look, I'm nervous enough about all this shit. I thought we would have time for me to at the very least figure out what I am going to say to her. I have had no time to prepare, and while flying by the seat of our pants seems to always work..." Nicky ran his hands through his hair. "I don't know if it will be enough this time."

"Piper still loves you." Dom solemnly dropped that breadcrumb of information before leaving the doorway with Nicky nervously straightening his tie in the mirror.

A chill had set in the October air as Dom and Nicky pulled up in the old ragtop Camaro. They had been thankful one of Dom's acquaintances happened to have shop an hour north and agreed to let them borrow the beauty for the night. While Dom thought it was a little too flashy for an event like this, Nicky wanted to catch everyone's attention. The car screamed class and money, therefore no one would look at the men and think they were out of place. As the men handed it over to the valet, they watched a kid no more than nineteen bug out. Yes, this was exactly what Nicky wanted.

Following the crowds of well dressed people, they made their way up the stone steps of the lavish venue. The two were surprised to see the packed place in such a small town. Fire breathers dressed in an Arabian nights kind of attire lined the stairs and entryway, giving a little show to what was to come on the inside. Every wall was covered with billowy silk tapestries and gold framed artwork. It was pretentious to say the least.

Nicky and Dom had spotted the open bar when they entered the room and figured it would be the best place to set up shop for a moment. With so many people moving in and around the room, it was difficult to retain their bearings. Whoever had planned the event, had done a wonderful job in Nicky's opinion. It was definitely designed to draw a certain kind of crowd.

Once they had ordered their drinks, they turned, keeping their backs to the bar. Scanning the room, Dom had noticed not much was different from the soirée he had been made to attend. Each section of couples had splintered off into smaller ones and then filtered into another. While the conversations might be a little different, the structure was all the same. Who had the biggest wallet in the room and what business they were in.

Nicky, on the other hand, looked carefully at each and every woman. While the masks would make it a bit challenging, he would know those crystal blue eyes anywhere. After several scans of the room, Nicky had seen a table with what looked to be a fortune teller and the group of women gathered around. A raven haired woman stood among them in a shimmering midnight blue gown.

Nicky elbowed Dom, who seemed more interested in the group of men that gathered on the other side of them. When he flashed his eyes back in Nicky's direction, Nicky pointed his chin in the direction of the table. Dom's eyes went wide as the smile widened on his lips. "There she is."

"I'm going to see if I can get a closer look. Make sure there isn't a look-a-like before I blow my cover." Nicky slammed back the whiskey he had ordered.

"I'll keep you covered." Dom knew this was going to go one of two ways, hoping for the latter, as Nicky made his way through the sea of people.

The women that had grouped around Piper started cackling over a joke one of their husbands had told on their way over.

"How can you tell a good English teacher from a bad one?" A woman in a bright green mask asked.

"How?" Piper asked, trying to blend into the group.

"When you know the difference between a man eating chicken and a man-eating chicken." The woman's laughter erupted again sending the whole group into a fit of giggles.

"Ah, good one." Piper tried to play along at what was yet another dad joke.

"Ladies, do you wish to draw a card for Madam Victoria." the fortune teller said, drawing their attention back to her.

"Choose mine." Piper spoke up, welcoming the distraction from the group.

Madam Victoria nodded and shuffled the deck. Pulling two cards laying them face down for a moment before revealing their truth. The group of women went quiet as Madam Victoria flipped each card over and gasps started to be heard. The Queen of Swords and Death. Piper frowned thoughtfully at the tarot cards arranged before her.

"I will say this is the most interesting one so far this evening." Madam Victoria's eyes glinted.

"Oh nothing good can come from Death being in a reading." one of the women said with a shocked expression.

"The Queen of Swords combined with the Death card is a powerful combination. It's telling you to embrace change, face the truth, and let go of anything that's no longer serving you." Madam Victoria said with a knowing look in her eye.

As if on cue, Piper looks up to see Xander rounding the corner with a heavily pregnant Nadia on his arm. Gritting her teeth, she straightened her back looking over the pitying looks from the other women standing around her. She would not make a scene and wouldn't stand for this any longer. If he wanted Nadia then she would do everything within her power to give that to him. Piper quickly excused herself, needing air and space.

Her resolve shifted as she walked toward the doors to the garden. Her father was standing there with John, probably chatting about some

221

business deal. When they saw the murderous look on her face, they froze. With both men having the same thought cross their minds, *What had Xander done now?*

"Evette, darling, what's wrong?" Larry finally found his words.

"Nothings wrong." Her tone was as cold as the north wind.

"What has that boy done now?" John knew all too well who was the cause of this.

"Nothing more than his usual. I mean if you call publicly showing off his heavily pregnant mistress, which he is telling everyone that will listen is our surrogate." the tears pricked the back of Piper's eyes but she wouldn't dare let them fall.

"He said what?" Larry stared at John.

"Oh father didn't you know. I can't have children." Piper's sarcastic tone dripped with venom. "I'm done with this. Either you find me a way out of this marriage or I will. Cason/Hulston group be damned." Piper plowed her way through the men that retreated back into the main ballroom to find out what was going on.

Once she was safely alone outside, Piper allowed one tear to fall. She had played the "happy" little wife for far too long. It was time for her to take action. Yes, she had gotten her escape every time Valence Sr. called for another job, but she still had to come back here. She still had to be married to that bastard. Enough was enough. Reaching down into her handbag for a cigarette, Piper had noticed she wasn't alone. Putting it to her lips, a man's hand, in a very nicely tailored suit, lit it for her. "Thank you."

"When will you stop running?" the man said and Piper closed her eyes taking a drag off her cigarette, begging the threatening tears not to fall.

"It's not safe for people to see us together." Piper's voice became hoarse, holding back all the emotions that she had bottled up and shoved down. She didn't dare turn to face the man, in case it wasn't who she thought it was.

"You became the person you pretended to be, so seamlessly drifting between the two worlds. You know you don't belong here, not like this at least. You belong with me, to me. As I do to you." Nicky ran his hands gently up her arm brushing the hair away from the spade tattoo and kissing it lightly. Repeating the same words he had told her time and time again.

"It's not that simple, when the men that promise you the world destroy you in the end. One showed his true colors, the other..." Piper turned to stare into his eyes with all the pain, fury, loss that his absence had caused her. "Well, I was just another job to you wasn't I? Some damsel in distress that would make you feel better about your life?"

Nicky reached out grabbing her wrists and pulling her to him. His voice went dangerously low. "I don't know where this is coming from, and you can bet that sweet little ass of yours I will find whoever filled your head with that nonsense." Nicky flexed his hands around her wrist giving him ideas the same way it had when he did it the first time.

"Nico..." Her voice was breathless, as it sent shivers down his back.

"I love it when you say my name." Nicky whispered in her ear, pulling her into his chest feeling the warmth from her body.

"Boss." Dom stepped out of the shadows. "I hate to interrupt, but there is a situation."

"Busy. Handle it." Nicky never took his eyes off Piper.

"I'm afraid I can't handle this by myself." Dom knew there happened to be too many witnesses for him to use his normal tactics.

"What is it?" Nicky snapped.

"An unexpected guest has arrived." Dom looked down, straightening his cuffs.

"Morang business." Piper finally found her voice.

"Unfortunately." Dom's voice was gruffly hollow.

"Go. I can't be seen or noticed. He'll blow my cover." Piper's heart broke at having to send him away.

"I promise this isn't the last time you will see me." Nicky gently kissed Piper's lips, while slipping a phone into her handbag. Nicky studied her face one last time before leaving the garden and rejoining the party.

Business called, and unfortunately, Dom and Nicky had been there to answer it. The one person who could lure him out, without kicking up a fuss, was also the same person Victor could blow out of the water, as he would remember her from previous altercations. This could present a bigger challenge. Piper was a high profile person at this event, and the boys couldn't jeopardize revealing who she happened to be behind the scenes. They would have to use a less savory tactic to deal with him. After all, Victor never could say no to a good whiskey.

CHAPTER 21
BATTLE WORN

The cold air hit her skin like shards of glass, but it wasn't the chill that made her shiver, as she stood on the balcony watching the dawn of a new day. It was the memory of him standing in front of her in the garden. His intense eyes, the grip on her wrists, and the smell of his cologne lingered on her enveloping her senses. The unexpected reunion had been so brief, so intense, and now, nothing. It had been so brief in fact, Piper thought she had imagined the whole thing.

Three days had passed, and the silence stretched into something unbearable. No messages, no calls, no sign of life, there was just her screaming into the void, looking for answers. Piper had tried to distract herself with work, but when not even Don Valence had reached out to her for another job, her mind began to spiral.

The phone she had found in her purse after returning home from the event was the only evidence she had that it was all real. It now sat on her desk next to her other two phones. Piper mentally begged the universe to make them ring and for her to hear his voice one more time. At this point she would have a pointless conversation with her lovable goofball, Dom, if it put her just one step closer to Nicky.

As she was lost in her thoughts beginning to shut down for lunch, her phone rang making her heart nearly leap out of her chest. Grabbing for each phone to see which one was ringing, praying it was the mystery phone Nicky had slipped her, Piper had seen her father's name lighting up her personal phone. Debating on sending it to voicemail, Piper had a sickening feeling she should answer it.

"Hello Father." Piper's voice was pleasant but with little feeling.

"How's your day going?"

"Well, no one has died today."

"Are those really your standards?"

"Pretty much. I mean no incident reports is a good thing isn't it?"

"I suppose you're right. Anyway, the reason I'm calling."

"Yes?"

"John and I would like to have a meeting with you this evening if you're free."

"I have a dinner meeting with the head of Callon Enterprise this evening." Piper looked at her desk calendar to check the time. "Or did your new secretary give me the wrong date and time again?"

"Oh, I'm sorry Darling." Piper could hear the shuffling of papers. "That dinner meeting was scheduled for Larry Jr.. last week. He had gotten the stomach bug and was rescheduled for tonight, but put on the wrong person's calendar."

"That's fine. I'd remind my brother though. You know if it isn't on his calendar it doesn't exist to him."

"I know all too well." Larry cleared his throat. "So, you will be able to meet us this evening."

"I suppose. What's this about?" Piper was becoming more and more annoyed by the conversation by the second.

"Something you had said the other night at the event."

"I was serious."

"So you will be at the meeting?"

"Time?"

"5pm. The office should be mostly cleared out by then, after all this is family business. We don't need to have too many ears listening in."

"Agreed." Piper huffed out, but something didn't feel right. She could smell a trap from miles away, but she didn't have a choice but to deal with his head on. "I'll be there."

"Very good. I'll see you in the third floor conference room at 5."

"See you then." Piper had disconnected the call, sitting back in her chair. Something was definitely up. Her father never wanted to meet her after hours, especially not on company property. If there happened to be something that needed her attention it was always a dinner meeting, or during working hours. She had hoped maybe they were taking her seriously, and found a way out of her marriage.

Piper had unfortunately found out after returning from their honeymoon, divorce wasn't an option for her. The contracts between the family wouldn't allow even a cut and dry no fault divorce. When they said till death do they part, someone took it very seriously. Piper had received a small portion of the papers but never the whole thing. What she had seen though, would allow her to walk away if she could prove prior or current abuse.

Thankfully, Piper had kept the pictures from 13 years ago. She wanted out clean without having to rehash the past but it didn't look like it was going to be that easy. Opening her office drawer, Piper had pulled one of three flash drives with the proof she needed. She would let all the evidence speak for itself. From the damage Xander had done to the record of the long time affair that both families knew about and attempted to cover up, Piper wouldn't be holding punches here. It was time for her to go to war.

The next four hours of mindless meetings and paperwork passed within a blink of an eye. Piper found herself at 4:30 pm packing up her office and slipping the flash drive into the pocket of her jacket. She had been smart about all this. If things went badly, she had a plan. The other two flash drives had been sent out by courier with letters attached to them. One to Dom's PO Box in Texas, and the other to Don Graves, both with letters that stated if they hadn't heard from her in three days time to turn the evidence over to the news and police.

It was a short ride up the elevator as her office was a floor below. She was calm, cool and collected until she had heard Xander's voice coming from the inside of the meeting room. This wasn't a sit down, it was an ambush, or an intervention of sorts. While both heads of the family understood her disgust with Xander, neither stepped in to help or rescue her. Any normal father would be gutting Xander like a fish for cheating on his daughter let alone having an open affair in public.

Piper quickly checked her briefcase for her weapons, on the off chance she would have to fight her way out of the room. Thankfully, she never left the house without her gun, and few people knew she had it, let alone carried it on her person. This would play to her advantage, or at least she hoped it would.

"You must be mad, coming here like this." Piper casually said walking into the room placing her briefcase on the table.

Xander didn't even look up to acknowledge her. He looked to be taking a very important phone call from who he suspected to be Nadia by what she could here. Before making kissy noises into the phone, he had told her that he would be going out for dinner with a client. Piper half heartedly wondered if the "client" was his new blonde secretary? Once a cheater, always a cheater, Piper thought as he ended the call and placed the phone down on the table.

"Well, well, well. Look what the cat dragged in?" Xander stood buttoning his blazer and walking toward her.

"I know. She could have at least had the decency to leave your ass in the trash where she found you." Piper retorted.

"How dare you look down your nose at me like that."

"But you make it so easy to do so."

"Let's see if you still have that smug look on your face when our father's get here."

"You honestly think, I give two shits about what they have to say, Xander? I'm going to get a divorce from you whether you like it or not. I'd rather it be quick and clean, but if you want to play dirty. Hey, we both know I'm more than game." Piper's blue eyes reflected the storm that was brewing just under the surface.

"If you leave now, you lose everything." Xander gloated.

"See that's what you seem to think, but even if that was true. I'd rather start from the gutter than be married to you for one more millisecond." Piper squared up preparing herself for the attack she knew was coming. "I might be too old to start again, but I welcome the challenge. It won't be the first time or the last."

Xander inched his way across the room, step by step coming dangerously close to Piper. She, already aware of his ill intentions, reached a hand behind her placing it on the loaded pistol. *One more step, you bastard, just one more damn step.* Piper remained calm at this advance, though her mind was racing as it analyzed each of his movements.

As Piper went to reach for the weapon, Xander drew back with his fist. Before either could complete the next move the door swung open wide revealing both Larry Cason and John Hulston. A combination of shock and horror etched on their faces, while Xander stood there like a child that had his hand stuck in the cookie jar. Piper's look of defiance never wavered, as she also never broke her eye contact with Xander.

"What in the hell is going on here?" John had said before Xander had the good sense to drop his arm.

"Just a conversation with my wife, father." Xander's eyes were smoldering.

"If this is the way you talk to her, there is no wonder why she doesn't want to be married to you."

"She was asking for it. She needs to learn to submit to her husband, to heel." Xander straightened his suit as he walked to where he had his things on the table. "Larry, you should have taught your daughter some manners. My mother doesn't talk to my father in such a way and I won't have my wife do anything less."

"Boy, I'd watch that tone. I already saved your life from my daughter once. I won't be inclined to do it a second time." John put his hand on Larry's shoulder as he spoke.

"No offense or anything, gentleman." Piper removed her hand from the gun. "It has been a long day for me, and I'm sure Mary has a lovely dinner waiting for me at home. Could we move this along. What you do with him after I leave is none of my concern."

"Evette is right, we are here to handle a serious matter and most of us have dinner plans to attend." John spoke glaring at Xander.

"Absolutely, John." Larry placed his briefcase on the table pulling a rather thick file from it. The two men were careful to stay between the feuding couple.

"Now for the reason we are here." John took a long shaky breath looking between Xander and Piper before beginning. "As everyone knows. There was a marriage contract between the Hulston and Cason family, that was due to result in the eldest son for ours to the eldest and only daughter of the Cason's. When Ethan died everything changed, resulting in Xander taking that role."

Piper's mind raced as the details she had not been privy to were laid out on the table. Leaving her with more questions than answers as she listened.

"When Evette ran away, thirteen years ago. That put us all in a lurch."

"Ran away...." Piper chuckled. "That's what you believe, don't you. I ran away. Cold feet?"

"That's what happened." Larry's disappointing tone was evident.

"Is that what Xander told you? I mean you only had his side of what happened that day. You've only heard his point of view. Did any of you in the last year think to ask for mine?" Piper folded her arms sitting on the edge of the table.

"What would it have made any difference? You left without a word. Hell, not even a sign of life." Larry's voice increased in frustration at Piper's petulant behavior.

"Because, I'm your daughter." Piper's body stiffened at the memories that let dance in her head to keep herself grounded in the situation. "You stand there and accuse me of running away like a scared child, but where were you at the time?"

"What is that supposed to mean?" Larry fired back at her.

"Nothing. Continue John, I have places to be." Piper sounded more and more detached.

"As I was saying." John looked to his daughter-in-law with a bit of questioning, that would have to be held to the end. "It put everyone in a lurch. Mostly due to money that was exchanged on the promise of the pending nuptials. Which is what formed the Cason/Hulston group, and made the Cason Oil group the controlling interest in Hulston Oil. Evette and Xander were due to become the faces of the business. After five years of operation, the business would have been able to stand on its own feet and become its own entity. Allowing the initial investment to be held in trust for the future of the company."

"You mean the offspring between Xander and myself, don't you?"

"Yes" John looked guilty as he answered.

"So, let me get this straight. You're pissed off and have no intent of letting me out of this marriage because of money and the fact I have openly refused to have that man child's offspring." Piper gritted her teeth.

"In your absence, young lady, your father was gracious enough to allow the deal to continue until you were found and brought back to face the consequences. The business greatly suffered and the clock didn't start until your "I dos." Now the company is hemorrhaging money and there is no way to pay anything back, until we can get it back on its feet. As you and your brother are the primary stakeholders in the company."

231

"So, how much are we talking here?"

"That doesn't matter. We are just here to tell you both that some sort of middle ground must be had here. I understand my son hasn't been the best since your return..." John began his rant, but Piper quickly cut him off holding up her hand.

"How much? I think I have the right to know how much my asking price was. If I was that much of a prize, how much was I sold into hell for?"

"Twelve million of your inheritance was invested into this project, leaving you twelve million in your trust fund." Larry finally spoke up, not meeting his daughter's eyes.

"A trust fund that could only be accessed after I said I do or the age of..." Piper pressed both men putting the information together slowly.

"You were 25." Larry confirmed.

"Okay..." Piper tried to gain some sort of control over her anger. "So, in the thirteen years of operation, I have been the controlling interest in this company, not Xander."

Xander sat at the end of the table still looking smug. "Well, technically I have been. As your Fiancé, I was handling things in your stead."

The realization of the motives he had in that hotel room flooded like a breaking dam. Had she not returned at all or been found dead the contract would have been void, but still would have been paid out. He had access to everything, running it all into the ground. Piper's body stiffened to stone, as she reached for the gun in her back. She had more than one reason to end his miserable ass life; this was just the tipping point. As she took the gun from her back and chambered the round, the room fell silent.

"So, after every damn thing this slimy ass worm had done to me and this company. You're telling me only till death will free me?" Piper played with the gun in her hand debating on if he was worth the bullet. "He's the problem here. I mean you see that right. I have all the proof I

232

need to claim, I was just pushed over the edge and snapped. Neither of you will be able to push this under the rug, if he's dead."

"Piper, there are other ways to handle this." John said, looking between the gun and his son.

"You are taking his side against me. You both are. Now, I'm going to give you ten minutes to rummage through those damn papers and find me an out clause." Piper turned the gun over in her hand. "Or let's just say I'm going to have to call some old friends to clean up this mess."

"This is extortion!" Larry screamed, never taking his eyes off his daughter.

"No, father, it's business. Ruthless, cut throat business. Survival of the fittest. And oh yeah..." Piper had almost forgotten the little insurance policy that she kept in her jacket pocket. "You might want to take a gander at this." Piper threw the flash drive down the table landing in between John and Larry. "Might answer some questions. After all, the only coward here is sitting at the other end of the damn table."

Larry snatched up the thumb drive and placed it in a computer that was connected to the room's projector. As the screen came to life, pictures dated days after her disappearance played on the screen. The horrible state of her face and body displayed for each man to see. While the fathers stood there stunned, Xander turned and dropped his head, refusing to look at the carnage he had caused.

With both fathers eyes glued to the screen, no one noticed she had made her way from one end of the room to the other, until it was too late. Piper quickly grabbed Xander's chair and swung him to look at his handy work. Piper grabbed his chin and forced his face toward the screen, placing the barrel of the gun to his temple. "Look, Darling. Look at what you left behind that night. The night we were supposed to be flying to Aspen for a getaway to reconnect after I called off the wedding the first time. Remember, you begged me to take you back after I landed from the Montana trip. Look at what you state you left me in, to go to Nadia. What don't you have the stomach to see the broken body you created? You know I still have the baseball bat. Keep flipping, gentleman. The next slides are the medical reports, and the best is yet to come."

They moved through each document, coming to the last set. The proof of the financial abuse of funds, all the forged documents, the cover up from the Hulston family on not only Nadia but on no less than six other women that all had children by Xander. Massive child support payments and hush money paid to the women, all coming out of the company funds. This was her end game and now the bomb had been dropped and detonated.

"How many more copies are there?" John looked pained by the realization it wasn't just Xander that would go down with this information. She was taking out the whole family in one fail swoop.

"Besides that one, three. Two are with trusted associates and the third is on one of seven computers. Anything happens to me or I don't show up in three days time... Let's just say it's going to get messy around here. Tick... Tock..."

"I can have the papers in twenty minutes and a judge's signature on them first thing in the morning," John pleaded.

Piper gave it a good long thought. "That's acceptable. I have a few conditions of sorts. You understand." She took the gun away from Xander's head and walked to the other end of the table. "Xander, go clean yourself up. I can smell the piss from here."

Xander's eyes were wide, but had been too terrified to move. John had walked over pulling his son from the chair and practically slung him out of the room.

"What are your conditions?" Larry stepped forward.

"There is a gag order put in the divorce. Neither family can say a word about me or how this came about. In turn I keep quiet. Next, I keep all shares pertaining to both Xander and myself, which will later be sold to my brother if he wishes to keep the Cason/Hulston group alive. At such time, all debt will be considered paid. Xander will be held responsible for all the bad deals that have left this company in ruins. I will instruct my brother to bring in a forensic accountant to see how much damage is here and if it can be repaired. Each family goes their own way and it's over. My house and car belong to the Cason Group, our finances were never co-mingled. There are no common assets. Open and shut."

"Done." John said, as Piper put the gun away.

"Good."

"I have one question." Larry looked at his daughter intently. "Why now?"

"My job is done here, father. It's time for me to be who I really am." Piper sat down in the chair looking as sincere as she could. "You taught me so much. Don't act surprised when I use what I have been taught to my own advantage. It's just business, sometimes it's good other times it's like a snake you have to cut the head off from. This is me killing the snake. You taught me that, remember?"

Larry had hung his head. All the signs that he missed, the excuses he believed, and disappointment he felt for his daughter, were gone. The student had surpassed the master and she had done it in such a way that made him proud. Larry hadn't done what was right by his daughter and he would now spend a lifetime trying to make it right. That was if she would let him, the choice would now be hers and there was nothing anyone could do about it. She had cleared her name, and put the blame on the right person.

Within the hour, papers were drawn up, signed and notarized. She had laid the wedding set that was presented to her on her wedding day back in her father's hands. Piper took her copies of the papers and headed down to her brother's office hoping to catch him before his dinner meeting. She had gotten lucky, when she had found him buttoning up his day's events.

"Got a minute?" Piper had poked her head inside his office.

"For my favorite little sister?" His crystal blue eyes danced with amusement. "Always."

"You do realize I'm your only little sister." Piper mused walking over to give him a hug.

"As far as we know." Lar mused. "How did the meeting go?"

Piper waved the paper's at him. "About as well as could be hoped for, but I have the divorce decree in hand."

"You want to talk about it?"

"Do you have time? I know you have that dinner meeting."

"They called and rescheduled. So, I have time."

The two settled onto the couch and into a long conversation. She left out as many details as she possibly could. Mostly for his own safety, than her own. He agreed to act in her best interest, if she needed a break to clear her head, but refused to allow her to sell him the shares. In his mind, that was her right, and the fact she got to hold it over Xander's head was a bonus. She had found out through the conversation; he had never liked Xander, but when Ethan died, he felt responsible to look after him as Ethan would have wanted.

Lar thought Piper was happy, and even though he had seen some things that were questionable in nature, he didn't want to cause a rift between them. He honestly didn't know if she would believe him, so he had gone to their father and mother, which told him to keep his mouth shut. He felt horrible about it. When she had gone missing after they had returned from Montana, Lar was the one that sounded the alarm, when he didn't like the explanation that Xander had been giving the family.

Piper couldn't stay mad at her older brother for doing what he thought was best at the time. Hell, they were both still relatively new at the whole adult thing back then. She was happy to know that he would get both companies back on their feet, and Lar had every intention of firing Xander midday to allow him the privilege of being escorted from the building with all staff there to watch.

He had told her not to be a stranger, and there was always a place for her at the company. Lar understood all too well, she needed to spread her wings. Too much had happened and some things needed time to heal. Though she was honest when she had told him about going no contact with their parents. He hoped she wouldn't be cutting him out too. He felt guilty over all the time that was lost, even though it was through no fault of his own. She promised to stay in touch when she had gathered her things and left his office.

By the time she had made it home, Piper's head was swimming. She was free or as free as anyone really could be after all that happened. Piper was even on solid ground with her brother, which she wasn't sure would ever happen again.

Mary, always reliable, met her at the door with a cigar and a very large glass of wine. Taking her coat and briefcase, Mary spoke. "So, productive day?"

"You could say that. What did you prepare for dinner?" The smells wafted to Piper's nose.

"Oh, I hope you don't mind but I ordered out."

"Please tell me Chinese or that good steak place around the corner?"

"Both." Mary giggled. "It just arrived. I figured it's such a lovely evening we would eat out on the patio, and you can tell me all about your day." Mary was always up for some good office gossip.

"That sounds wonderful." Piper took a drag off her cigar and went to head for the back door kicking off the ridiculous high heels, when the phone rang. Her stomach knotted when she realized it was the mystery phone she had placed in her back pocket, after getting out of the car.

"Johnson." She answered, earning her a knowing look from Mary. There was something she would have to explain later.

"Piper?" Dom's voice sounded strained as she heard blood curdling screaming and wailing coming from the background.

"What's happened? Is Nicky, Okay?" Piper panicked.

"Piper, Darling, you need to get your ass here NOW! Nicky has gone off the rails and I can't control him."

"What's happened?"

"Don D'Angelo is dead."

"Shit. Sit tight, I'm on my way." Piper went to disconnect the call when she heard Dom say something else.

"Piper?"

"Yeah?"

"Plane will be at the airport in 15 minutes. Wheels up in 30. I sent a car will be there in 5."

"Roger that." Piper hung up the phone with tears welling up in her eyes.

"What's going on? What's wrong?"

"I wish I could explain everything right now Mary, but I can't. I need you to stay at the house. Same protocols as always. No one in or out until you hear back from me. Understood." Piper rushed up the stairs to grab her always packed luggage and came back down again.

"I understand. Duty calls." Mary smirked. She always knew there was something different about her boss, but it was much more fun not knowing.

CHAPTER 22
LONG LIVE THE DON

It was late into the night before Piper had pulled up at the compound with dozens upon dozens of vehicles lining the front. Some she recognized, others she didn't. With the death of the head of the Valence family, they were closing ranks fast. Normally, protocols would have been put into place when he became sick, but this was quick and sudden.

Her appearance was supposed to be kept quiet, but when Nicky had boarded himself in the old man's office, things got complicated quickly. So quickly, in fact Dom had to find another way into the office, while they had sent Kendrick to drive her back from the airport, and Manny had to guard the door.

 Piper didn't even wait for the car to come to a complete stop before making a run for the front door. She might have marveled at the people that were looking at her like they had seen a ghost if it wasn't for the wailing, Piper heard echoing down the hall. Most made a path for her to make a run for it, others possibly took a harder than necessary trip into a nearby wall. Nothing was keeping her from getting to Nicky.

Manny had many different emotions play out on his face as Piper came at a dead run down the corridor. She had guessed Dom hadn't told anyone she was coming as Kendrick had the same expressions when she appeared at the waiting car. All Dom had told Kendrick was "He called in the big guns."

"Move away from the door, Manny. Let me see him." Piper wasn't in the mood to be playing games after the day she had.

"I don't think it's safe." Manny almost froze in place not believing she was really standing there.

"Manny, I don't have time for this. Let me in or I will find another way in, come back here, and kick your ass." Piper glared at him.

"I don't need to add myself to the body count." Manny stood to the side, shouldering the door open. Piper nodded her head as she entered the room.

She would have sworn a tornado had blown through the office, or someone had robbed the place leaving the scattered items in their wake. But it was much worse than that, the only father figure Nicky had ever known or respected was now gone. The worst part, Piper didn't see Valence Jr. anywhere in site.

Dom was crouched next to the grieving Nicky, when he noticed she had entered the room looking around for them like a mad woman. Breathing a sigh of relief, Dom ran to Piper giving her the biggest hug and lifting her off her feet. "Thank god you're here."

"It's all good. What happened? The last time I talked to Valence Sr. he was fine."

"How long ago was that?"

"I don't know about two or three weeks ago. He had donated to the galla I hosted that you two crashed. Not the point, he was fine."

"Piper, he had a stroke. He died in Nicky's arms. There was nothing anyone could have done." Dom choked back tears as he explained.

She looked over at Nicky, who more than likely wouldn't have moved from the spot where it happened. "I got this. Do me a favor?"

"Whatcha need?"

"Keep everyone out of here. We all know he won't hurt me. And something to eat. You interrupted my dinner."

"I'll handle it. Thank you for coming so quickly." Dom hugged Piper again before leaving the room.

"Nico..." Piper called out walking over to see Nicky hugging onto one of the couch pillows. She sat down on the floor allowing him time to understand she was not only there but real. "Nico, baby. I'm here."

Nicky looked up from the pillow he gripped with swollen eyes. "He's gone, Piper. He's really gone."

"I know, baby." Piper tried to sooth him as she fought back tears. Reaching out to touch his hair, Piper's voice became shaky. "You know he loved you, and in his own way he tried to protect you. Sometimes things just happen. We have no explanation, it's just their time."

"We were arguing. Arguing about you actually, and he said he was trying to wake me up. That if I loved you, I would have never let anything stand between us. I must have not loved you that much if I had allowed you to marry that asshole. When I pointed out everything we had found in the files, and he was the reason you weren't here. He went to go say something and it just happened. He fell over. I thought he had a heart attack. I started CPR and Dom called the ambulance. By the time they had got him to the hospital, they had found he had a stroke and he was gone." Nicky had recounted every minor detail.

"Then you came back here and decided it would be a great idea to barricade yourself in his office?" Piper found humor in the situation.

"My office." Nicky's voice was barely audible.

"What?" Piper was caught off guard.

"I'm Don Valence now."

"Wouldn't your father?" Piper was a bit confused.

"Pops didn't trust him to blow his nose. Safeguards were put in place, if anything was to ever happen to him. One of which was the designation of power, everything went to me as the eldest grandson."

"Well I guess it's a good thing I already swore my undying devotion to you." Nicky cracked a smile at her words.

The office door swung open revealing a distraught Valence Jr.. "You must be mad, coming here like this. This is all your fault."

"I know you would really like to believe that Angelo, but I was sent for. The best thing for you to do is go to your office and down a bottle of that top shelf bourbon, and grieve. I'll cut you some slack right now, but if you keep talking I'm going to make sure you don't have a good arm to carry your father's casket. Do you understand me?"

"Nico, are you going to do something about this bit..." Angelo didn't get to finish the sentence before Piper backhanded him, knocking out one of his crowns.

"See I warned you. Now look at what you made me do." Piper rubbed the back of her hand. "Manny. Kendrick."

"Ma'am" They appeared around the corner.

"Did Dom not tell you we were not to be disturbed?"

"Yes, ma'am but we were dealing with the kitchen."

"Alright, Do me a favor, take Angelo back to his office and keep an eye on him. Someone bring me some ice and ring the doctor." Piper started barking out orders.

"Why the doctor? Is Nicky okay?"

"Nicky is fine. I think I just broke my hand."

"Yes ma'am. We will have the doctor come at once." They tried not to snicker as they removed Angelo.

It took a little coaxing, a promise she wasn't going anywhere, and food to get Nicky to leave the office that night. It was all a disaster, but Piper was certain with some food and sleep, Nicky could at least think. He had to be smart about the transition. Most of the other families would fall in line, but there were some like the Morang family that would look at this as an opportunity. Especially, since Piper wasn't one of their favorite people, and the drama with her and Xander would soon come to light.

It hadn't even dawned on Nicky to ask Piper how she got there, or how she knew to come. He didn't question his good fortune. All he needed to know was she was safe and literally within his grasp. Everything else was details.

After a half bottle of wine, Dom had to help carry Nicky to bed. Piper told Dom she would tuck him in and asked him to prepare her room for her. She wasn't sure if it was the best idea for her to sleep in the same room with Nicky. They had been apart for so long, she didn't want to assume things would go back to the way they had always been.

Pulling the covers up around his shoulders, Piper bent down to kiss him on his forehead. "Good night, Nico."

Before she could walk away from the bed, Nicky had grabbed her wrist and pulled her on top of him. "You're not going anywhere." His voice was raspy but she understood.

"I'm just going to be down the hall." Piper tucked a loose strand of hair behind his ear. "I promise, I'll still be here in the morning."

"I'm never sleeping alone again, and neither will you." He turned trapping both in between the layers of blanket.

"Fine. Fine. I give." Piper weaseled her way out. "But I still need to change out of my clothes."

"No, you don't. You just need to take those off." The evil grin, she loved, played on his lips more in temptation than warning.

"Nico, we are just sleeping." She shot a warning look at him as she dressed down and climbed up next to his warm body.

You never know who you'll bump into at a funeral" was what most people remarked when they saw Piper with Dom flanking Nicky as they entered the church. While most of the men had rotated out so the majority could be at the church, two people Piper hadn't expected to run into right off the bat after entering were Kris and Mark. The look of terror in their eyes gave her a certain satisfaction.

243

"I thought you'd be happy to see me," she said with a wry smile. "Why the long face?"

"What are you doing here?" Mark whispered fear evident in his eyes.

"Dom got a hold of me. I'm here to pay my respects."

"Piper, we need to talk." Kris stepped forward mirroring Mark's expression.

"And what would you have to talk to her about?" Nicky's voice was low enough for only them to hear.

"It's just business, Nicky. We just need a word with her." Kris looked like a two tailed cat in a room full of rocking chairs.

"We can talk back at the house after the funeral. This is a time for all of us to pay our respects and mourn. There will be time for business later." Piper wanted them to stew on what her presence meant for the two of them.

"That's fine." Both men exchanged a look as Piper passed with Dom and Nicky to be seated at the front of the church with the family.

After what seemed like an hour of up downs, communion, and a dozen or so prayers by the priest, the eulogies finally started. None of the three could keep it together, when a middle aged man stood at the podium and started, "He was a successful, attractive and charming man, but people of that age and position almost always had secrets, most of which I hope he took to his grave."

They had to excuse themselves because they were laughing too hard. They understood it was slightly inappropriate, but they knew D'Angelo better than most in the room. He would be rolling in his coffin if he could by the pompous display of concern and affection towards him. Nicky knew his grandfather as a loving, fierce, and terrifying man. He was firm but fair. Even in the situation that landed Nicky separated from Piper for a whole year, Don Valence had taught him the greatest lesson of them all. "You protect and fight for what's yours."

The three stepped out of the church to get some air. Finding a shady spot in the Texas' sun was a little easier than expected. It was all too much to handle in the short amount of time. Catholic funerals were normally three days, but Valence Jr.. insisted it was all handled as quickly as possible. Everyone believed it had more to do with the will and the changing of guard than his concern for his late father's wishes.

"How long do we have?" Nicky took a cigarette out of his inner pocket of his suit jacket.

"Figure about another hour for the rest of the eulogies, last prayer, the blessing of the pallbearers, then show on the road." Dom retorted, taking a drag off his own cigarette.

"Well, my feet are killing me. Why hadn't I remembered to grab my flats." Piper leaned on Nicky to try and take some of the pressure off, while also rummaging through her purse. "Damn it to hell."

"What? Did you forget something?" Dom poked fun at Piper digging like a raccoon looking for her something shiny.

"Yeah, I did. I left my cigarettes in my other hand bag." Piper sighed, taking Nicky's from his lips and kissing him. "Thank you."

"You know that would normally aggravate the shit out of me, but it's sexy as hell when you do it." Nicky placed a kiss on her neck.

"Eww. Come on guys, we are at a funeral." Dom made gagging noises. Inside, he would be eternally grateful for Piper's return.

"Nicky, Dom it's time." Val's voice echoed from the top of the church steps. A smile reached her eyes when she had confirmed the beauty on his arm was none other than Piper.

"Hey, let me straighten your ties. You don't need anyone thinking you two are a bunch of slobs." Piper made quick work of making sure the men were presentable before walking back into the church.

The rest of the day's events paced in a blur of condolences, crying, and people needed to speak with the new man in charge. Which Nicky did politely explain, he would handle back at the main house after the burial. Decisions had to be made quickly and with no time to put affairs in order, Nicky was a little out of his depth.

One of the changes, Nicky had enacted fairly quickly, caused more than a few to go into a tizzy. Piper, not Dom, had been named Nicky's Consigliere. For Nicky, there was no other choice. She was the level headed one that kept him in line, and regardless of her future plans, he selfishly wanted to make sure she never left his sight. Hell, she had been doing the job for D'Angelo and Nicky for years. It was just now her official place in the family.

After what seemed like hundreds of meetings, assurances, and even proposals of new agreements, it had come time to deal with Mark and Kris. Both Nicky and Piper needed answers and this time no one was going to leave the room without them. Especially since, they were the only ones that knew what the direct orders had been.

Dom had a cheeky smile on his face, as he escorted both men into the room. Piper was thankful, at least with this encounter, she hadn't had to track them down, as she had the entire day. Dom had volunteered, Piper believed it was more out of the ability to torment than saving one more round of her on her feet. Dom took a lot of pleasure in making people squirm.

As both men took their seats in front of Nicky and Piper, they visibly flushed. Piper could see the fear in their eyes. Whatever was going to be spilled, had both men wishing they were anywhere but where they were. Kris fidgeted in his chair while Mark's leg was going about a mile a minute.

"So...." Nicky cleared his throat bringing all attention and focus onto him. "I'm going to give you one chance to speak about the events of the last year. You know what will happen if you lie to me, I don't have to explain that part. I would say to choose your words wisely before you speak. So, what do you two have to say for yourselves?"

246

Mark and Kris knew their asses were in a sling, and the things they had done would cost any normal person their lives. They had hoped maybe Nicky and by extension Piper were in a forgiving mood.

"Where do you want us to start?" Mark said, cringing at the sight of Piper playing with the knife D'Angelo used as a letter opener.

"From the beginning would probably be the best place."

"Okay, you see what had happened was...." Kris took off like a rambling chipmunk.

It took about ten minutes for both men to let the whole cat out of the bag, leaving Nicky, Piper, and even Dom shell shocked. As both sat there, chests heaving, and praying for anything but their lives being ended, Nicky looked between Piper and Dom for clarity.

"We are so so so very sorry," Kris stammered.

"I swear, we were just following orders. Hell, we couldn't even go to confession over this. Please understand, this was never our intent to hurt either of you. But when the big man said make it happen and keep our mouths shut. That's what we did."

"I don't care what we have to do. Just please don't kill us." Kris had tears streaming from his eyes.

"Oh dear lord, enough." Nicky rubbed his temples. "You two are almost too pathetic to deal with. I understand you were following orders, and I'm sure I'll come up with an appropriate punishment for you later. For now you're causing a migraine."

"We will do whatever we need to prove our loyalty," Mark confirmed.

"You'll be paying a smaller price compared with what she's went through. But for now, get out of my sight."

Mark and Kris both excitedly jumped from their seats and kissed Nicky's ring, hauling ass out of the room. As soon as the door closed, Dom busted out laughing. This started the infectious laughter to be spread through the room, and before too long the three were trying to catch their breaths.

"You know I can't stay mad at their goofy asses." Piper wiped her eyes.

"Their good men, just not the brightest crayons in the box." Dom retorted.

"If brains were dynamite, I still wouldn't trust them to blow their nose. The old man put them in a tight spot and for all intensive purposes, they did what they were told to do. Piper stayed safe and it's all over now." Nicky shrugged. "Piper, make sure they get all the shit jobs for the next six months. If they can make it through those without anything major happening. We will readdress their punishment."

"Sounds better than hearing them whine." Piper rubbed her neck as a ball of tension started to form.

"You okay?" Nicky observed her cringe when she hit a certain spot on her neck.

"Just been a long day. Hell the three of us haven't even eaten yet."

"Speak for yourself. Every time I leave the office I stop by the kitchen." Dom stuck his tongue out at Piper.

"Don't make me cut that off before you learn how to use it properly." Piper stretched.

"Awe there's my spicy pepper."

"I'll give you some heartburn in a minute you keep fucking with me. Nicky, deal with him."

"This is between y'all, but please no blood on the carpet it's Italian."

"What in this room isn't?" Piper shot back.

"You." Both Nicky and Dom blurted out.

"Where the hell is my knife?" Piper looked around as Dom's eyes went wide and ran from the room. "I swear that man is a child."

"What's that make you for indulging him?"

"Apparently, the fucking Mother." Piper huffed.

"I think someone needs a hot meal and a relaxing bath. Whatever's left can wait till tomorrow." Nicky had come to stand in front of Piper tucking a loose strand of hair behind her ear. "You know I couldn't do this without you."

"And as long as I'm here you'll never have to worry about that. Let's go before I give Dom a permanent piercing." Piper wrapped her arms around Nicky's neck and kissed him softly.

CHAPTER 23
IT WILL ALWAYS BE HER.

Standing on the balcony in the balmy Verona late afternoon, Piper looked out over the streets of the city with a sigh of relief. The last six months had not been easy but they had made it through relatively unscathed. While most fell in line with Don D'Angelo's choice for a successor, there were a few that bucked against the new head of the Valence family. Valence Jr.. being among them.

It was no secret Angelo had no stomach for the darker side of the business, and everyone knew it was his pride more than anything that had him plotting against Nicky and Piper. Thankfully Kris and Mark, who had been assigned to watch Angelo, took their jobs seriously. They quickly reported back to the three when the first signs of trouble got too much for them to contain. Which led Nicky to have to make a decision no one saw coming.

Nicky sent Valence Jr.. to "keep an eye" on the family in Sicily, under the guise of both heads of the monarch being gone. Nicky had told him, "I needed someone I can trust to oversee the business, since I can't be in two places at once." This act seemed to sate Angelo enough to agree. After all, Nicky knew his cousins would straighten him out if he stepped on too many toes.

Even with the wars that sprung up as the results of Angelo's dealing, Piper had quickly shut them down. Though the stress took a toll on her, it was nothing compared to the damage control she had to deal with back in New Mexico from time to time.

She had been lucky to remember after everything was said and done, to contact Don Graves. Thankfully or not depending, there had been a snow storm that had delayed the package. He had no idea until Piper had called, that there was even a possibility of her being in trouble. They had a good laugh about it, but Piper did instruct him to keep it safe in case it was needed for later.

Xander, on the other hand, had gone off the rails when she vanished without a trace once again. No one currently knew where he was, but it did make it through the grapevine that Xander disappeared hours before he was to marry Nadia. Whether he had helped escape the church and 250 wedding guests had yet to be determined. In her state of shock of being left at the altar, Nadia's water broke, ushering in Xander's fourth child by her. Needless to say, the Morang family was now on the hunt for the missing father/groom. Piper chuckled at the thought of him getting exactly what he wanted, just to run like a scared bitch when it was time to live it.

Mary was amazing at keeping her up to date on all the good gossip. So much so, when Piper had come to collect the rest of her important things she had given Mary a choice. She could continue living at the house, making a very good salary, and keep things running for her. Or Piper would pay her a hefty severance package allowing her to leave, go and do whatever Mary wanted. She ultimately chose to stay even if Piper wouldn't be there.

The only problem that wouldn't resolve quickly was the badgering from her parents. Lar was currently keeping them at bay, but Piper knew that wouldn't last forever. Boundaries were not their strong understanding, and if the last two years had taught her anything, sometimes a woman had to do what a woman had to do. When she got back from Verona, Piper planned on approaching the topic of Nicky meeting her parents. Though she was pretty sure it would not go as well as any of them would hope.

Looking back, life had not turned out the way it had been planned, either time if she was being honest with herself. But through it all she finally ended up exactly where she wanted to be. Piper was looking out over one of the most beautiful places in the world.

"Am I interrupting?" Nicky walked out onto the balcony fixing the cuffs of his shirt.

"Nope. I was just thinking. Everything okay with Dom?" Piper had heard part of the conversation before taking her wine out to the balcony.

"Yeah, Tootsie called from Nashville and needs a sit down when we get back."

"Probably, to make sure all the protections are still in place from D'Angelo."

"It sounded like it, but as I told Dom, no business while we are on our vacation. Whatever it is will wait until we get back home." Nicky slipped his arms around Piper's waist holding her close to him. "I missed moments like this more than anything."

"I know. I did too." Piper turned in his arms to face him. "If we don't leave now, we are going to miss our reservation. I didn't shimmy into this dress for nothing."

"I think it would be more fun shimmying you out of that dress, but you're right, we need food." Nicky conceded but let the thoughts of her dance in his head.

Taking her by the hand, he led her down the stairs to the waiting vehicle. Piper knew about the reservation, but had no idea where they actually were going. All Nicky would tell her was "it was going to be the biggest surprise of her life." He knew she hated surprises but it never stopped him from doing it.

Flying through the streets, Piper loved the thrill it gave her. The freedom she never knew she would feel again. Nicky squeezed her hand, which sent butterflies through her stomach. After almost 14 years, she still felt the heat and passion he had invoked in her sitting in that bar. Piper hoped that would never change, but there were certain habits Nicky had reverted back to over the last few months. Piper had chalked it up to Nicky being Nicky.

She didn't want to upset the status quo and while he hadn't been outright dismissive of her, Nicky didn't put a label on what they had. Piper didn't want to push anything with everything they had been put through in two years. She didn't have a problem being his comfort but without a defined understanding this left her stoic to the possibility of a future. Piper tried to push it from her mind and enjoy their time alone from the rest of the responsibilities.

Pulling up at the metal gate, Piper's heart began to flutter with excitement. They were having dinner at one of the oldest Vineyards in the area. A place that Nicky said he could get them a private tour of, well this was one way for him to pull that off. As the car came to a stop outside what Piper presumed to be the main home, two men came to open the doors.

"Don Valence." The well dressed man shook Nicky's hand. "Don Graves, sends his regards and gave us all instructions for this evening."

"That explains so much." Piper snickered.

"What?" Nicky feigned innocence.

"How Dana knew we were leaving town." Piper rolled her eyes at Nicky.

"Well it's only polite to ask permission to use someone else's property. Not that I wouldn't have come anyway but I actually asked this time."

"This time?" Piper raised an eyebrow at him as he took her arm. "I might or might not have broken into here when I was a teenager taking some very expensive 1928 Merlo."

"Nico." Piper scolded.

"I didn't get far. Pops was hot on my heels. I didn't ever get to pop the first bottle open. Hilarious that it was given to me as a 21st birthday present, though."

"Irony wasn't lost on that man. Either of them." Piper was paying more attention to Nicky than her surroundings as they walked through the house and into the garden.

"It certainly wasn't. As it is not lost on me."

"How is this ironic?" Piper chuckled.

"Every time we were supposed to come here, something came up, putting us everywhere else." Nicky carefully brushed the hair away from the tattoo on her back. "Now we are finally here not being pulled into a thousand other places. But..." Nicky's voice trailed off as Piper's eyes lit up with delight.

The entire garden had been set up with fairy lights, candles, and even violin players. It looked like a scene taken straight out of a fairy tale. The sky was even starting to turn pinkish orange with the setting sun. Everything was perfect. Except the last word she had heard.

"But what?" Piper's eyes held a look somewhere between confusion and anger.

"We can't keep going on like this." Nicky's words hit her like a ton of bricks.

"I see. Well then we didn't have to come all the way to Verona for you to tell me that. Thank you for protecting me. Thank you for giving me a purpose, but I can't..." Nicky's mouth crushed hard onto hers, smothering whatever words that were fixing to come out of her mouth to ruin the moment he was trying to assemble.

"Look here you little hellcat, I have given you a little too much liberty but you never listen." Piper stood there with a mix of emotion not only swimming through her mind but also her blood, as she was being scolded.

"Now, as I was saying. We can't go on like this any longer. I can't allow it. I have made many mistakes in not saying certain things to you, and if I did I'm the one that didn't fulfill my end of the promise." Nicky swallowed hard. "It killed me, Piper. It fucking killed me, when you were gone."

"Oh Nico." Piper went to touch him but he held up his hand.

"I can't go through that again. I won't go through it. Til fucking death or nothing less. I am yours, you are mine." Nicky took the black velvet box from his pocket. "I know I'm a lot to deal with. I know Dom is a man child that will probably be the fun uncle we have to tell no when it comes to our kids. I know you will always need me to be there and sometimes I won't be able to be." It was now Piper's turn to shut him up by placing her hand on his chest.

"Are you going to ask me or not?" Piper's voice was stoic but full of all the hope, and anticipation of what this would mean.

"I was trying to." Nicky smiled. "Evette Cason, will you marry me?"

"Under one condition."

"Whatever you want."

"Never call me Evette again." Tears poured from her eyes, as he slipped the diamond ring on her hand, the music started, and Nicky spun her around the garden.

Special Notes:

To all that wish to do that something crazy or out of the norm, do it. January 1st 2024 the weekly writing challenge was born. I was told it was an amazing idea but no one really wanted to do anything with it. So, I did, as any past football player would. I ran with it. In October 2024, we came up with our own name, The Hold My Pen Promptcast.

While we have been through a lot in the last year, My Co-Host Izzy Krause along with fellow Authors PA Power and C.R. McCormack can be found every Saturday Night on TikTok displaying everyone's talents by reading the weekly submissions.

Just know when a writing challenge, meets a string of prompts that all go together, and a bunch of people that needed to know what happened in Mexico, you get Crossroads

www.ingramcontent.com/pod-product-compliance
Lightning Source LLC
Chambersburg PA
CBHW030108260626
47156CB00008B/2568